DISSERTATION MOST DEADLY

DISSERTATION MOST DEADLY

Elizabeth A. Seitz

iUniverse, Inc.

New York Lincoln Shanghai

Dissertation Most Deadly

iUniverse, Inc.

For information address:
iUniverse, Inc.
2021 Pine Lake Road, Suite 100
Lincoln, NE 68512
www.iuniverse.com

ISBN: 0-595-31782-0

Printed in the United States of America

For Jorge

Alice sighed wearily. "I think you might do something better with the time,"
she said, "than waste it in asking riddles that have no answers."

—Lewis Carroll

Acknowledgments

I owe a debt of gratitude to so many people. First, I'd like to thank our writer's group, Kevin Daley, Bella English and Brad Pritchett, for giving me great advice and support throughout the process. I'd also like to thank my friends, Annie Gwee (a.k.a. Nina Greeley), Teresa Neff, Cynthia Perras, Kim MacKinnon, Raymond Rubin, Adrian Roscher, Gwenn and Paul Gebhard, and John Daverio for their input and advice at almost every stage of writing.

Thanks also to my aunt, Iris Chekenian, a wonderful writer herself, who helped with everything from copy editing to advising me on how to write my bio! When she took on another "full-time job" I was most appreciative. I'd also like to thank my father, Roland Seitz, who really does know everything about WWI (and WWII, for that matter).

Lastly, I'd like to thank my husband, Jorge, who has supported me in all my endeavors. I would be lost without him and our son, Alejandro, and of course, The Goose.

It is to Jorge that I dedicate this book.

CHAPTER 1

▼

I couldn't believe he was dead.

The cheerful voice on the line said, "Is there anything else I can help you with?"

"Ummmm, yeah," I replied. "Could you tell me how old Dr. Brownsten was? I mean, he just finished his dissertation in 1999 or so, didn't he? How and when did he die?"

"Well," the receptionist paused. She must have been at a loss.

"Weeellll," she repeated, more slowly this time.

I came to her rescue. "Is there anyone else I can talk to about this? Anyone specifically assigned to music history?"

"Oh yes," she replied, instantly becoming cheerful again. "That would be Caroline Berk. I'll transfer you. In case we get cut off, her extension is 2134."

Click. Nothing. Dial tone.

I called back. "Extension 2134," I said as another equally chipper voice answered the phone. This time it rang and rang and rang. What was Archana Publishers doing anyway? Obviously nothing. I decided to be stubborn. I'm very good at it. I hit the speakerphone button and continued cleaning my desk, a futile exercise, especially with a sixteen-pound cat splayed all over it. The phone droned in the background. I didn't care.

After about five minutes, a very annoyed voice answered.

"This is Berk."

"Caroline Berk?"

"Yes, may I help you?" The voice was still annoyed.

"Well, Ms. Berk, my name is Leigh Maxwell. I'm a graduate student at City University in Boston and am writing my doctoral dissertation on Enrique Dadi. I understand Archana Publishers contracted Dr. Jack Brownsten to do a complete biography on Dadi and I was just trying to contact him."

"He died," she cut in.

"Yes, yes, I know. I was told by the secretary or receptionist in your department, but what I'd like to know is if you have any materials he was using or that he had already submitted. I'm sort of getting stonewalled by the Dadi archive in Spain. I was trying to connect with someone here in the States who may have manuscripts, microfilms or anything else helpful." I hoped I sounded a bit pathetic at that point. "Is there anything you can do to help me out?"

"Look," she answered. It wasn't a good beginning. She paused and began again. "Look, I took over the Music History department only three months ago. All it says in my files is…" pause, paper rustled. She was looking at something. It may have been her paperback for all I knew, but at least the edginess in her voice was gone. "All I can tell you," she continued more authoritatively, "is that he died in 2000, manuscript unfinished. We have nothing in our files. He does have a widow. She might be of help. I can't give you her address but you can write to her care of me and I'll forward it. That's the best I can do."

"Well, thanks," I replied. "I'll write to her today. Could you give me your address?"

She did.

"One more thing," I added. At this point, I was definitely trying her patience. "Ummm…wasn't he a young man? I mean, well, how did he die?"

"Oh, yes, it says here Dr. Brownsten was born in 1965. He was in his mid-thirties when he died, no idea how. Is there anything else?"

"No. Thanks for all your help."

With a firm click she was gone. I slowly placed the phone in its cradle. I couldn't believe it. Brownsten was dead too. This was the third scholar I had tried to contact about my work on Enrique Dadi and all three were dead. Of course, I was frustrated. My dissertation was stalled because the archive wouldn't give me access to their materials, and everyone in the States who was even remotely working with Dadi seemed to be gone. First there was the graduate student from Chicago who died in a car accident. Then the Spanish historian from Kansas, missing, presumed dead in a skiing accident. Now Brownsten was gone too. Brownsten was only in his mid-thirties. I was thirty-four. This hit very close to home. I felt like I was in the Twilight Zone.

I looked at my computer screen. There was the icon for the Dissertation Bibliography and an outline and abstract. That was it. I had read all the secondary information I could get my hands on already, not much, by the way. What I needed was to see all the primary source stuff: sketches, letters, notes and manuscripts.

I guess it would be helpful to explain who Enrique Dadi was. I tend to get so caught up in my work that I'm surprised when people don't know exactly what it is I'm working on, much less what a musicologist is. Dadi was an interesting composer, born in Spain in 1877 and died in Puerto Rico in 1949. The turn of the century was a great time for musicians. So many exciting things happened then. Composers like Debussy, Stravinsky, Schoenberg, Ravel all knew each other's works but each was so different from the other. Dadi is especially interesting to me since he lived in France during World War I and returned to Spain after the war, while most people did just the opposite. He also traveled around the United States, living first in Florida and then Puerto Rico during the Spanish Civil War. What has always struck me about Dadi has been the lack of stylistic coherence between pieces. I mean that when I hear Mozart, even without knowing the exact piece, I know it was written by Mozart. I can't say the same thing about Dadi. The early pieces that I've been studying are, quite frankly, pretty bad. I could probably write better, but they do have stylistic coherence and I can always tell authorship. After Dadi studied in Italy and France, I can't tell if it is his work at all. Each piece is so different from the other and each is brilliant. I also knew from the grad student that some of Dadi's pieces have never been published. He had seen some of them, and wanted to edit and then publish them. My goal was to pick up where he left off. I needed to find those pieces, but the troubling thing was that the people who already had were turning up dead.

I kept staring at my computer screen and suddenly felt very old and tired. Nothing like graduate school to make you feel wasted. After six years of classes, exams, more classes and more exams, here I was ABD (all but dissertation) and I wasn't getting anywhere. Eight months of reading and note-taking hadn't gotten me far. In fact, I vaguely considered switching my topic to Beethoven–at least everyone had written something about him. Maybe I could find a new angle. Ach. I needed encouragement.

I hit the speakerphone and called my advisor. He also happened to be a good friend.

His answering machine kicked in.

"Jack, pick up," I said into the machine. Pause. "I know you're there. You don't teach today. You're hiding."

I was rewarded with: "What's up? I wasn't hiding, just reading."

"Jack, Brownsten is dead."

"Who?"

"Brownsten. The guy writing the biography on Dadi. He's dead too."

Jack just chuckled. "Well," he finally said, "You should title your dissertation 'Do Dadi and Die' or maybe 'Deadly Dissertation.'"

"This is serious, Jack. I don't know where else to turn."

"Well, you better do something soon, before, you know, you die or something…" More laughter.

In spite of myself, I cracked a smile. "Okay, so my dissertation is called 'Do Dadi and Die.'"

Jack added, "'Maybe Death Dance with Dadi' or…"

"Jack, seriously. What should I do now? I'm no further along and I have to keep going. I have to get this thing done. You know what they say. 'A good dissertation is a done dissertation.'"

"Well, you can always go back to the Beethoven piano concerto stuff you were talking about a year or so ago."

As soon as he said it, I knew I couldn't begin again. "Jack, I'm eight months into this already. My abstract's been accepted. The proposal is finished…" I trailed off. "Well, okay, I guess I'll contact Brownsten's widow, try the archive in Spain again and go to work. How's that?"

"Sounds good. Why don't you follow up that lead on the family in Puerto Rico? Why not look them up and try to contact them? Your new boyfriend should be able to help. His family is from Puerto Rico, right? Maybe they can do some searching for you."

Of course, I didn't want Jack to know I'd forgotten about Dadi's family in San Juan. Dadi had two living children. Maybe they had some of their father's papers. That had been on my list of things to do. Jack remembers everything. It's frustrating at times. "Yeah, I'll do that. I've got to go to work. Shit, it's two o'clock already. I was supposed to be there at one thirty. Are we still on for lunch tomorrow?"

"Sure, we'll talk about this more then. Okay? Are you all right?" Concern edged into his voice.

"Yeah, sure, it's just that the guy was in his mid-thirties, you know, and just finished his dissertation…well, whatever. I'm fine. I'll see you at the Pizza Palace at twelve or so? Okay? And thanks Jack, we'll talk more tomorrow."

I hung up. I was still uneasy but felt better. Jack's gallows humor was what I needed, I guess. I went into the bathroom and washed my face and hands. Looking at myself, I realized that I had more lines around my eyes and mouth than yesterday. When you are in your mid-thirties and still in school, you tend to age much faster. I put some undercover stick on (much needed) then some mascara, hoping that I would look more human. My boyfriend, Carlos, says that my skin is so white I glow in the dark, so blush was in order. I also put a little gray eye shadow on to bring out my gray eyes. I brushed out my hair and put it back in one of those ties with the different color balls on the ends your mother always used when you were a kid. I have a zillion of them but can only find one or two at a time. Afterwards, I definitely felt better.

I finally looked at the clock, wondering if I should call in sick to work, but I thought better of it. I shouldn't fritter away precious sick time. Who knows when I would really need it?

I threw on my jacket, grabbed my purse and headed for the door.

Boston in October is absolutely gorgeous. As I hit the street, I looked up. In between yellow, red and green leaves, the sky was a light blue with little puffy clouds. It was chilly enough for a jacket but warm enough that people still ate outside at night on Newbury Street. When the wind blew, there was a hint of the cold winter ahead, which made everyone appreciate the warmth during the day even more. Walking in the sun, I felt my energy returning.

I live in a small, one-bedroom apartment in the South End, a funky neighborhood behind Copley Square, complete with a great mix of people, a smattering of restaurants and small businesses. Best of all, there are basically no students. Recently, the prices for apartments were getting outrageous, but my landlord seems to have forgotten all about me, and I hadn't gotten a rent increase in four years.

I turned from Columbus and walked down Massachusetts Avenue, past Symphony Hall and the Mother Church, and then left onto Commonwealth. I got to the Music Library exactly one and a half hours late. As I hurried in, the music librarian looked up and raised her eyebrows.

"Sorry, Helen. I was on the phone to Archana Publishers. I'll stay an hour later to make up the time."

"Okay, Leigh, but try harder next time. I understand all about the funk you're in."

That's what I like about Helen. She got out of grad school just a few years ago and knows what it's like. She's covered for me, made excuses for me and has yet to seriously bug me. In other words, she's the perfect boss. On the other hand, I do lots of work for her. I'm probably, no, make that definitely, over-qualified for the job, but it pays the rent and my health insurance, so I don't complain about it more than once a day. Helen also puts up with my whining, so I guess it's close to ideal.

I sat down at the desk and went through my e-mail, then the job postings on the internet. There was a good opportunity if I wanted to live in Montana and work eighty hours a week as a flute, piano and choral conductor and at the same time teach all the music history courses they offer. I passed. Don't get me wrong. It's not that I don't like Montana, but I just need to live in a city. If Moose Creek, Montana had a great record store or two, bookstores on every corner, a great movie theater along with at least a few museums, a good symphony orchestra, not to mention a first-class health food store and some good restaurants, I'd be there. But since it probably only has a McDonald's and a Wal-Mart, I'll pass.

Work seemed piled up all over my desk. Actually, it was stuff I hadn't wanted to work on and so, today, I just gritted my teeth and went at it. NPR was droning in my headphones, something about a crime bill. Since becoming a musicologist, or at least a musicology graduate student, I can't even have music on, even in the background. Voices talking, talk show hosts in particular, I can zone out, but music demands that I stop and listen. I used to like the music in restaurants, but no more. My boyfriend, Carlos, is always surprised when I say something about it when he doesn't even realize there's any on.

Work was particularly slow today. Not that I didn't have work to do, but *I* was slow. Having gotten through a small stack of CDs and processed a few requests from patrons, I looked up as Helen stopped by to talk.

"So, what did Archana say about Dr. Brownsten? Did you get his number?"

"Helen, you'll never believe it. He's dead too. I know I'm beginning to sound like a flake. He's now the third person who has turned up dead or missing. What do you think? I mean, it's weird, isn't it?"

She seemed to consider it for a moment. It was nice to be taken seriously. "So, who else? I remember the grad student in Chicago, car accident, right?"

"Yeah. Barry and I had been writing back and forth on e-mail and it stopped suddenly. Then I found out, car accident down in Puerto Rico. Having been there and seeing how they drive, I understand it. But it seemed like a freak accident. No other cars were involved. I didn't get the details. And then there was the historian from Kansas—Cutridge his name was, I think—who is still missing, by the way. And now Brownsten. I don't know. Brownsten got his Ph.D. a few years ago. He was almost my age. Helen, tell me I'm crazy to be worried. Please. I'm getting anxious."

Instead of reassuring me, Helen invited me to dinner. Staying an extra hour was forgotten, at least for now, and we walked down to Cafe Luna for some good pasta. After ordering, Helen turned our conversation immediately to Dadi and the deaths I had stumbled upon. Helen has intense green eyes, eyes that have always held my attention. She placed her hand over mine while she was talking. "Leigh, I know I read too many mysteries and this is probably just in my mind, but what seems strange to me is that all these people were in good health, young and working on the same project. All my mystery books say the same thing. There is no such thing as a coincidence. You've got some vacation time accrued at work. Carlos has some money that he can lend you so you can take off. Just go to Puerto Rico and do your research. Don't you have a lead down there? Wasn't that where the grad student from Chicago died? Follow the lead on Dadi but at the same time ask around about the car accident. And be careful. Do me that favor, okay?"

I thought about it. After three glasses of wine it sounded like a good plan. "Carlos is out of town until Wednesday on business. I'm actually not sure where he is, though. Mexico or something. I'll talk to him when he gets back. And don't worry about me. I'm just a bit anxious, nervous, whatever."

We then turned to other subjects, books and music, and how boring work was. Helen's a professional librarian, which means she's got more interesting stuff to do than I do, but of course, more of the annoying things as well, like dealing with other librarians. After dinner, I decided to walk home. Instead of going at my usual breakneck speed, I just strolled along. Lots of people were out on the street doing exactly what I was, savoring the weather before the zero degree temperatures hit us. I turned onto my street and up to the front door. The door was slightly ajar and I grew vaguely annoyed that no one had bothered to shut it properly. As I shut the door behind me, I saw my cat, Jabba, on the stairs. He seemed a bit twitchy and jumped a foot in the air when I opened the inner door and called his name.

"Jabba, you bad cat, how did you get out?"

He came down to me but didn't look so great. Carlos always complains that I project my feelings onto the cat. That's not necessarily true. After twelve years of living together, Jabba and I know each other very well. I can always tell when there's something wrong. I knew it as soon as I came up to the second landing and saw that my door was wide open. My immediate thought was that Jabba had gotten it open somehow but looking into his eyes, very pretty and very blank, I realized that Jabba had had nothing to do with this. I stood at the threshold and couldn't will myself to go in. I craned my neck around and saw a mess. From my front door I could see my living room and bedroom. No one was there. My adrenaline was in high gear, and I began shaking from head to toe. Things were scattered all over the place. I'm not exactly a pig but I do tend toward mess. The chaos in the apartment now was none of my doing. Papers had been thrown all about; books were pushed out of bookcases. I noticed with some degree of smugness that the stereo was still there and the thought occurred to me that maybe it was just junkies looking for quick cash. I began to get angry and barged into the place, picked up the phone and dialed 911.

The police in my neighborhood are great. They've always come within minutes of my calling, and believe me, I've had occasion to call. Even so, it felt like an hour until they arrived on my doorstep. I glanced at the clock and saw that it had been twelve minutes. Not a real emergency to them, I guess. The crime had already happened. As soon as they showed up, I relaxed somewhat and showed them around the apartment. I hadn't been in the bedroom yet, but it was far worse than the living room. Almost all my files had been pulled out. They were everywhere. I gasped as I realized my computer was gone. The monitor sat clumsily on its side as if it had been carelessly tossed there. All my music books were on the floor or thrown on the bed. Articles had been carelessly ripped out of their folders. It seemed senseless, almost mean. Don't get me wrong, all robberies are mean. I've had six in my lifetime, three in this apartment alone. The pattern is always the same, though. They always take the stereo, maybe the TV, and once it was the blender and food processor. But they never touched anything personal. Those things aren't worth anything to anyone. They leave pictures or books or letters. But this robbery was different. This one upset me more than any of the others. This one hit at my being.

I started to explain to the cops everything that was missing, and then I realized my backup drive was gone also. The modem and monitor were still there. But then all the computer diskettes that I always threw in a corner of the desk were gone too. All my backups, my letters, taxes, correspondence, they were all gone. I sat down on the bed, my knees were really rubbery by now, and I felt like throwing up. The lump in my throat prevented me from talking for a bit. I didn't want to cry in front of the cops, so I just tried breathing deeply. They were patient.

Finally, the shorter one said, "Ummm…Miss Maxwell? Is there anything else missing?"

I looked around. "The alarm clock is still here." I opened the top drawer, "All my jewelry is still here but it's all junky stuff anyway. Maybe files, but who knows? It is such a mess. Why would anyone want to take Xeroxed articles with notes in them?" My eyes rested on a highlighted passage, "Associative tonality is used by Wagner in three ways…" I felt like crying.

After my experience with the blender and food processor, I checked out the kitchen. It was such a relief to find something that was exactly as I had left it. Here, at least, was something that was still mine. I sat at the small breakfast table next to the window. "I think that's it. They didn't even take the stereo."

"What would you say was the value of the items lost?"

"Invaluable, at least to me," I paused. They waited. "Oh, I don't know. Let me think, probably about a thousand bucks. The computer is a few years old already. I had been thinking of replacing it but I couldn't afford it. Well, now I'll have to. I was hoping to get out of debt some time in the near future. I'll need a police report for the insurance. At least I have that."

"You can pick it up tomorrow at area B. Do you have anyone who could come by and help you clean up? Or would you like a ride somewhere?"

"I'm fine, really. Thanks for your help." I shut the door after them and looked around. Jabba was already settling in for a nap. I picked him up and cuddled on the sofa. He started purring, and I felt better immediately. I picked up the phone and called my friends one by one. After the fourth explanation, I began to calm down. Everyone was sympathetic; everyone invited me to stay the night. I finally got around to calling the management company, and they said they'd send over a locksmith right away. I sat there and wanted Carlos to come home. Right now he was somewhere in Mexico, though I wasn't exactly sure where. I went over to the answering machine and noticed the light was blinking. I hit "play." Carlos' voice was clear: "Hi. Hoped to catch you in. I'll be home a day early. I'm coming home tomorrow about six. I'll call you then. Love you. Bye." Relief surged through my body. Carlos would be here in eighteen hours.

My buzzer sounded and I went downstairs. At two o'clock in the morning everyone looked like an ax murderer to me but the man outside had a toolbox and a cap that said ASAP Locksmith, so I let him in. He changed my tumblers and then when he noticed I still seemed nervous, put another dead bolt into the door and a chain for the inside. When he left, I felt better. I threw the new brass dead bolt in place, put the little gold chain across the door, picked up the cat, threw everything off the bed in a heap and lay down. I needed sleep and was absolutely exhausted but I tossed and turned. I imagined getting home just ten minutes earlier to stop the thief. I imagined myself demanding the computer back and actually getting it. I finally drifted off dreaming of dark alleys, stormy seas and huge boats being tossed ashore. I woke with a start at four o'clock. Jabba was awake and hungry as usual. I padded into the kitchen, fed him and got back into bed. This time, I slept deeply and without dreams. I didn't know it was going to be the last deep sleep I got for a while.

CHAPTER 2

▼

About nine o'clock, Jabba woke me up again. Time for breakfast. I called Helen as I spooned cat food into the bowl. I explained what had happened and said that I needed a day to get my life back in order. She was very sympathetic and offered to help, but I declined. In some ways, I'm like a cat that likes to go off and lick its wounds all by itself. I needed to sort my life out and I needed to do it alone. I started with the living room, picking up books and putting them back on shelves, for once not alphabetizing them by author. When the books were done, I fixed up the coffee table and threw the five-month old magazines and newspapers into the recycling bin. I finished that at about eleven when the mail came. I could hear Max, our mailman, outside, opening the little metal doors to our boxes. I took out the vacuum and had a go at the floor. Cleaning always makes me feel better. There's nothing like having the house spotless. It lifts my spirits and I love sweating over the vacuum cleaner or scrubbing the kitchen sink to take my mind off my troubles. I don't do it often, mind you, but today it was therapeutic.

I washed the windows, at least on the inside, and scrubbed the kitchen floor. The kitchen and living room sparkled. I felt good, virtuous and clean in spirit. Then I turned back to the bedroom. The shades were still drawn and it looked dark and menacing. I couldn't face going in there, so, instead, I picked up the mail. Jabba dutifully followed me down and then I scooted him back up. It was our daily ritual. Jabba wants to fight with every cat within four blocks of the house–dogs, too. I've seen him go after the German Shepherds who live a few doors down. He always wins, but for the sake of the vet bills, I like to keep it at a minimum.

I settled on the couch in my spotless living room with my back toward the bedroom. Two catalogues, one from Lillian Vernon and one from Victoria's Secret, two charities, and a letter, finally, from the archive in Spain. It was a simple letter, neither helpful nor obstructive. Basically, they would be happy to help my research along if I got to Spain. I'd tried desperately to get them just to acknowledge my existence and finally, they had. This particular archive is devoted to 19th-and 20th-century Spanish composers and is centrally located in Madrid. They have quite a bit of Dadi's work in all of its manifestations: printed, written, sketched, everything. Librarians, Helen included, have told me that getting permission to see things would prove to be difficult, and frankly, it has been impossible so far for me. This letter was the first glimmer of hope. They said they were "willing to help" me. I got so excited I picked up the phone and called immediately. Forgetting the time difference, I only got hold of a security guard. He told me there had been a fire in the building and part of the reading room had been severely damaged. He suggested that I wait until after January to come to visit. That was over three months away.

I was initially discouraged but mostly worried about the books and manuscripts that were housed there. Some things were truly irreplaceable. My missing hard disk was now put in perspective. Generally, archives have important materials in fireproof rooms, or at least microfilmed or computer scanned in case anything should happen to the original. Who knew what they did in Spain? Things might be different there than in other archives I had worked with. I decided to press my luck and called back to tell the security guard to leave a message that I was coming within the next few days. I had to see for myself. Maybe I'd just jump start the dissertation and get to Spain and then go to Puerto Rico. Helen was right. I hadn't taken a vacation for two years. I had over six weeks of free time accumulated.

Once my phone calls were done, I felt strong enough to face the bedroom, and by six o'clock I had reestablished a semblance of order. The files all seemed to be there but they were in complete disarray. The monitor was still functional and the modem hadn't even been touched. Maybe it was time I got out of the dark ages and bought a computer that actually had a modem built-in. I put the books back on the shelves and cleaned. Then I hit the bathroom and cleaned Jabba's box, something he always appreciates by immediately going in it. By that time, it was seven o'clock—just in time for Carlos. I took a shower, got dressed and waited on the couch with my new mystery novel. Jabba curled up with me and I finally felt like I was at home.

Carlos called at eight thirty from the airport to say the plane had been late and he was coming straight over. Carlos and I have been together for six months, but it seems as if we've been together forever. I've never felt so comfortable and happy with someone. It just feels right. All the clichés about knowing who the "right one" will be were true, at least for me. We met about six months ago at a concert at the graduate school. A friend of mine was doing me a favor and performing some of Dadi's songs on his recital. There were only a handful of people at the performance and the only person in the audience who wasn't a friend or acquaintance of mine turned out to be Carlos. We met that night at a small reception after the recital and we've been together ever since. I couldn't believe my luck that I actually found a wonderful man who was gainfully employed in the computer field and also interested in music! For the last few months, we've been basically living together. We still maintain our own separate apartments, but I think that will probably change soon, too. Boston is too expensive a place to pay for an empty apartment. If I didn't have to pay rent, I could certainly afford to buy a new computer.

As I was at the sink, rinsing my coffee cup, I glanced down at the street and saw Carlos getting out of a cab. I was so glad to see him. Even though he had been away only four days, it seemed like an eternity. I grabbed a cold Harpoon Ale out of the fridge and put it next to his favorite chair. Then I ran into the bathroom to brush my hair again and make sure that I looked presentable. I heard him and his bags banging his way into my apartment building, but he had to knock at my door. I had forgotten all about the new locks.

"Hey, what happened? What's with the new lock?" He said through the door.

I yanked the door open and hugged him and his luggage. "Oh, have I got things to tell you. Boy, do you look good."

For that I got a big, long kiss, which came to a crashing end when the garment bag slipped off his shoulder and smashed into my side. We dragged everything into the room and shut the door.

"Tell me," Carlos said while he was taking off his coat. And I did, all of it: my worries about Brownsten and the grad student in Puerto Rico, the worries Helen had spoken about, and last, the robbery. Carlos is good that way; he listens patiently while letting me babble on. I talked as he unpacked a few shirts and things. He keeps most of his stuff in my apartment. As we only live two blocks from each other, it wouldn't be a crisis if he forgot something anyway. By the time I was finished, he was settling comfortably into my rocking chair with a beer in hand, munching on Tostitos chips.

"Well, you can do what you want," he began. (He always says this, which is part of the reason I love him so much.) I waited for the "but." It was a long time coming.

"But, is the topic all that important? If you're running into brick wall after brick wall, then change topics. What about the Beethoven concerto paper you toyed with a year ago? You said you had a new analytical perspective."

"Everyone does Beethoven," I replied peevishly. After a minute, I added, "That's not really it. I've put almost a year into this. It's a good topic. The idea of starting over again makes me sick. I've already been at this degree six, no seven years. If I don't keep going now, I'll just run out of steam. Does that make sense? I feel I'm running on empty, and if I change course now, I won't have enough to finish. Did you know that eighty five percent of all people who start Ph.D. programs don't finish? I read it in the New York Times a month or so ago. If I don't finish this thing, I'll be in that eighty five percent. I'll feel like a total failure."

Carlos raised his hand, "Okay, okay. Don't beat me up about it. It just doesn't seem like this is a good subject for you to tackle. What the hell, it's already taking you too long."

"It hasn't been all that long. This program is brutal and you know it. I had to take four years of classes and then all the exams. I already passed everything I need to—comprehensives, language exams, theory exams, piano skills. I just have to finish writing this thing. Actually, I could write some kind of document now on some of Dadi's work, but I need more research to make it truly interesting. I want my dissertation to be something really good. I want to write something that is truly worth a doctorate, something that would make me really proud."

"I would write up what you've got already and forget about Spain. Make the dissertation mostly analytical and forget about the historical."

"Trust me, it's not enough. And besides, I'm really interested to know what all these other people saw. Barry even mentioned pieces that haven't been published yet."

"Well, I don't know why you're so hell-bent on this degree anyway. There are no jobs for you, even when you're done. Why not just dump it and do librarianship full-time? At least it'll pay the bills."

I was beginning to lose my temper. "Carlos, I want to be a musicologist. I want to teach. As Captain Kirk says, 'it's my first best destiny.' I don't want to do anything else." It crossed my mind then that I shouldn't be angry at him. Maybe we hadn't ever discussed this before, but how could he be so unaware of my strong feelings toward my career? It wasn't just a job—in some ways, it defined who I was. Of course I realized that there were no musicology jobs, but I kept hoping I'd be one of the lucky ones. I hoped that I'd be at the right place at the right time with the right topic in hand. And Dadi *was* a good topic. No one had really done it right before. This conversation was making me realize that we had, in fact, only been together for six months. Maybe Carlos didn't know me as well as I thought. Maybe I didn't know him as well as I thought.

Carlos sighed. "Okay, then. Let's figure out what you need to do to wrap this all up. I take it from your story that you're interested in what happened to the grad student down in Puerto Rico. I don't know that I'd go poking into things like that; you'll only be wasting valuable time. What can you possibly see there, a dark conspiracy or something? About Dadi?" He sounded so amazed that I had to laugh in spite of myself. "Even if there isn't a crazed musicologist killing people, and you're all crazed from what I can see," he added quickly, "then you've got a bunch of unfortunate accidents and a very inefficient and stubborn archivist. What do you have in mind anyway? I assume you want to go to Spain in person and demand to see things, to get the New Yorker in you going."

"That's the general plan. I also want to get to Puerto Rico. Maybe I can stop off on the way back from Europe."

"Have you tried contacting the people down there?"

"No. That's for tomorrow. I had all the information about the family on my computer and now it's all gone. I can retrace my steps, but it may take some time. My first problem is getting in touch with the people at the archive in Spain to make absolutely sure I can get in. Then I have to make plane and hotel reservations, get some money and ultimately, a new computer. Do you think that you could call your family and ask them to look around a little and get me some information about Dadi's children?"

"I don't think that'll work. I'm not really that close with my family."

"But you just went down there a month or so ago to visit them, no?"

"Even so, I don't really think I can do it. Don't you have any information at all?"

"With the computer gone, everything is gone. My outlines, bibliography, correspondence was in that thing. It is irreplaceable."

"Don't you remember I told you to back the hard disk up and keep it offsite?"

I felt like a bad little girl being scolded by her mother. I shifted uneasily in my seat. "I didn't do it. It was a good idea, but I was too lazy."

"Well, getting the information the second time around will be easier, I guess."

For the rest of the evening, we hammered out reservations and other arrangements. I have a large overdraft account at the bank, which amazingly hadn't been touched in months. I set my alarm so that I could try the archive again at three o'clock in the morning, my time–this time no answer. Not even the security guard picked up. Since I had woken up Carlos too, we put the time to good use and fooled around, pushing Jabba off the bed by accident. I got up again at four thirty and fed Jabba to make him feel loved. Then I called again. I finally got through to an assistant librarian and I told her who I was and that I was coming. I didn't ask, I just told her. She was polite and said she'd try to help me as much as she could, but with the fire and all it would be difficult. I told her that I wanted to see the archive itself and that I wouldn't be in the way of the clean up.

In the morning, I had a list of errands a mile long. My flight was in the evening so I had to make every bit of the day count. After stopping by work, the bank, the post office and the dry cleaners, I went home to pack. Carlos dropped by in the middle of the afternoon with lunch, and his computer and tons of floppies from his apartment. The cartons of Chinese food from Chef Chow's were a welcome sight. I've been going there for years and always order the same thing. Those spicy green beans are to die for, but then again, so is Carlos.

I gathered my papers and called Helen again to make sure this impromptu vacation was fine with her. Helen told me to be careful and wished me luck. I also called Jack and told him. Of course I had forgotten all about meeting him at the Pizza Palace and profusely apologized. When he heard what I had been through in the past twenty four hours, all was forgiven. Jack was the first person who was pleased that I was going to Spain. Maybe he just wants me to finish and get out of his hair, but I was happy for the encouragement nonetheless.

I then put in a call to Puerto Rico. Dadi had two children who were still living. The older child was a woman, and I had no idea where she lived or if she was still alive. But, the younger was a son and a Cardinal in the Catholic Church. He was easy to locate. I called the Catholic Diocese in San Juan and got the number to his office. Once connected, they told me that he was not in. I then found the number for the Cardinal's residences and again was told he was out, but I could talk to his personal secretary. I was put on hold for quite some time, and then a man's voice came on.

"Yes, may I help you?"

I explained who I was and what I was working on. Then I added, "Even if Cardinal Dadi doesn't have any of his father's materials, I would still like to talk to him. I could possibly get first hand accounts of premieres, compositional habits, that sort of thing. I would like to fill in our background of Enrique Dadi."

"The Cardinal is a very private man. I'm not sure that he would want to discuss family matters with you."

"Oh, yes, I understand. I certainly don't wish to pry into anything personal, but his father was an important composer, and I would just like a more complete picture of musical life at that time. You know, the music he preferred at home, things like that. I'm not going to ask anything really personal."

"I am sure there is nothing here that would interest you, Miss Maxwell. I certainly will forward your message to the Cardinal, but I can assure you that he will not be able to help you with your research."

"Well, thank you for your help. Is there a convenient time when I can speak with him myself?"

"You can try his office in the mornings. You may be able to reach him there. And I strongly suggest that you refrain from calling his private residence again." With that he hung up. I would try calling the Cardinal at another time, but hoped I wouldn't have to deal with his personal assistant again.

Carlos dropped me off at Logan Airport that evening, promising to kiss Jabba at least once a day, leaving me with my garment bag, his laptop, a briefcase of materials and my mystery. For some reason, when he pulled away from the curb, I felt very alone and uneasy. As we were boarding, I took a deep breath and got in. I don't particularly mind flying, but I hate turbulence. I had to will myself onto the plane. As I sat down, I just wanted to cry. There had been too much going on in the last few days and I had not gotten enough sleep. I wouldn't get any on the plane either. I started to read my mystery and immediately felt better knowing V.I. Warshawski was catching criminals. If she could be strong, then so could I.

C H A P T E R 3

▼

The flight was less than memorable. I tried to sleep but just couldn't. I even had a few beers but nothing made me sleepy. When we finally landed, I was grateful to be on *terra firma* again. It was about seven in the morning Madrid time and the city was just waking up. I grabbed a cab and was deposited in my hotel around eight. Of course, I couldn't check in yet, since they usually didn't allow you in the room until two or three in the afternoon. I washed my face and changed into nicer clothes in the public bathroom. I then left my things with the front desk and went in search of good, strong coffee and some breakfast. I don't know what it is but coffee in Europe is so much better than it is in the States. Even the Starbucks that now dot every street corner in Boston don't make it nearly as well as a corner bar in Spain. Maybe it's the water or the air. All I knew was that I really needed some. The strong coffee and tostada, Spain's equivalent of toast, really revived me. With caffeine in my veins and a full stomach, I felt human again. At a pay phone, I called Carlos to tell him I had gotten in safely, but he wasn't in, so I left a message. Since the hotel still didn't have my room ready, I decided to start working right away. I gathered my computer and briefcase and trekked out to the archive.

The archive was in a beautiful building with a large courtyard in the center; it was very old and stately. But as soon as you walked through the archway and entered the courtyard you could smell the fire. Smoke stains marred the outside of the building's west wing. The stench of burnt paper and wood was overpowering. There were piles of blackened books scattered outside that section of the building. My heart sank; it was worse than I had feared. I took a deep breath and picked my way to the door leading to the archive. Surprisingly, it was open–I always expect the worst. I made my way to the front desk, where a frail old man sat in a starched pristine uniform, sipping coffee from a thermos. I had an immediate picture of his wife, with her bowed back and strong, heavily veined hands ironing the uniform carefully and leaving his lunch and thermos on the kitchen table.

I explained to him who I was and why I was there. He seemed sympathetic and just slowly shook his head. I began wondering if he hadn't understood my Spanish, but he interrupted me when I started again.

"No, Miss," he said. "The Archive is closed during renovations—you see the mess outside? They are still trying to find out what is gone. I do not think you would even be able to see anything, even those things that were not burned. The water from the fire trucks made everything soaking wet. It is a real shame. So terrible, so terrible."

He shook his head sadly and looked down at his folded hands. Since he seemed willing to talk, I took the seat right opposite his little desk.

"So, I noticed that the west wing of the building was harmed, but not the east. How exactly did the fire start? What was in the west wing?"

"Well, Miss, that is the terrible thing. The east wing of the building has all the administrative offices—study rooms, conference rooms, some offices. But in the west wing we have all the materials, manuscripts, books, everything. Yes, we even had an original Goya in there—now damaged, but, thanks to God, not destroyed. We had people working on microfilming everything, but had only gotten through the C's—got everything by Chapí on film. They were going to begin the D's soon. It's such a shame, such a shame. So terrible, so terrible."

"But what started the fire?"

"I truly do not know. The fire department called the fire suspicious; I do not know what that means. How could it have started? Everything is secured on that side. We have all been so upset. The librarians have been working overtime trying to sort everything out. It will take years, believe me."

"Perhaps I could help in some way," I chimed in. "Could you speak to Rafael Gazza please? I contacted someone in his office several days ago by phone and she encouraged me to come. I work in a library back in the States, so maybe I could be of service while I'm in Madrid for the week."

The guard considered it, and picked up the phone. He punched a few numbers and spoke quickly, much more quickly than he had when talking to me. I only understood every other word. When he replaced the phone, he said, "The director will be with you soon. You may have a seat over there." He pointed to an old orange sofa in an adjoining room. "In the meantime, you may fill out the visitor's information card," which he pulled out of the desk.

I sat down where I was told, filled out the card in a few seconds and waited. The smell from the fire was overpowering and was slowly turning my stomach. After waiting for about twenty minutes, I began to get restless. My head was pounding and I was close to losing breakfast. I started to sweat a little and had to concentrate on breathing through my mouth. Just as I was about to go outside and clear my head, a handsome young man in an apron came into the waiting room.

"Dr. Maxwell?"

"Yes," I said, without blinking an eye–no point letting him know I was only ABD.

"Dr. Maxwell, it's so nice to meet you. I'm Rafael Gazza. I'm afraid we really can't help you. Everything is in such disorder, as you see."

"Well, can *I* help you? I have come such a long way. I spoke to someone here just a few days ago on the phone and explained who I was. They said to come, so here I am. If you don't want my help, could I just see the area where your Dadi pieces were kept?"

He seemed to think about that for a while. "I'm not sure who told you to come, but I assure you we didn't realize the extent of the damage. Normally we don't let anyone into the West Wing; our librarians bring the materials you wish to see to one of the conference rooms. Our books and scores have to remain secure. These are extraordinary circumstances, and our situation is terrible back there. The librarians are all busy sorting out the books and I cannot really spare any of them to help you right now. I realize you've come a long way, but I am sorry." He looked at me again. Just then, another woman came from the back, spoke quietly with the security guard for a moment and then crossed the room. She smiled at us and stopped for a moment.

She held out her hand and said "Hello, I'm Elena Rodriguez, assistant librarian."

"Leigh Maxwell. I've just come from Boston to work in the archive."

She nodded, "Yes, I heard you were coming." She glanced at Gazza, hesitated, and continued again. "Everything is in total disarray, but I overheard that you'd be willing to help us out. Well, Rafael, we could always use another hand, no? Even to pick up some of the books that weren't damaged and place them back on the carts. And you, Miss Maxwell, can get some work done at the same time."

Gazza's expression was unreadable. I couldn't tell whether he liked or disliked her, but I could tell that two minutes ago he wasn't going to let me into the West Wing and now there was a faint chance.

He looked back at me again. I tried to look trustworthy and pitiable at the same time.

"I'll do whatever you'd like. I can sort books; that's no problem. I'm a librarian, you see."

He just looked at Elena and then said hesitantly, "Sure…sure, follow me. You'll get awfully dirty. We're all in work clothes, but why not?" He smiled at me then, but I wasn't sure that the smile reached his eyes.

I looked down at my green silk suit and cream colored blouse–both favorites. No matter, I was getting into the archive at last and I didn't want to blow my chances by leaving, changing at the hotel and then coming back later. Maybe Gazza would have changed his mind by then.

Gazza, Elena and I walked down a long hallway and into the main room at the end of the west wing. It was huge with large, formal windows. Every five or six feet there was a large bookcase, but several of these were completely crumbled and reduced to rubble. The rest were standing, but books and papers were scattered about. The floor was still a sloppy, wet mess and my little Italian pumps made a god-awful slurping sound with each step. The devastation was overwhelming. I wanted to cry. It was all such a waste.

As we paused, Elena looked over at me. "Yes, I had the same feeling when I first saw it. It is tragic. I cried for an hour yesterday and again last night when I got home."

Gazza shook his head and said, "It's really not as bad as it looks. Let me bring you around and introduce you to some of the other librarians and show you what's where."

He brought me to some of the smaller rooms that were directly off the main hall. He introduced me to several people who were picking up the books, wiping them off as best they could and placing them on moveable book carts. Gazza showed me to the rooms in the back, mostly holding rare books. These rooms had not been touched. The offices to the side were now being used to house the books least damaged in the fire. These were stacked according to the composer's last name. The first name that caught my eye was Albéniz. Some first editions had been burned around the edges. A folder with some loose sheets had been tossed on top. My eyes wandered down the stacks. Bardí, Chapí, and then came the D's. My heart started racing; there were only a few D's. There were some small books, all out-of-date biographies on Dadi, most written during his lifetime, but nothing more. I knew all of these volumes already.

I turned to Gazza. "This is all the D's? No more on Dadi?"

"I'm sorry Dr. Maxwell," he said, "but the fire started near the D section. Everything has been laid to waste in that part of the archive. It was not just what we had on Dadi, but almost all the other composers from D to G. Thankfully we sent all the Manuel de Falla papers down to the Falla Archive in Granada several months ago. You're free to look through this material here and then out in the main storage area. I'm truly sorry you had to see the archive in this state. We've never had anything like this happen before. I must get back to work now. If there's anything more I can do for you, please let me know."

Once he left, I took off my jacket, and put my purse and briefcase down. I took out my Dictaphone, just in case I came across anything interesting. I started through the small pile of D's. Indeed there were the few monographs on Dadi I had already read and nothing else. I turned my attention to the A's, B's and C's, to see if anything had been misplaced. As I looked through the piles, I began to see all the dissertation topics just waiting to be discovered. Although I was exhausted and jet lag was beginning to set in, I forced myself to concentrate. I didn't know when I would ever get the chance to see these things again. For all I knew, Gazza might change his mind tomorrow.

When I finally looked up, six hours had passed and I was losing my second and third reserves of energy. Two cassettes from my Dictaphone were full. I straightened up, noticing that my four-hundred-dollar-suit was completely filthy and that my creamy silk blouse now looked tie-dyed in charcoal. I needed a shower, food and sleep. I gathered up my belongings and went looking for Gazza. In six hours, none of the librarians had disturbed me. I saw them all still working away.

Gazza was surrounded by several carts filled with books and papers. I explained that I'd be back the next morning to help. He graciously walked me to the door, explained to the security guards to let me in the next morning at nine o'clock and then left.

I got back to my hotel at about five and checked in. The bellhop sneezed loudly and looked at me as though I had leprosy. I guess I had gotten used to the sooty smell all around me at the archive. The clerk at the front desk looked up and down at my ruined clothes and asked if there was anything he could do for me. All I wanted was a room and a shower. The bellhop never even asked if he could help with my bags.

The hotel I had booked was just off Gran Via, a major road bisecting Madrid. It was cheap, but clean. The only problem was the noise. My room was right on the third floor overlooking the street. With the windows shut and the curtains drawn, the sound was still deafening.

I called down to ask about restaurants in the neighborhood and got a few recommendations. I took off my clothes and shoved them into a plastic bag, took a quick shower and changed into jeans and a sweat shirt that didn't smell.

I went to a nearby pizzeria. Being a vegetarian is sometimes difficult in the States, but being a vegetarian in Spain is even worse. I usually end up eating Italian and feeling guilty about not partaking of the local cuisine. No matter, the pizza was warm and had lots of cheese on it.

When I returned, it was just about eight o'clock. I threw myself onto the bed and shut my eyes for a moment. I must have fallen asleep because I was startled by the ring of the phone. I glanced at my watch—ten o'clock. I felt like I was being dragged out of a deep cave. I grabbed the phone, hoping it would be Carlos "Yes?"

The voice on the other end said something quickly in Spanish. Having just woken up, I didn't get it right away. I was still a bit confused as to where exactly I was. "What?" I said eloquently. "Who is this?"

There was a pause and the person said in slower Spanish, "We have a call for you."

"Yes, yes, put them through."

There was a click and then silence. "Hello?" I asked. Perhaps the lines were crossed. "Hello?" I said more loudly.

This time I was rewarded with a voice, vaguely familiar, but somewhat muffled, saying "Leigh Maxwell?"

"Yes?" I said in Spanish.

"Stay away from the archive. It's for your own good."

"Who *is* this?" By now I was wide awake. I was also getting angry and I switched to English. "What are you talking about?"

The soft voice then switched to unaccented English. "I said stay away from the archive. It's for your own good. I can't and won't explain myself further, but I wouldn't want anything to happen to you. I'm serious. You know it. Go back to Boston."

"But why would…" I began. Then I heard the click and shortly after a dial tone. I was stunned. Who knew I was here? Who knew where I was staying? Why would they call me? Was this a threat or were they really concerned for my safety?

The whole conversation sounded like a cliché in a bad murder mystery. Agatha Christie was probably laughing up a storm.

I went over and over in my mind all the people whom I had met in the archive, including the security guard. It didn't sound like him. The voice was one that I had heard before, but where? It definitely sounded muffled, as if the person had held a handkerchief up to the mouthpiece. I thought back. Yes, I had put the name of the hotel on the archive papers when I was filling out the visitor information card, but I hadn't told anyone else.

Then I thought about the call itself. Was it local? Was it long distance? I got up in a hurry and went down to the receptionist. She had no idea where the call originated. I explained it all to her and she insisted on calling the police. By the time they arrived and listened to my story, the urgency had gone, and I wasn't too sure whether it was someone concerned for me or threatening me. Since there was basically not much they could do, they kindly told me to go back to bed and forget the whole thing. By their standards nothing had really happened.

By that time, I was so tired that I readily agreed. The whole story was sounding strange to me too. Was it really a mad musicologist defending his work on Dadi? Still, I couldn't shake the feeling that something serious was going on. I went back upstairs and sank into bed again. Two o'clock. If I was to get to the archive at nine it meant I should be up by seven, and that would mean only five hours of sleep.

I tried to sleep, but couldn't. My father always used to say to me that he had to "sleep fast" if he only had a few hours. Even though that old joke was comforting, I was still on edge. I turned on the radio and shut my eyes–still no sleep. I started to read my book, and around five o'clock I finally drifted off. It was a disturbed, anxious sleep, full of dark alleys and missed trains. I was grateful when my wake-up call came at seven. Though not rested at all, I felt better to see the sun through the curtains. I dressed in jeans and a sweater, ate quickly in the hotel and was at the archive at nine o'clock sharp.

CHAPTER 4

▼

The security guard was again at his post and waved me in as soon as I crossed the threshold.

"Good morning, good morning, Miss. You can go right in. A few people are here already, I think."

I went into the main room and, unable to find Gazza, sat down for a chat with Elena Rodriguez. She seemed a little less harried than the day before and we talked in general about the collection. She then gave me a mini-tour of the rare books in the rooms off of the main holding room. She also showed me some wonderful sheets of manuscript written by Barbieri, a Spanish composer famous for his *zarzuelas*. In all, we spent a wonderful hour talking and sifting through some of the exciting materials the archive held.

I felt very comfortable with her and at the end of our impromptu tour we began talking about our personal lives. I found out that she was a single mother of two with the equivalent of a master's degree in singing. She was lovely and open and I felt relaxed with her. I decided I should ask her about some of the Dadi things I had been hoping to find at the archive. At the mention of Dadi's name, however, she completely withdrew. The smiling open face was replaced by a somewhat shifty expression. She absolutely refused to look me in the eye.

"Can you tell me anything about these pieces I've been looking for? Anything at all? Were they all destroyed?" I asked after a bit of a pause.

She looked around the room as if there were someone stalking her and then looked down at the floor. She was quiet for a long time.

"Please, I've come such a long way, and I really need to find these materials." I hoped to add an element of guilt to the scenario–it always seemed to work on me. I knew she could tell me something, but I just didn't know what.

Finally, she let out a small sigh as if she had lost an inner battle.

"Okay, let me tell you all I know about this." Her voice was barely a whisper, but now she looked right into my eyes and I could tell from her serious expression that she was deeply frightened. "I started working here about a year ago–you know there's not much work available for performers. This seemed ideal at first. I only work twenty five hours a week, but I make enough money to live. I also sing when I can get jobs, so I'm doing fine. About six months ago, we got some additional funding to catalog some of these rare manuscripts that I've been showing you. I was given the job since I was familiar with the collection by then and we hired another part-time person to shelve books and the like. You know, she does the boring parts of the job. It was wonderful, finally going through all we have. You're a librarian, you know. If people don't have access to the material, you may as well not have it." She slowed down so I nodded and murmured something reassuring, I hoped. She took another deep breath and continued.

"I started with the big composers, the ones more people wanted to know about. I was told I could start where I wanted, so I began with Albéniz. It took over a month just to get him organized." She paused again.

"To make a long story short, I got to Dadi three months ago. I'm a fan, you see, so I was particularly looking forward to working on his scores. We had quite a bit of it, but I got a few strange phone calls after I started. I told Rafael that someone had called and told me to leave the Dadi papers alone. I couldn't figure out how this person knew what I was working on. Rafael told me to do more on Barbieri, but I had already started Dadi and didn't want to stop. And, you were there, writing to us about once a month, if not more," she paused and smiled at me, "and I wanted to see if we had the materials you needed. You see, we couldn't give you access until we knew what we had, so I decided to keep going. About a month ago, I received another phone call. It sounded like it was long distance and I didn't recognize the voice, but the person said to lay off Dadi or something terrible would happen. I told Rafael about it again. He seemed puzzled and started going through everything himself to see if there was anything particularly disturbing or harmful to anyone. I don't know. But he told me to leave it alone and get on with the other work. Frankly, we had a fight about it. I was getting frightened and wanted to know, first of all, how anyone knew what I was working on, and second, what did it matter that I was going through the material? I supposed I thought that if I knew what the problem was, I could just fix it. So, I kept going, even after he told me to stop. This time I kept detailed notes on everything I was doing. I also took photographs of some of the important pages. Rafael doesn't even know about that. I'm sure it's against the law or something." She looked at me again for a long time and took my hand. Hers was clammy and cold, but I held onto it firmly nonetheless.

"I feel so much better telling someone this," she whispered. "Thank you for listening." She barreled on, "Several days after, I came home to find my house robbed. They had taken some notebooks and things, but nothing really valuable, except my camera. That scared me. The police didn't have much hope of recovering anything. My daughters cried all night; they were so frightened. Nothing like this had ever happened to them. Luckily, I didn't have the pictures at home. The film was being developed. My camera was a loss, but nothing more than that. After I put the house in order, I came to the conclusion that they were after my Dadi notes so I stopped working on them. Why not take the TV or jewelry or something? In the Dadi papers were manuscripts for music he never published. Song cycles, sonatas, a solo guitar piece. I sang through some of the songs. They were very different from his usual style, but beautiful nonetheless. In fact, a few were in French and really sounded unlike anything he'd done before. I thought this was a major find. No one had even touched these things before. Along with the papers were some letters, personal letters that have never been published. They were love letters to Dadi, signed simply, 'Your true love.' They were moving and beautiful and very poetic, often quoting from various Spanish and French poems. I copied them in my notebooks, all lost now. But I remember being intrigued about who the writer could possibly be. You know Dadi's biography? These letters were dated before and during his marriage. I checked some of the correspondence we have from his wife and the handwriting didn't match, not at all."

Elena paused again. Rafael chose that moment to pop in. We were startled and Elena must have looked a bit guilty or frightened or both. I laughed, if a bit forced, and said "Oh, you caught us chatting. I was just hearing about Elena's family."

Rafael looked at me then at Elena, then back to me. He said, "Well, we should be getting to work. All of us are in the conference room. We were waiting for you to begin the morning meeting, Elena. We didn't realize you were in this back room." He turned on his heel and left abruptly.

I turned back to Elena. Her cheeks were red and she seemed very uncomfortable. I took her hands in mine and she seemed to study them. "Thank you for telling me all this," I said quietly. "I know it must be hard and because of all that's happened, you probably don't trust many people anymore, but you can trust me. I'm going to continue my work. I don't know what all this means, but I'm going to find out. I'm stubborn that way. I really appreciate all you've done." When I finished, I let go of her hand. She looked up then, her dark eyes had tears in them and she seemed grateful to me.

"Leigh, please come to my house this evening for dinner. I can pick up those photos for you. You can have them. I'm not going on. The robbery, now the fire. You see, I'm sure the fire started in the D's. I'm sure it was no coincidence. I'm truly frightened now, and, frankly, I have to think of my daughters."

"I've thought the same thing about the fire, Elena, but really what could be so important that people would set fire to an archive or steal notebooks, or my computer for it? But I'd love to come tonight."

"Your computer?"

"Yes, I had a robbery also, but I'll tell you all about it tonight."

Elena nodded and then gave me her address. It was close to my hotel. She told me to be there at nine thirty or so, the typical dinnertime in Spain. She got her purse and left for the meeting. I continued working in the back room, sifting through material. Finally, many hours later, Rafael came to tell me they were closing.

On our way out, he asked if I had had a pleasant chat with Elena. I became immediately wary. All day it felt as if he had kept an eye on me. Once outside, I left him with a curt goodbye and told him I'd be back the next day. I went straight to the hotel to change and shower, and maybe even have a little nap. My lack of sleep was making me edgy and probably a little paranoid.

CHAPTER 5

▼

I got to my room and started to transcribe some of the notes I had taken using the Dictaphone. I was concentrating so intently that the ringing of the phone startled me. I glanced at my watch. Damn. Almost nine o'clock already. When I picked up the phone, the operator said that I had a call. She put it through, but all I heard was a click. My first thought was that the operator probably had made some kind of mistake and disconnected the caller. While I waited for the return phone call, I dressed quickly and got ready to go to Elena's. I often joke with my friends that I can dress, put on makeup and look put together in under eight minutes. Sometimes, I'm not sure they believe me. That night I broke my own record, six minutes flat, and I was ready to leave. No one had called back, and I really needed an evening of relaxation, if not sleep, so I left the room and made my way downstairs. Homemade food, a nice family and maybe some robust Spanish wine, the kind that takes the enamel off your teeth, was just what I needed.

I thought of walking to Elena's since it was fairly close to the hotel, but when I got to the lobby I realized it was raining steadily. Of course, I didn't have an umbrella, much less a hat, so I decided to take a taxi. I had to wait for one to arrive. It seemed that the entire population of Madrid had decided they needed a taxi at the same time. I spent my time sitting by the bellhop in an overstuffed red velvet chair that was so comfortable that it very quickly lulled me into a meditative state. I kept going over in my mind all the things that had happened in the last few days. I sorely missed Carlos and wished he had been there with me. I really wanted to talk with him, but had been unable to get in touch since I had landed in Spain. I realized then that wanting someone along to help you was not necessarily the same thing as being clingy, dependent and weak. I had spent the last several years trying to convince myself that I didn't *need* anyone, much less a boyfriend, but since we started seeing each other about six months ago, I realized that Carlos was different. I just *wanted* to have him along.

I always want to do things just to prove to myself that I can do them, my doctorate being the most obvious example. I am always trying to convince myself that I am strong and that I don't need anyone, that I can be a wonder woman and take care of myself and everyone else around me. Carlos has tried to convince me that depending on people is not a sign of weakness, but in fact one of strength. I'm not sure about that and I guess I still have my doubts. As I mulled over my relationship with Carlos, I hadn't noticed that my cab had come and was waiting at the curb. The bellhop signaled to me that my cab was there. As I snapped out of my reverie and started through the front door of the hotel, a tall man came out of nowhere and folded himself neatly into my small, yellow Fiat taxi which pulled quickly away from the curb. As soon as I realized what was happening, even my best New York "Hey" couldn't stop it. Luckily, another cab was pulling up and I quickly jumped in, probably absconding with someone else's ride. I told the driver where I was headed and glanced at my watch. I could still be on time.

I looked out of the window as we pulled away only to see the same tall man getting out of the first cab that I had missed. He glanced my way and I had a strange feeling I had seen him before. I was frustrated that I couldn't place the face and tried all the tricks I knew to wrest it from the far recesses of my exhausted brain.

I'm not that great at remembering faces–or names either–but voices are another story. No one really believes me when I can figure out who the actors are under the makeup they use in *Star Trek*, but it is the voice that I recognize. Who else would have figured out that one Cardassian was actually the Evil Being from the movie *Time Bandits*? Carlos bet me a nice dinner at Hammersleys on that one and I enjoyed every scrumptious bite of it. But faces are hard for me. I sometimes feel like Humpty Dumpty when he says to Alice that she looks like all other human beings because she has two eyes, a nose and a mouth.

The tall man stood at the curb as my taxi slowly pulled into traffic. As soon as he glanced my way, some instinct told me to be afraid of him and I sat back, afraid that he would notice my stare. I huddled in the corner of the taxi and listened to the hypnotic sound of the wipers as I waited for inspiration to come. When the ride ended a few minutes later, the driver stopped on a small, dark street with rows of dark apartment buildings on either side. I glanced at my watch; it had taken us about ten minutes to get here.

"Are you sure this is the address?" I asked the driver, while looking about on the dark street.

"Yes, yes. 1200 pesetas," he replied, sounding somewhat annoyed and rushed. I looked up and down the street, reluctant to get out of the car. I had no umbrella and the rain was coming down in sheets. I didn't see one street sign, no movement, no cars, nothing. We seemed very far away from the bustle of the Gran Via.

I paid the driver and asked him to wait until I got inside the house. As I closed the door he peeled off and there I was in the rain with the address on a small piece of white paper clenched in my hand. I had absolutely no idea where I was.

I walked to the nearest building searching for a number. My feet were soaked immediately and water squelched through my toes. First, my favorite Italian pumps were ruined by the soot at the Archives and now my comfortable flats were soaked through. I was quickly running out of shoes.

The first building was actually boarded up and I began to shake. I glanced around but there was still no sign of life. I started walking up the street only to notice a man walking toward me on the opposite side. He had a large umbrella that covered his face, but I could tell that he was tall and thin and he had on the same tan color raincoat that the taxi thief had been wearing. I decided to try some aggressive body language I learned in my self-defense course, so I stood up even straighter and started literally marching down the sidewalk, trying to appear tough and sure of where I was going, instead of uncertain and scared. As I neared the man, I sped up so that I was practically running. He hesitated for a moment, looked up and down the street and started to cross to my side. I picked up speed, but knew he would be behind me any second. Should I turn and face him? Should I confront him and scream? How good was my self-defense course anyway? The first thing they taught me was to avoid situations like this, but when actually confronted with one, would my training kick in? As I thought all these things in a split second, I knew at once that I would be absolutely worthless if I had to get tough. I'd love to be strong like that and able to kick someone to defend myself, but I wasn't sure I could actually strike. My mother had always said that violence in any way was deplorable. That lesson had stuck and while I may have been an imposing figure at five foot nine, in spite of my self-defense training, my knees were so weak and shaky that in fact, I probably couldn't have kicked a tin can. I felt like I was just a big marshmallow inside.

Luckily, at that moment, a car turned into the street and began making a three-point turn. I ran toward it and knocked on the driver's window. He almost jumped through the roof with surprise, but he did open his window a crack.

"Please help me," I panted, "I believe I'm lost and have just flown into Madrid yesterday. Would you please drop me at the nearest metro station?" I glanced nervously over at the man with the umbrella. He had stopped completely and seemed to be waiting for the outcome of my conversation. The driver took a look at me, and must have figured I was just what I appeared to be, a cold, drenched, scared American. He sounded like an angel when he said, "Okay, hop in the car."

My mother always said, "God protects fools and drunks." Since I hadn't had any wine yet, I was definitely the fool. I got in and we drove away. The man with the umbrella crossed the street and disappeared from my line of vision. As soon as we were back on a main thoroughfare, I began to breathe easier. My knees were still shaking, but I was safe, out of the rain for a few minutes and on my way to a metro stop.

The driver's name turned out to be Javier. He was twenty two and a new grad student at the Complutense in Madrid. He, himself, had been lost and had turned into the street to get back on the main thoroughfare going in the opposite direction. He had a map in the car and, seeing how upset I was, insisted on driving me to Elena's house, which we managed to reach in just five minutes with me directing him from the passenger seat. We exchanged addresses and I thanked him at least twenty times for helping me out. I decided that I would send him flowers or something nice since I felt that he had truly been a knight in shining armor. And, like a real gentleman, he waited until I got into the front vestibule and waved good-bye before he left the curb.

I rang the doorbell and Elena let me in. Her apartment was small, but warm and inviting. When she opened the door, she let out an exclamation of disbelief. "Oh, no. I hope you didn't walk over; it's pouring outside. You're wet." The words reminded me suddenly of the *Rocky Horror Picture Show,* when Riff-Raff says to Brad and Janet as they are standing in the rain, "You're wet." Maybe I've seen the movie too often, but I laughed aloud when Elena echoed Riff-Raff's line, partly since I've always loved the movie and partly out of sheer relief to be there. Elena was the perfect hostess. She took my drenched coat and gave me a glass of strong red wine and a towel for my hair. I went into the bathroom to get as dry as possible. I toweled off, combed my hair, got as much of the mascara off my cheeks as I could and took off my drenched shoes. I felt much better afterwards.

Elena was very sympathetic when I told her all about my ordeal. She kept shaking her head and exclaimed that it was terrible what taxi drivers were like nowadays, but she seemed to believe that it was all a simple misunderstanding. I, on the other hand, was convinced the whole thing had been staged. The taxi driver was probably in on it too. Why had the tall man taken my cab and then gotten out only one block later? How had he appeared just a minute later on the street where I was dropped off? True, I hadn't seen his face the second time, but it seemed like too much of a coincidence. I decided to drop it for the time being, since I would probably upset Elena with my grand conspiracy theories.

Dinner was wonderful. Elena had made lots of different dishes because she wasn't sure what I ate. So, I had salad, bread, cheese and olives–my favorite kind of dinner. Elena ate the sausage she was so fond of, and when I declined because I didn't eat meat, she graciously said that it would make a great lunch the next day. The wine flowed, Elena's children were animated and excited to have a guest all the way from America. After they were put to bed and the last of the dishes had been cleared away, Elena and I got down to business.

She brought out some photographs and even from these I could tell she had discovered something of great value. Sheaves of notated manuscript paper were depicted. They were pieces I didn't recognize. Several different styles of hand-writing were evident on a few of the compositions I looked at. All along the margins of the paper, and even in between the staves, was writing in a language that I had never seen before. Unfortunately, the photos were so small I couldn't be sure of what I was looking at sometimes.

"Elena, these are marvelous but I don't know these pieces. I thought I was familiar with everything Dadi had written, but I just don't know these."

"Yes, these are some of the ones that were unpublished. I started taking photos, and I got through about half of them. There are over one hundred fifty photos I took and here are all the negatives. You take them all. I really want nothing to do with it any longer."

As I looked through the photos, I could tell that this was a significant find. I just couldn't place the year or the time when these pieces had been written. A few piano works seemed to be in a handwriting I recognized. Some of it looked like Dadi's but some looked like another person's. The photos were too small, the standard 4x6 from the photo shop, so I just couldn't tell what all the writing was around the edges.

"Elena, these are terrific. I'm so glad you have them. Maybe we should keep a copy here so that if anything happens to me…"

She abruptly cut me off. "No, you take them all. I don't want anything to do with it. Please just take them. I feel better now knowing that they will be out of here and in good hands."

I looked through them some more.

"Elena, when were these written? Could you tell? The handwriting seems to change often and with the writing on the sides and bottoms, well, it's just weird, I don't recognize the language. Russian maybe, I'm not sure."

Elena grew a little animated and leaned toward the photos. She pointed to one in particular. "Leigh, this is the interesting part. I believe this was all written during the Great War, you know, between 1914 and 1918. Dadi was in France most of the time. We can't pinpoint his whereabouts for some periods, but he was there. He seems to have disappeared for months at a time and no one has really dealt with this issue. I've looked in the biographies, but they are vague and all they say is that he had been living in France just outside of Paris those three years. I've discovered some letters, though, that indicate he was gone and unreachable.

"One letter was written by Manuel de Falla from Spain to Dadi's friend Maurice Delage, who also had remained in France. Falla was complaining that Dadi was to have been in Madrid for a concert or something, but didn't show. Delage wrote back and said that Dadi had left two months before and that everyone assumed he had been heading for Spain. The paper these pieces were written on is French, mostly. There's some other paper with a watermark I don't recognize. And again, there's a whole sheaf of things on German paper."

I was somewhat startled at that. "German paper, Elena? You couldn't get it during the war, except of course in Germany. There was no trade of that sort of thing. German." I paused to think this through. "Elena, did you check out when and where that paper was sold and made?"

A proud smile lit up her face. "Yes, I did. It was only available in Berlin between 1915 and 1920. One piece was dated July, 1916. Did you see it? That's one of the dates when we can't confirm Dadi's whereabouts. Now what do you think of that?"

This was getting very interesting. I shook my head and mused out loud. "What was Dadi doing in Berlin in July of 1916 and what is all this writing around the edges? What could he have been doing? And how in the world did he get in and out so easily? No one knew where he was."

Elena looked thoughtful. "Yes, I asked myself these same questions. I got some people in Berlin involved with trying to find Dadi. Several were working on it just before the fire. I haven't heard from them, but we'll see. I can write down their names and numbers and you can contact them if you wish. You could tell them that you were working with me on the project. I don't have much hope that they'll find anything since lots of stuff was lost during the bombing in World War II. That's probably why they haven't responded yet."

Elena wrote everything down. It was getting late and I was tired. Lack of rest, good red wine, and a filling meal had taken me past sleepy straight to exhausted. Probably the remnants of the mascara on my cheeks made me look even worse than I felt. Elena suggested that I stay the night with her, but I wanted to get into my own T-shirt and figure out my next move.

We called a taxi and I made it back to my hotel without incident. I had at least six hours to get some much-needed sleep. Before leaving Elena's house, I had put the pictures in a plastic bag underneath my damp coat so that no one could see that I had taken anything with me. I thought it best to be cautious. I got into my hotel room, locked the door, slid the safety bar in place and then pushed a chair in front of it, something I had never done before in my life. I checked if there were any messages from Carlos–still nothing. I then unplugged the phone, got into my favorite *Star Trek* T-shirt with Picard's face all over my chest saying "Make it so," and slept soundly for the next five hours. It was not as long as I needed, but it felt good nonetheless.

CHAPTER 6

▼

I woke up the next morning and decided not to go to the archive. Besides, it was Saturday and I wasn't sure if Elena would be in or not. I didn't want to go in if she wasn't there. My work now was clear. I had to sort through the photographs Elena had given me, figure out their significance and then maybe even try to transcribe some of the pieces. I had to figure out what Dadi had been doing in Berlin during World War I and what in the world the scribbling around the margins of the pieces meant. I had seen Dadi's handwriting numerous times, and even though I couldn't decipher what the words meant, or even what language it was, it seemed to me that this was his writing. The music was another story. Some of it was beautifully written and looked almost printed. Others looked thrown on the page by Jackson Pollock. None of it looked like Dadi's hand. So, I called the archive and left a message for Rafael Gazza to say that I wasn't feeling well and would not be in. Then, I drew up a list of things to do. Making lists always helps me organize and get ready to do work. I'm anal about it. I even include things like 'lunch' and 'dinner' to make myself feel better when I get to cross them both off. Of course, I may skip 'post office' or 'bank' but I never do skip 'lunch' or 'dinner.'

First, I had to get copies of Elena's photos made and enlarged. I got out of the hotel early, found a camera store and waited for my photos to be done. I paid a premium to have them done right away, but figured American Express would like the business. I had two regular sets made and one enlarged–each picture blown up to 8 x 11. The two smaller sets I sent express to the U.S. I sent one set to Carlos and another to Jack.

That done, I went back to the hotel and began to look carefully at the enlarged photos. I wished that I had the originals to see if there was anything that the camera missed–watermarks, erasures, imprints, whatnot–but instead of complaining, I felt grateful to have the photos at all. The originals were probably a blackened soggy mass right now anyway.

After several hours, I wasn't much further along, so I decided to call Carlos and tell him all about my adventures so far. It was good to hear his voice.

"Jabba's fine. You shouldn't worry about him so much," he said when he heard my voice. "He's white and fat and sleeping as we speak."

"Carlos, I miss you, too," I said somewhat sarcastically.

"Yeah, you miss the cat more."

"Well, at least the cat doesn't go on business trips every other day or snore too loudly. But, seriously, I want to tell you all about what's been going on. First of all, I sent you a package of photos of Dadi's music. Can you believe it? It's music that hasn't been published. They were taken by one of the librarians here before the fire. No one knows about them. They don't seem to be by Dadi. In fact they're kind of simple and not in any style I recognize, but they are new. This is what I've been looking for! There's also some writing all along the edges of the pieces. I can't figure it out. At any rate, there are about one hundred fifty photos. Keep them safe. One interesting thing, though–it appears Dadi was in Berlin for some time during the first World War. What do you think of that?"

"That's odd. A Spaniard living in Paris going to Berlin during World War I? But which librarian took the photos? Did he give them to anyone else?"

"No she didn't. But keep the copies I sent you safe, okay? They're really important, I think."

"Who was it, and what's on the papers, Leigh? What does the writing say?"

"Carlos, I don't know the language at all. It looks like Russian maybe, but I'm not sure. Something Slavic, but I can't tell what. I've got some manuscript paper and I'm going to be transcribing a piece or two. I'll call the librarian in Berlin in a little while and see what's up there and if anyone got any further on the question of what Dadi had done in Berlin. I'm thinking of going to Berlin myself. What do you think?"

Carlos paused. "Leigh, why don't you just come home now? I mean, you have some pieces that haven't been published. Just come home and figure it out from here."

"Carlos, I think it may be important to go now, since I'm already halfway there. I'm going to call the librarians in Berlin today. Even though it's Saturday, they might be open. I'll take it from there and see what they say. I'll be fine.

Everyone's been really nice here and these photos are great. Once the dissertation is done, I'll be famous! No problem finding a job in musicology then!"

Carlos laughed. "Well, let's cross that bridge, you know. But let me know your plans. Do you want me to meet you in Berlin? I could, you know. I've got time at work and plenty of frequent flyer miles."

My defense mechanisms kicked in. "I can do this myself," I said more sternly that I had intended, but I continued anyway. "I'll see what the people in Berlin say and then make up my mind. I'll let you know."

"Leigh, I never said you couldn't, but do you *want* my help?"

I softened up. "Carlos, I love you and you'll be the first person I ask when I need help, okay?"

"Okay, okay. I love you, you know. I just want to be there for you."

"You always have been; you're a doll. But, I should go. This is costing a fortune. I'll call and tell you my plans. Look for the package. I mailed it to your office. Don't tell anyone what you have. I've got to go. Love you."

"Bye Leigh." With that he was gone. I began to feel that I might have been too hasty turning down his offer, but if I really needed his help, he would be there; I just knew it. Right now, I needed to call Berlin and figure out what I was going to do. If Berlin had nothing, then I might as well go home with my booty.

I called the librarians in Berlin, but only one was working on Saturday and he was not available just then. I left my name and number. I made a mental note that I should call back in an hour or so. As soon as I put the phone in its cradle, it began to ring. I jumped a foot off the bed, making me realize just how on edge I was. The operator patched me in and I heard Elena's voice.

"Leigh, are you okay? Rafael said you called to say you were sick and wouldn't be in to work at the archive. Is everything all right? I was afraid some of the food was bad."

"No, Elena, everything is fine. I think it's a combination of too much red wine and jet lag catching up with me. I've got a terrible headache." That wasn't too far from the truth.

"I'm sorry to hear that. I was sick all last night. Some stomach flu or something, maybe food poisoning."

"Is there anything I can do for you Elena?"

"No. I called the doctor and he said it was probably the sausages that were bad, but I just bought them yesterday afternoon. No matter. I'm so glad you are a vegetarian and didn't eat them. I'm much better now, but I am still at home."

I wondered if the food poisoning had been a coincidence too. "Is there anything I can do for you?"

"No thank you. Do you need anything?"

"Elena, I have a call in to Berlin to speak with a librarian named Johann Spurber, but I haven't heard back from him yet, so I'll wait here today. Thanks again for last night. It was really wonderful."

She interrupted me; "I'll put a call into Berlin for you too. I'll tell them that we are working together. I'll talk with you later. Bye."

I put down the phone and continued working. It was a while before she called back.

"Leigh, I'm sorry it took so long. Believe it or not, Johann Spurber from Berlin called the archive too. He was checking to see if it was all right to talk to you. He's got some information and will call you at your hotel in just a bit. I should go. I may go to the archive for a bit later. Rafael sounded a bit lost without me. I'll talk to you later. Feel better." She hung up so quickly, I didn't even get to say good-bye. I was pleased, though, that the people in Berlin had tried to call her. Leave it to the Germans to be efficient.

Ten minutes later the phone rang and the operator put Johann Spurber through.

"Dr. Maxwell?" he asked in heavily accented, though perfect, English. I didn't tell him I wasn't a doctor yet, since I figured that Germans, including my own father, just loved titles of any type.

"Yes, this is Dr. Maxwell. Is this Johann Spurber? I've just gotten off the phone with Elena Rodriguez."

"Oh, that's good. Did she tell you our findings?"

"No, she said that you would fill me in."

Johann paused. "Well, Dr. Maxwell."

"Please call me Leigh."

"Well…Leigh," he said somewhat reluctantly; being a German official he must have found it very difficult to dispense with formalities, "In our collection, there are many things that will be of interest to you. Miss Rodriguez sent us quite a number of photocopies as well as a few originals on loan." I realized Elena hadn't told me that some of the originals were in fact safe. Maybe she just forgot that she had loaned them out.

Johann continued, "We've managed to find out where the paper was manufactured. Also, we've deciphered some of the writing along the outside. On my own, I took the originals to a friend who is a handwriting specialist. It is Dadi's handwriting on the outside, but the music is in six different people's handwriting here. I could show you all this, but it is difficult on the phone. Perhaps you have access to a fax machine."

"Would it be best for me to come to Berlin? I could arrange that in a day or two."

"Well, yes, of course, that would be best. Then you could take back the originals to Miss Rodriguez or maybe Dadi's heirs."

"Dadi's heirs?" I asked. Since getting stonewalled on the phone, I figured that there was nothing for me in Puerto Rico.

"Oh, yes. His son is quite interested in gathering his father's material. I believe he may be starting some type of archive himself. Some of these materials may be on loan from the family. I'm not sure. Miss Rodriguez could tell you."

I was surprised by the fact that Johann thought Dadi's son had some of his father's materials. The Cardinal's secretary had led me to believe that the Cardinal did not seem interested in his father's work. Why had he lied about it? Maybe there were other family members I didn't know about.

"Is the son Cardinal Dadi? Was there more than one son?"

"No. Enrique Dadi had just the one son and one daughter, both now living in Puerto Rico. Have you been in contact with the Cardinal? He's a very pleasant person. He came personally to Berlin to see some of our things about a year ago."

"No, I've never met either of them. I called Puerto Rico, but the Cardinal's personal secretary told me there was nothing of interest for me there. I'll have to call again and see if I can talk to the Cardinal himself. Maybe he'll be more helpful than his secretary. But first, I'll make reservations for Berlin and will be there in a few days. I could travel on Sunday and be at your office on Monday. Will you be available?"

"Yes, I will be in on Monday morning. Do you need any help with reservations or anything?"

"No, no. I have a few family members who live in the area and will probably stay with them. Thank you again for your help. I'll call when I have the reservations and all."

I called several airlines and booked overpriced flights for the following day. I also called a cousin who actually does live in Berlin. I hadn't seen her in five years since my father's sixty-fifth birthday party in Florida.

She answered the phone on the fifth ring. "Uebler."

I never get used to that–answering the phone with your last name.

"Steffi? This is Leigh Maxwell." I said in very rusty German.

"Leigh, is everything all right? Is your Dad well?" She responded in beautiful English with a slight German/British tint to it. I hate that. I always feel so inept in languages, and my relatives in Germany always speak English better than I speak German.

"Everything's good, Steffi. Don't worry, Daddy's fine. Running around too much as usual, but doing well. He keeps laughing every time it snows in Boston. He just doesn't understand that I actually like snow. I can't believe it has been over five years since I saw you."

"It doesn't really feel that long. Your Dad keeps us up on all the current events. How's the dissertation going?"

I guess she didn't know that was a no-no question to ask doctoral students, but it did give me an in. "Well, it's going fine. I'm actually calling from Spain right now and am planning to come to Berlin for a few days. I just found out that I need to see some things there. I know you still work at the Pension Schwartzer Adler and was wondering if you could get me a room there like you did seven or eight years ago when I last visited."

"Sure, Leigh. It's off-season anyway. It will be nice to see you and I'll get you the family rate. It's gone up a bit, but still it's only 35 Euros for family. But, you know you can always stay with me and Heinz at the apartment instead."

I knew Steffi and her son Heinz lived in cramped quarters, so I declined and said that I would love to stay at the Pension where she worked. It's a wonderful little place with feather beds, clean crisp white sheets and big old tubs with plenty of hot water. Steffi has worked there for over twenty five years. I just couldn't imagine staying in a job that long. While talking to her, I realized I was really looking forward to seeing her. There is nothing like having family that you actually like. Steffi is a lot of fun. She visits my Dad in Florida about once a year. All she does is sit in the sun and tan. No use telling her it isn't any good for her skin—she does it anyway. I was looking forward to seeing Heinz too. Last time I was in Berlin, he was away with his father and the time before he was only seven. My Dad tells me he's now six feet tall and into Techno music and black leather. Not a lot different from some of the students I've taught. I couldn't wait to see him.

I gave Steffi my flight times and she promised to pick me up. Good thing too, since the airport is quite a ways from downtown and a cab would have been very expensive. I got off the phone and felt that I was making headway. Thank God American Express doesn't have a credit limit, since I sure was spending money like water. I had no idea how I would pay for it all, but decided that there was nothing I could do but just keep going.

I started to look over the photographs again, but what I had told Elena wasn't far from the truth. Jet lag was hitting me hard or maybe it was just a week of too little sleep. The wine from last night had left me with what I call "my red wine headache," right behind the eyes. So, like a good scholar, I pushed the papers to one side of the bed and settled in for a nap.

CHAPTER 7

▼

My nap was so successful that I woke up with my mouth wide open in a pool of drool that spread all over the left side of my face. My bones felt as if they had been pulled into the bed by extra gravity and subsequently unable to move. I uncurled my aching body slowly and sat up. It was nine in the evening. I was just in time for dinner. I went to a small Spanish bar right around the corner from the hotel. It was very old and cramped, with worn wooden floors and large windows with flaking gold writing claiming that it had been in operation since 1758. I didn't doubt it. I decided to eat lightly to save both calories and money, so I ordered a caña–a small glass of beer–and just feasted on the tapas that came with it. Spanish bars have the right idea; they give you a little to drink and a little to eat at the same time. My free food was *ali oli*, a wonderful mix of mayonnaise, garlic, and potatoes. Okay, I guess not so light in calories, but delicious nonetheless. I had a few beers, each one was only about forty cents, and watched the people in the seats near the window. It was smoky and dim inside the bar. I swear every person in Spain smokes. RJ Reynolds is making a fortune here. I noticed the sawdust on the floor needed changing; cigarette butts and crumpled white napkins dotted the worn, wavy wood. I ordered another beer and was beginning to relax amidst the press of humanity. I then began scrutinizing the people standing along the bar as I was, and finally stopped short when I reached a tall man in a tan raincoat with his back toward me. He was obviously there by himself, not speaking to anyone. A squirt of adrenaline surged through my body. He was the only one in the bar wearing a coat, and he had what appeared to me to be only a glass of mineral water in front of him.

I didn't want to believe it was the same man from the taxi ride. After all, lots of people have tan raincoats. But, there was something in his stance that seemed familiar. I trusted my gut instinct that told me I was in danger and I knew instantly that I should get out of there. I asked the bartender where the bathroom was. Luckily it was toward the back of the building next to a rear door. I decided to walk past the tall man and look him in the eyes. I had caught a glimpse of him when I was in the back seat of the cab, so maybe I would remember the face. I needed to know if I was getting too paranoid or if I had reason to fear for my safety.

As I walked past him, he turned toward the bar and away from me again so that I couldn't get a good look at him. I was sure that as soon as my back was turned he would look to see where I was going, so I stopped and bent down, supposedly to check the shoelaces on my Reeboks. I glanced back and saw his face. It was the same one as the other night–pale skin and black eyes with a flat look that made me shiver. His eyes seemed to chill the entire space around him. Even the people next to him at the bar gave him a little extra room by leaning a bit too far toward the people they were with.

I hurried to the bathroom, noticing that the rear door was locked and bolted, and tried to decide what to do next. I had to get out of the bar and back to my hotel room somehow. The next day I'd be off to Berlin and safety. As I stood in the bathroom, trembling, wondering what I should do, two women came in chattering loudly. One was dark and tall with big hair and the other was a smaller, somewhat washed-out version of her friend. They spoke in Spanish so quickly that I had trouble figuring out exactly what they were saying. They were also using lots of slang that I just didn't know.

"Oh, I can't believe he asked me that. How incredible. And he's been sleeping with Angela's sister all this time? I'm leaving as soon as I'm done here," the dark one said to the other. It was clear from her tone of voice that she was utterly excited by the idea that "he" was sleeping around and had obviously propositioned her.

The other one twittered while dabbing hot pink lipstick on her thin lips. "Oh, Felicia," she trilled, "I've heard he also slept with Angela just last week." The last few words in her sentence were punctuated by small breaths in between "last" and "week." She seemed a bit breathless from all the excitement.

I have never understood twittering girls. I've never been able to master the technique. Sometimes I feel that I just don't fit in with other women. I like cars and stereos and drinking beer. Growing up, I never read *Tiger Beat Magazine* or *Seventeen*. I never cared, and still don't, I guess, about how much weight I could lose by eating only grapefruit or what shades of nail polish were "in" this year. Ever since I can remember, I've read *Car and Driver*, much to my father's glee and my mother's disapproval. I don't fit in. Maybe that's why I chose musicology; we're all just a bunch of kids who were never picked for kickball. But right now, I needed help and they were my only option. I decided to butt into their conversation and ask for it.

"Um, excuse me."

Their talk immediately stopped and they turned toward me, giving me the once over and obviously not liking what they saw. A dirty-blonde American, taller than the two of them, no make-up, Levi's jeans, a pair of Reeboks and an oversized man's shirt (one of Carlos' rejects) topped off with my requisite black cardigan. My garb certainly didn't live up to their spiked heels, painted-on designer jeans, and satin shirts. They were obviously annoyed that someone had interrupted their excitement. The dark one lifted her sliver of an eyebrow and crossed her arms in front of her to indicate her displeasure, while her partner shifted uneasily on her heels and looked to her friend for guidance. It's too bad that I can't affect my famous New York accent in Spanish, or even approach the type of banter these girls had been engaged in. I was lucky enough to be able to speak Spanish at all.

"Um," I said even more eloquently. I knew I couldn't explain what was going on to them, but decided on another tactic. "Could you help me? I just broke up with my boyfriend outside. I'm going back to America tomorrow and I don't want to talk to him again. Could you walk with me outside or make sure he doesn't see me when I leave?"

"You afraid of him?" the dark one asked expectantly. A bit of excitement crept into her voice. She put her hands on her voluptuous hips and leaned slightly toward me.

"Yes, I am," I answered honestly. "I really need your help. I've got to get out of here."

"Oh, we have to help her, Felicia," the other one said, putting her hand on Felicia's wrist for emphasis. The two friends looked at each other.

"My name's Felicia. This here is Dulce," the dark one said with a jerk of her thumb toward her shorter counterpart. "I don't want to get in any trouble, you understand. What'd he do to you?"

"Well, my, ah, boyfriend, he's been following me and I'm scared." Felicia nodded knowingly and waited for me to continue. I guess that wasn't enough information for her and I'm sure that my hesitant Spanish wasn't up to the task.

"Um, he's just someone I can't really talk to again. I don't know," I continued. I'm not very good at lying, so I began to falter.

Felicia interrupted me. "So, what does he look like?"

"He's tall and has dark hair. He's standing at the bar. He's wearing a tan raincoat."

"Oh, that one," Felicia interrupted, waving her hand dismissively. "I noticed him already. He looks very strange. I would not have gone out with him."

"Well, I just want to get out of the bar without his noticing me. I really have no other plan. I wanted to go out the back door, but it's locked."

Pointing to the round cruise-ship size window in the bathroom, Dulce said, "What about the window?"

Felicia looked over at her friend with a disapproving look on her face. "Dulce, get real. Even *you* couldn't fit through there, much less her." She pointed disparagingly at my one hundred and fifty-pound body. I must admit, while not fat, I certainly don't have the waif-like body of today's models. I wasn't particularly insulted. After all, most of the world's women are my size and not size two petite, but the thought did cross by mind that maybe I should read those articles on grapefruit diets.

Felicia wrinkled her brow and seemed to be considering her options, and then she smiled. "Just count on us. We'll create a sensation out there. Are you with me Dulce?" Dulce nodded in agreement. "But, first, I've gotta pee." And with that Felicia went into the lone booth with a flourish.

Dulce turned back to the mirror while she continued to dab on the ghastly pink goop. Her shirt was a horrible shade of loud orange and the color of her lipstick was a sorry choice. I noticed she had chipped purple nail polish on. She said to me when she was finished, "Where are you from in America? I've never been there."

"I grew up in New York but now live in Boston. What about you?"

Dulce giggled–a sound not wholly pleasant. "You can't tell? I'm from Galicia. Everyone knows because my accent is so heavy. Felicia is trying to get me to speak correctly the way they do in Madrid. She's so well-spoken."

"Oh, yes, she is," I began. "I'm sorry about my Spanish accent. It's probably pretty bad."

"To be truthful, it is. You speak like someone from South America. The accent is just not the way it should be."

"Well," I began, but was interrupted by a loud flushing sound accompanied by Felicia banging open the booth door at the same instant.

"I feel much better now. Too much beer. Christ."

Very eloquent, I thought.

Felicia turned to me without washing her hands, I noticed. My mother would have been horrified. She said, "Now, follow us out in about a minute. Ready, Dulce?"

"Thank you. Thank you so much," I said from the bottom of my heart. "How can I ever repay you?"

"No problem. We'll have fun," Felicia said with Dulce nodding vigorously in agreement. And with that they were gone.

I counted to thirty, but could wait no more. I peeked out the door. Dulce and Felicia were all over the man with the tan coat and were creating quite a stir. I don't know what happened but his pants were wet with something and the two girls were giggling and apologizing all the while they were trying to wipe it off in the most suggestive way that made the rest of the men in the bar both jealous and uneasy at the same time. Dulce caught my eye and winked at me. I scurried out of the bar while no one, and I mean no one, paid the least bit of attention. I had lucked out again. Felicia and Dulce were my guardian angels that night.

I got back to the hotel without incident, went straight to my room, and barricaded the door again. I was hoping the beer would have made me sleepy, but instead, I was still high on adrenaline, and it made me incredibly jumpy. So, I tried reading my book. I turned the pages but I wasn't concentrating, often having to read the same page over and over again. I finally gave up.

I turned on the television and found MTV, but it was a local dating show that made my blood boil. These shows always portray women as being incredibly desperate. I'd rather watch music videos, but they were hardly on anymore. I wondered where the music was in Music Television? I switched to CNN Headline News and watched the same half hour segment countless times, with very few changes. I was trying to lull myself to sleep but the nap had been so successful, and I was still so wound up from the incident at the bar, that I couldn't even think about rest. Nor did I want to work. So I just lay on the bed switching between MTV and CNN, all the while getting more and more anxious.

I must have dozed off at about six because I woke with a start when the remote control fell from my hands. I jumped up and decided I could sleep no more. I made sure everything was packed and left. My flight was at nine o'clock, but I couldn't stand to be in the room another minute. I went downstairs, checked out, and got a cab to the airport. After my experience of the other night, I asked to see identification before the driver pulled into traffic. He looked at me like I was crazy, but showed me his driver's license, and his license for the taxi. Satisfied, I sat back and let him drive.

I was not sorry to be leaving Spain. The last several days had been stressful and I was emotionally wound up and physically exhausted at the same time. I felt like I was going to get sick any minute. I was even anticipating that little tickle in the back of my throat that signaled we were in for ten days of hell. I got to the airport with no problem and I tipped the driver well. It was only seven by then, but I checked in at the Lufthansa gate and went to find some breakfast.

As usual, the coffee was strong and tasty and the bread was fresh. I sat in the small cafeteria with about ten other people who were all drinking beer and waiting for the flight to Berlin. I've never been able to drink alcohol in the morning, even beer. It turns my stomach. My German cousins say that beer is not really liquor, but one of the four food groups. I have my doubts.

I went to the gate around eight o'clock and decided to call Elena and tell her where I was going. She answered on the third ring.

"I hope I didn't wake you," I said when she picked up.

"Oh, not at all. The girls have been up for hours. I'm always up early with them. How are you feeling? The headache better?"

"Yes, I'm fine. I wanted to call since I've decided to go to Berlin. In fact, I'm at the airport right now. I'm meeting up with Johann Spurber at the library tomorrow and will see in person what he's got. He told me he even had some originals that you had loaned him."

"Oh God," she cried, "I completely forgot. I'm so glad they have them. They weren't part of our original collection. Carson Barry gave them to me. He was a graduate student from Chicago. He sent them to me right before his car accident in Puerto Rico. He actually got them from Dadi's family."

"Where is Dadi's family now? Is his son still in Puerto Rico?"

"Yes, and so is his daughter. Have you heard of Cardinal Dadi or met him?"

"I'm not Catholic. I only found out what a mass was when I started studying music history."

"Well, Cardinal Dadi is a very important man in the church. They say he's in line to be the next Pope–the first Latin American Pope. He visits Spain fairly often. I heard him say mass at the cathedral in Toledo. He's a very magnetic person. He even kissed one of my daughters, Lisette, as we were leaving the church. He was such a passionate speaker. I truly believe he's been touched by God. Rafael Gazza told me to drive to Toledo for the mass. He knows the Cardinal very well through all the work he does for the church."

"I hadn't realized Rafael was religious," I replied, trying to take in everything she was saying.

"Oh, yes. He goes to mass every morning at seven, that's why he's always early to work. Rafael was going to go into the Seminary but changed his mind at the last minute. He's still very active though. Didn't you notice the pictures he has up in his office? Rafael with the Pope, then with Cardinal Dadi, and more. You must have noticed the large crucifix he has over his desk."

"Elena, with all the mess at the Archives, I'm not sure I even got to his office. I don't remember any crucifix, though. That, I think, I would have noticed."

"Well, Cardinal Dadi is the younger of Enrique Dadi's children. The other child was named Maria, I believe, after Dadi's wife. The biographies are so sketchy; they never really say anything about his personal life. Carson Barry gave me some letters and a few pieces that I believe he had gotten from the Cardinal, though Carson didn't make that very clear. The daughter, Maria, is still alive and may even live with her brother. She could have been the one who gave them to Carson. I'm not sure."

"Johann Spurber told me that I should take the originals back to you. Do you want me to do that?"

"You know, Leigh, I'm not sure. I didn't even tell Rafael about the things Carson had given me. I don't know why. I think they should go back to Cardinal Dadi or Maria. Maybe I can send them by messenger back to the family."

"Actually, Elena, I was planning a trip to Puerto Rico myself sometime soon. I'll let you know as soon as I know my plans and we can figure it out from there. For the time being, tell everyone that I'm visiting some relatives and will be back soon. It's actually true. My relatives live in Berlin and you can get in touch with me through them. My cousin's name is Steffi Uebler. You can find the number in the telephone book. Uebler is not a common name."

At that moment, a voice over the loudspeaker broke in and announced that our Lufthansa flight was boarding. I continued, "Elena, I'll talk with Johann Spurber and see what they've uncovered. Then I'll look through the materials they have and call you, okay?"

"Sure, Leigh, let me know what you find out. Have a good time with your relatives and give the librarians in Berlin my best. They have been very helpful. I'll talk to you soon. Don't miss your plane. Bye."

I hung up the phone, satisfied that she had, in fact, just forgotten about the originals that were still safe in Berlin. I shouldn't have doubted her. I began to wonder if Cardinal Dadi had more of his father's materials. Maybe he even had some of the compositions that were rumored to exist. Perhaps he would be so grateful that I returned some of the letters and manuscripts from Berlin that he would show me whatever he might have. I had to get past his personal secretary

first. I'm sure the Cardinal was inundated with requests from people and the secretary had simply been protecting his boss.

I stepped onto the plane, still in my reverie. The blonde flight attendant
handed me a menu and left. I had my choice of soft drink or juice. It was only
about an hour and a half ride so I settled in with my mystery and munched on
stale peanuts and mineral water, not the greatest combination at nine in the
morning. We ran into some turbulence about half way there and I was ever more
grateful when we hit the runway in Berlin. I looked at the gray, efficient buildings
lining the spotless runway and thought that I must truly be in Germany now.
Although somewhat austere, it was a welcome sight.

CHAPTER 8

▼

I picked up my bag and went through customs and a security check that lasted over an hour. As soon as I was through the glass sliding doors, I heard a low voice cry, "Leigh, over here." My cousin (or was it second cousin, or first cousin once removed?–I can never remember) loomed before me.

"Heinz?" I asked, not believing that this big, husky, handsome man had been my seven-year-old cousin with whom I used to play Zelda on the Nintendo. "Heinz?" I asked again. He laughed. It was the beautiful, low, self-conscious laugh of a teenager.

He gathered me into his arms and said in perfect English, "It's been too long. Why do you not visit more often?"

It was so nice to be there I just laughed and hugged him very hard. "Well, you were on vacation with your father the last time I was in town, maybe seven or eight years ago. And besides, it's really expensive and I'm still a starving student." I looked around and added, "Where's Steffi?"

"She had to stay at work. There was a crisis with the hot water or boiler or something." I couldn't stand the fact that he knew the word "boiler." His English, though slightly hesitant at times, was better than my German would ever be. He continued, "We are going to meet her at the Pension, get your room and take you around the city. It has changed a great deal since you were here. We're having dinner with our cousins Oskar and Barbara tonight. Your father already called and spoke to everyone."

"Oh no, Heinz. I thought maybe just the three of us could have dinner. Oskar and Barbara are fine, but I haven't seen you both in so long."

"You know your father has already called Oskar and Barbara. He wants you to call as soon as you get in." Heinz smiled at me. "It's really good to see you again. The car is just over here."

We got to a small green Peugeot. "New car?" I asked. The last time I was in Berlin, my cousin drove her big, old, black Mercedes. I loved it; it was the kind of Mercedes with big bug eyes for headlights and the large fat tail end.

"No, this is my car. I bought it a few months ago with the money I earned at my job. Do you like it?"

"I love little European cars. Love Peugeots, too. Great choice, Heinz. Too bad there aren't any dealerships in the U.S. anymore. A friend's mother still drives her big 405 station wagon and loves it. They're wonderful cars."

Heinz beamed and slid into the small car with the ease of a seventeen-year old. I clambered into the cramped passenger side still carrying my computer, briefcase and pocketbook. The car was spotless inside and gleaming, obviously taken care of with the pride of a first car owner.

We drove down the highway and Heinz started to play travel guide. "You can not believe all the construction going on. You can count into the hundreds the amount of cranes over the city. We have the largest construction site in all of Europe. It is in between the old East and West portion of the city. It used to be the border or, how do you say, no man's land? You'll see."

I was tired from the flight and lack of sleep the night before, so we drove for a bit in companionable silence. As we neared the city, I realized what Heinz had been talking about. Large construction cranes dotted the landscape like giant praying mantises. It was positively surreal. I counted on the right side of the highway at least twelve as we drove in; there were many more in the distance. We pulled up to the Pension a few moments later. It was only a few blocks from the main bustling shopping center, the Kurfürstendam–known by every Berliner as Ku-Damm. The lobby was small and dark, but welcoming, with a small waiting area next to the reception desk. I saw Steffi on the phone at her desk in the back. She waved to me as she was speaking to someone on the phone. I waited while Heinz extricated my bag from the small trunk of the Peugeot and brought it in. Steffi slammed down the phone and came from the back around the front desk to hug me.

"Leigh, you look great. It is so good to see you."

"Problems, Steffi?" I asked, gesturing toward her rear office.

"Agh, the boiler's out and the plumber says he can only make it at five this afternoon. That means we've only got lukewarm water all day. I can just hear everyone complaining already. But never mind. Here, you're in room twenty seven like last time. I'll get the key."

She stepped behind the small dark counter and plucked a large medieval-looking key with a huge round wooden key ring that said plainly "Pension Schwarzer Adler–Zimmer 27" on it. So much for all the new-fangled security cards they use in many hotels nowadays, but at Steffi's place, I felt very comfortable with just a key.

The three of us took the two-person elevator up to the third floor, managing to squeeze my bags into the tight space. It was the old style lift with the inner grate that had to be shut before the car would move. Steffi stepped in and closed it with the smooth move of experience, and the car started slowly creeping upwards. It took us longer to get there than if we'd taken the stairs. When we finally got to the room, Heinz easily hefted everything onto the bed and said, "Leigh, why don't you unpack and meet us downstairs. We can have something to eat together. I'm hungry."

His mother laughed, "You're always hungry."

"Well, so am I," I replied. "Sounds like a good plan. Thanks, Heinz, Steffi. I'll be down in a bit; lukewarm water is fine with me."

They were heading out the door when Steffi turned at the threshold and said, "Leigh, why don't you give me your computer and I'll put it in the hotel safe downstairs. You never know." I nodded and she grabbed the bag and shut the door. I took out some clothes, washed my face, and brushed my hair. I didn't want to take a lukewarm shower. Besides, the water temperature was not really lukewarm, more like lukecold. Steffi was going to get an earful from the other guests.

After changing my shirt, I went downstairs with my sooty clothes in a plastic bag. Steffi would know a good dry cleaner that could probably have them done today so that I could wear them when I met up with Johann Spurber in the morning. Heinz was lounging in the small waiting area reading a car magazine and Steffi was on the phone again. I could hear her voice trying to soothe a Herr Pickelman that the water would be piping hot later today and that she was terribly sorry for any inconvenience. She got off the phone and looked over at the woman sitting behind the lobby desk. "Sorry, Christa, you'll have to deal with all this now. I'm going out to lunch."

Christa's smile was resigned. "Have a good time," she said as the phone began to ring.

As we started out, Steffi stopped short. "Oh, I forgot, we should call your father. I told him we'd call as soon as you got in." She turned back to her office and I trouped after her dutifully. She looked up the number and dialed quickly. "Onkel Herbert? Steffi. Ja. Ja. Here she is."

"Hi Daddy. Yes, everything's fine. Yes, we're seeing Barbara and Oskar tonight." I noticed that Steffi rolled her eyes. "Yes, I'm in room twenty seven. Yes that's fine. Carlos is taking care of Jabba. He's fine...work's going well...Okay...Talk to you later. Bye." I looked over at Steffi. "Can we go now?"

"Good, let's go." And we did. The three of us talked and laughed and had a wonderful time. Steffi had chosen an out-of-the-way vegetarian restaurant–a rarity in Berlin–that was absolutely wonderful. It was my first real meal since getting to Europe. Heinz talked about his soccer team, his school, and his hatred of math. Steffi told me that after being divorced for fifteen years, she finally had a steady boyfriend whom she really liked. Heinz grudgingly admitted that he actually liked "the new guy." When we finished catching up, I recounted every one of my adventures during the last week. I told them all about the man in the tan raincoat, the robbery, the fire at the archives–everything. It felt good to tell someone the whole thing from the beginning and it forced me to re-analyze all that I had been through.

Heinz looked very concerned, and said slowly, "Do you want me to help you? I could be a body man for you."

He was so sincere I laughed. "You mean a bodyguard? No, thanks. I can take care of myself. Don't worry. I just wonder who he is and what he wants."

We went straight back to the Pension after lunch. Steffi explained that she had to get back to take care of the plumber, and I said that I needed a nap since the beer at lunch had made me very sleepy. Steffi took my clothes to the cleaners, crumpling her nose in disgust when she opened the bag. "My cleaner is great, but I'm not sure what he can do about this," she said thrusting the bag farther away from her nose and toward me. "I'm sorry I can't spend the afternoon with you, but I should really be at the desk. Heinz, what are you doing this afternoon?"

"I'm sorry, Mutti, I have football practice at three. I'll see you this evening though. We'll go to Oskar's together." Steffi rolled her eyes again when he said that.

"What's wrong with Oskar and Barbara, Steffi?" I asked. "They've always been fine to me."

"Once every five years is enough," she replied quickly and then shook her head. "No, that's not really it. You know, all my life my mother wished I was more like Barbara. Barbara has a lovely house, Barbara has great clothes. Barbara this, Barbara that. So now, going over there always makes me feel, I don't know, like I'm not good enough, would you say?"

I hugged her. "You're great. Your house is great. Your son is great. Forget it. I hate Barbara's house anyway."

A smile lit her face. "It is kind of...I don't know how to say *grell* in English."

"Garish?" I laughed. "It's the perfect word." I started toward the steps and turned around, "I'll see you at—what, seven o'clock?"

"Sounds good."

I stopped by the front desk to get my key, but it wasn't on the hook and Christa was nowhere to be seen. Steffi was already at her desk with the phone in her hand.

"Steffi," I called loudly toward the back. "Do you have the key? Did you take it? Where's Christa?"

"No Leigh, I don't have the key. Christa must be in the bathroom." She came out of the back toward the front. As she reached the front desk, Christa came down the stairs holding my key in her hand.

"Oh, hi." She said, "I'm sorry. I just got a complaint about noise from your room, so I checked it out. Everything is in order." She handed me the key.

"That's strange."

Steffi looked concerned. "Do you think that this has anything to do with what you were telling us about at lunch? Why don't we go up together."

We walked up the two flights. When we opened the door, everything looked fine, but the minute I opened my suitcase, I could tell it had been searched. I got a sinking feeling in my stomach and my knees started to shake.

"Steffi, someone has been in here. Wait, my photos." I began to search frantically through my briefcase as more adrenaline coursed through my body. I stopped. "Wait a minute. I put them in the front pouch of my computer case. Let's check if that is okay."

We practically ran downstairs and checked the safe. There were the computer and the photos, safe and sound.

"All right, Leigh. You shouldn't stay here. Just stay with me at the apartment," said Steffi.

I shook my head. I really wanted and needed my own space, and I didn't want to have to sleep on Steffi's sofa. "No, I'll be fine. And besides, if anyone is really after me, then I'll probably be safer in the hotel surrounded by lots of people."

"Well, then, if you're going to be stubborn, I'll change your room right now." She looked over the registration book—no computers used in this hotel—and picked out another room. "I'm listing you here as still being in room twenty seven, but your new name will be, what, Marilyn Monroe?" she asked with a wry smile.

"Too obvious. Romi Schneider?"

"Too obvious *here*," she said shaking her head. "Why don't we use your father's real last name, you know, before he changed it to Maxwell? I'll never understand why he did that."

"Daddy always said that Maxenschein would have been too hard to spell for most Americans. Did he ever tell you how he chose Maxwell?" She shook her head. I continued, "He told me that the first billboard he ever saw when he arrived in New York was for Maxwell House Coffee. Maxwell sounded a little like his name, so he took it. Frankly, I like it. It does make my life easier in the States."

"So, do you want to use Maxenschein now?"

"How about using my great-grandmother's name? Virginia Krause."

"Sounds good." She penciled me in as Virginia Krause and handed me a key for room fourteen. "Let's get your things, leave something behind as though you're still in room twenty seven. Turn on the light and keep the key for room fourteen with you. Don't hang it back on the hooks here. Christa," she said turning toward a very confused receptionist, "Leigh is still in room twenty-seven, in case anyone asks, okay?"

Christa nodded in agreement though she looked a little bewildered. We then made the switch. I left behind some dirty underwear and a T-shirt, strewn on the bed. I turned on the light by the dresser and then transferred everything else to room fourteen, which had a better view, bigger bed, and nicer bath. There was even a small television parked on the dresser.

"Are you sure this is fine? This room looks more expensive than number twenty seven," I asked Steffi.

"Sure. Don't worry about it," and knowing me for the Trekkie (sorry, Trekker) that I am, she added, glancing at her watch, "If you're interested, *Star Trek* starts in ten minutes."

"Great. Thanks for everything," I said, as she left the room. I was hoping that I could turn on *Star Trek* and fall asleep. I knew all of the episodes by heart. I've probably seen each a hundred times—no exaggeration. I own all of them on video. My sister and I used to time each other to see how long it took us to figure out which episode was which just from the opening music. It always took me under three seconds.

I settled into the clean, crisp bed, propping feather pillows behind my head. I had double locked the door and put the security bar over it. I found *Star Trek* on channel four, but of course it wasn't really *Star Trek*, but *Das Raumschiff Enterprise,* with Kirk and Spock speaking to each other in strange, German voices. I listened for a while but didn't know the German words for "universal translator," "warp drive," or "photon torpedoes," and gave up halfway through. Besides, it was the episode where the cloud-like monster eats people's blood. I hate that one; it's so cheesy when Kirk says, "I smelled…home" that it always makes me laugh. In German it wasn't so funny.

I frittered away the rest of the afternoon reading my book, dozing a bit and switching on more dubbed American shows. I finally turned off the TV with disgust when The Beverly Hillbillies came on. I just can't stand Ellie May.

At six o'clock I got up and got ready. I put on a nice skirt and blouse and made sure my hair was in a semblance of order. My Dad would hear all about what I wore, what I did, what I said, so I took extra care to assure that I wouldn't have to hear about it later. Steffi was right. Barbara always had perfect hair, nails, clothes, house, husband—a regular Stepford wife. I wouldn't be surprised to find she was actually a robot or maybe even a psycho-killer.

At quarter to seven, someone rapped quietly on the door.

"Who is it?" I asked more shrilly than I had intended to.

"It's me, Heinz. Mom told me to pick you up. Is something wrong? She sounded a little nervous."

"No, everything is fine." I said as I opened the door, shut it and locked it behind me, stashing the large key in my pocketbook. Berlin was a lot colder than it had been in Spain and my raincoat was not really up to the job. We got into Steffi's big, black Mercedes and headed to Oskar and Barbara's. Steffi turned the heat on high for me.

"How many miles do you have on this thing anyway, Steffi?"

"I don't know," she replied, but glancing at the odometer, she said "It says seventy-seven thousand kilometers. Is that all, Heinz?"

"*Two* hundred and seventy-seven," he answered. "We've gone round twice already. The old Benz still has some life left in it."

"I love this car," I said as I patted the worn black leather of the front seat.

"So do I," replied Steffi with a smile. "I remember when I bought it. Everyone thought I was spending too much money. You were the only one in the whole family on my side."

"I've always loved cars. One of these days I'll have a Porsche Cabrio in dark gray. I'll pick it up myself from Stuttgart and drive it all over Germany on the autobahns before sending it back to the U.S."

Steffi skillfully maneuvered through traffic as Heinz and I discussed which ten cars in the whole world we would have in our stable—if money were no object. He shook his head in disgust as my list included more Italian cars than he would have liked.

"What's wrong with Ferraris and Lamborghinis?" I asked at one point.

"Porsches can beat them hands down."

And so it went.

Steffi parked in front of Barbara and Oskar's. "Here goes," she said, as if steeling herself for the onslaught. As soon as we were out of the car, the front door of the pristine house flew open and Barbara seemed to glide gracefully down the stairs, looking every bit the put-together wife of a successful computer salesman.

"Hello, hello. Come in. We've invited a few more of your father's friends to join us. It will be a regular party," she trilled.

"Great," mumbled Steffi under her breath.

My German was slowly coming back to me. Maybe Kirk and Spock had helped me get acclimated to the sound of it that afternoon. Since I was in foreign language mode, I slipped into Spanish twice while being reintroduced to all my father's friends.

Of course, we had to take a tour of the house, which looked more like an over-stuffed museum. I absolutely loathed it. Large, dark, German antiques were positioned side by side with modern furniture. Every bit of every wall was covered with framed pieces of "art." We toured rooms after rooms that were obviously never used, but whose sole purpose was to be opened for guests and then shut again. Barbara beamed each time I stopped to admire something. Frankly, I picked things at random just to be polite. The full suit of armor was their most recent acquisition and I looked at it closely. I was sure it was not a fake. I couldn't imagine the hours and hours that it took for Barbara to clean the thing. I knew from my father that Barbara wouldn't allow anyone to clean the house except herself, don't ask me why. They certainly had enough money. If I could afford it, I wouldn't hesitate for a moment to hire a cleaning service. Hell, they could even take the Woolworth's "silverware" if they wanted. I looked at the armor more carefully. Each chink in the chain mail absolutely shined. I wondered how many hours of dead labor it cost her to make the thing gleam like that.

We finally sat down in a room in the basement that had been made into a large Bavarian den, complete with bench seating for twenty. It was the least cramped room we had seen so far, but it was still full of pictures on the wall and large dark furniture that looked old, solid, and stern. One piece of furniture served as a type of buffet table. There was plenty of beer and food spread out and so we all sat down. Barbara looked at me and said, somewhat disapprovingly,

"Leigh, I know from your father that you are a vegetarian, so I made some extra salads just for you."

"Thank you, Barbara. That was very sweet."

She dished out bratwurst for everyone else that frankly smelled delicious. Me, I got potato salad, which unfortunately had bits of bacon all through it, a cucumber salad with cream and fresh dill, and a beautiful fresh green salad that was absolutely amazing. With bread and beer, I was very happy. We talked and ate and the conversation flowed smoothly. Every once in a while I caught Steffi's eye and smiled at her. She seemed completely uncomfortable the whole evening.

The only problem with Bavarian benches arises when someone has to go to the bathroom. While I was on beer number three, nature called, and being the guest of honor, I had several people to my left and four to my right. So, they had to scoot out so that I could leave. Barbara had the great idea that we'd all switch places whenever someone moved. It felt like the mad tea party in *Alice in Wonderland*, but with one exception—we all took our own plates with us each time we moved. As the beer reached our bladders, the whole thing took on a kind of party-game air with someone having to go every five minutes or so. Oskar moved four times in an hour, Werner twice. Heinz, being somewhat shy and out of his element, didn't drink much beer, so he never gave up his seat closest to the door and therefore never had to move.

When I managed to get the chair opposite from where I had been sitting originally, I noticed a beautiful illuminated manuscript hanging on the wall. It was a page from a chant book and looked to me to be from the fourteenth century. Of course, being a musicologist, I was instantly intrigued.

"Oskar, that manuscript. Where did you get it?"

Oskar looked extremely proud. "That's new, too. I found it on my latest trip to Heidelberg just two months ago. Isn't it beautiful?" He took it down and handed it to me.

"Oh, yes, Oskar, it is." The manuscript was illuminated with pictures from the Bible along the left side of the page, all in beautiful colors highlighted with gold. On the bottom of the page was a filigree design of blue, red, and yellow that was absolutely stunning. I could tell that it was parchment from the small hair marks left on the page. "What's on the other side?" I asked.

"Oh, I don't know." Oskar replied in an offhand manner. "I had them paste it to a cardboard back so that it fit well in the frame instead of crinkling up around the edges. It was of no importance. This side was much prettier."

The musicologist in me flinched. How much of our art was lost to things like this? Were lost works by medieval composers like Machaut hanging in houses throughout Europe gathering dust? I couldn't say anything, except, "Well, Oskar, it's a beautiful music manuscript. Fourteenth century, I'd say, maybe even slightly later."

Oskar looked surprised. "No, Leigh. It isn't music. It's the Hippocratic Oath from the eighteenth century."

I was stunned. He didn't even know what was hanging on his wall! I quelled the desire to snatch it and run from the house. I had taken an entire year-long course in graduate school on the History of Music Notation, so I knew what he had. "What?" I eloquently answered.

"Oh, yes, the dealer in Heidelberg told me it was the Hippocratic Oath in Latin from the eighteenth century. It's pretty with all the gold, no?"

"Oskar. Look at the words. They're Latin all right, but look at them. *Glorificamus te. Adoramus te.* 'We glorify thee, we adore thee.' It's part of the Gloria from the mass. I'm sure of it. Besides, what do you think all the dots are all over the page and the four red lines? It's notes on a staff."

"It's just decoration, Leigh. Besides, music staves have five lines, not four. You of all people should know that," he answered smugly. With the exception of Steffi and Heinz, everyone around the table chuckled at Oskar's little dig.

I couldn't believe he still thought it was some type of decorated Hippocratic Oath. "Trust me on this one, Oskar. It's a music manuscript. Here you have the custos," I pointed to a particular squiggle, "and the rostrum marks up and down the page, and you can tell that it is parchment, not paper by..."

Barbara interrupted me. "If Oskar says it's the Hippocratic Oath, then it is, Leigh. He knows all about antiques. Isn't that right, Schatzie?" She looked at her beloved Oskar proudly.

I answered with a small laugh, "What do you think I've been studying for seven years anyway?"

I looked around the table and noticed that I had managed to convince no one except Steffi, who sat looking both smug and superior at once. For the first time since we got out of the car, Steffi looked comfortable, at ease, and downright happy. Heinz smiled too and then winked at me.

Barbara wrested the framed piece out of my hands, leaned over and placed it back on the wall. "It looks nice there, don't you think?"

Everyone murmured agreement and that was that. For the rest of the evening, I kept casting furtive glances at the beautiful manuscript. I wanted it. I really, really wanted it. I would appreciate it and, frankly, I knew what the hell it was. I kept thinking about lost manuscripts, history gone forever, on walls in basements, in attics, and finally in blackened burnt piles outside of buildings. I felt sorrow and loss, but mostly I felt frustration. The conversation ebbed and flowed around me, but I couldn't concentrate anymore. I kept thinking about the monks who had spent years writing out manuscripts only to have them ripped apart, glued to cardboard and placed on basement walls. I was definitely tired. I was suddenly aware that Steffi was saying, "Well, I've had a hard day and must get up early in the morning. We had a crisis with hot water at the Pension."

With that we all filed out, thanking the host and hostess profusely.

Once back in the car, we waved good-bye as Steffi moved the Benz expertly into the street. Once on the highway, she slapped the steering wheel.

"Oh, that was great! What idiots! That was wonderful. Thank you. Thank you, Leigh. That was the most fun I've ever had at Barbara's."

Heinz laughed. "You've made my mother very happy. Great going. She was really not looking forward to this evening."

Steffi laughed again. "They don't even know what is in their own house! What idiots!" She slapped the steering wheel again as we sped toward town. I smiled at the two of them. It was the reaction I needed to snap me out of my reverie and the three of us laughed together.

CHAPTER 9

▼

We got back to the Pension and Heinz walked me up to my room and made sure that everything looked all right. He kissed me goodnight and left. I double locked the door and settled into bed, but I couldn't sleep. The incident with the manuscript had left me pensive, and I kept thinking about what I was doing with my life. Why was I in Berlin chasing ghosts? Why wasn't I safely back in Boston sleeping between Jabba and Carlos? I just kept thinking and thinking, and I came to the conclusion that what I really needed was to speak to Carlos. I had been a bit abrupt with him on the phone and I shouldn't have. He only wanted to help and I had been a snit. I dialed home. It was about eight at night in Boston when I tried to get him, but there was no answer. I tried his apartment, too, but I knew he wouldn't be there and he didn't even have his answering machine turned on. Then, I dialed home again and left a loving message and hung up. Afterwards, I felt even more alone. My life seemed out of kilter and I needed some kind of balance.

Finally around three in the morning, I turned on the television and watched Dallas–a show I never saw when it was popular in the States. I fell asleep after a while but had terrible nightmares that woke me up every half-hour or so. I kept dreaming of darkened oil fields filled with bubbling sludge and oil-laden, blackened birds. From behind dark glistening trees with no leaves, large men in raincoats tried to find me, but when I tried to run, I began to sink in the black ooze. It was almost with relief that I finally woke with a start at seven.

I got up and took a long, hot shower–Steffi was good at her job–and got dressed for my appointment with Johann Spurber. I even put on makeup to appear more professional. Then, I went downstairs for breakfast and had wonderful crusty bread with sweet creamy butter and strong coffee. I was slowly reviving from my restless night. I noticed that Steffi wasn't in yet, and so I waved hello to Christa who was again behind the receptionist desk.

"Hello, Virginia," she said with a wink.

After breakfast I took my computer from the safe, but left the photos behind and headed out. The library where Johann worked was in what used to be East Berlin. I decided to take a taxi since it was quite far from the Pension and the last thing I wanted was to be late for my appointment. Being late in Spain was normal; being late in Germany was a big no-no.

I may have been imagining it, but as soon as we entered East Berlin, the buildings took on a gray, abused look. More cranes were evident on this side than anywhere else in the city. The buildings were a patchwork of newly restored or, literally, falling down. Large potholes dotted each street and on every corner, mounds of sand and gravel were piled on the sidewalks next to large cement pipes. My Mercedes taxi seemed to glide over the bumps in the road with very little trouble. The entire section of the city had the air of a gradual awakening.

Graffiti dotted the construction site walls that we passed and I noticed one in particular. Painted very carefully, and with much more detail than any other drawings around it, was a fist next to a swastika. Underneath, someone had inscribed, in German, "We will fight again." It made my blood run cold, an inauspicious start to the day.

On certain buildings you could see little dots, which the driver informed me were bullet holes. I thought of the people who had lost their lives trying to go the same distance I had just gone in a few minutes and the futility of the whole situation. I thought back to Le Carré's *The Spy Who Came in from the Cold*, a book I re-read every few years or so and wondered if the next generations would truly understand it. I shook my head and decided I was getting too pensive again.

We finally pulled up in front of a large building at the end of a square, which was now filled with construction vehicles instead of the usual trees, grass, and flowers. The building had huge columns at the end of an imposing staircase, and I wondered if Hitler had ever made a speech from here. It looked vaguely familiar to me; possibly I had seen it in old newsreels on PBS. I paid the driver, got out, and started the long walk up to the entrance. Before going inside, I turned to look at the square. It had once been beautiful, and I hoped that it would be again. As soon as I entered the building, I could see that the renovations on the outside of the city were reflected here on the inside. Scaffolding obscured the large entrance, and workers were already busy scraping and filling in jagged cracks in the walls. I headed to the security guard who, in turn, called Johann Spurber and told him I was waiting. I glanced at my watch and realized I was exactly five minutes early.

"Please wait over there. He'll be right down, Miss," the guard said as he pointed to a beautiful, new, black leather couch sandwiched between the workers. How different from the musty, orange plaid sofa at the Madrid archive. I looked around and imagined how grand the building would be once everything was finished. From far inside, I heard jackhammer sounds and the whine of a table saw. Just then, a tall, pleasant-looking man came round the corner. He was young, maybe in his late twenties or so, and good-looking with a body that was so thin it looked concave. His belt seemed to be the only thing that held up his pants and I couldn't imagine that they were any bigger than size twenty-six.

He extended a narrow, bony hand to me and said, in a soothing voice that would have been perfect for reading to children at bedtime, "Doctor Maxwell? Johann Spurber."

"Nice to meet you. Please call me Leigh," I answered, standing up. "Thank you so much for seeing me on such short notice."

"A pleasure. Please come this way." He led the way past scaffold after scaffold, worker after worker. The sawing sounds grew louder as we went left, then right, then left again. Though I usually have a good sense of direction, I was lost within two turns. It seemed to me that the building was nothing more than a huge maze of construction sites. At one point, Johann turned back to me and said, "I'm sorry about all the renovation, but we finally got funding six months ago, and we were more than excited. This building was in complete disrepair. We were concerned about our collection because of all the leaks in the roof, and along some of the window sills."

"Yes, I can imagine."

"Our collection is wonderful. I think you'll be impressed with our holdings. In the music section, we have some wonderful pieces. There are many scores of Brahms, Bach, and the like. We also have a Beethoven sketch book, one that was thought to have been lost after the war. The rare book room is quite remarkable."

We passed through a set of heavy glass doors and I was struck by the smell of new. New carpet, new chairs, new lights, new paint, new plaster. It was all high tech, quiet and efficient, yet inviting with a nod toward the splendor of the past. As soon as the doors were shut, the sounds from the outside were gone.

"This is beautiful, Johann."

He beamed. "Yes, this is the rare book section and where many of the librarian's offices are located. We renovated this section first, since our collection is invaluable. You're lucky. We finished everything about two weeks ago. You're the first music historian to visit our new space and my first visitor. Come this way; we can work in here."

He led me down a corridor to a beautiful conference room with an antique wooden table big enough to seat ten people, and modern, comfortable rolling chairs in an abstract pattern of teal, orange and emerald green that was surprisingly pleasing to the eye. Johann motioned me to one of the seats. The new chairs were ergonomically correct as well as beautiful and as soon as you sat down in one, you knew that this was a chair you could be comfortable in for hours.

I placed my purse and computer beside me on the large table.

"I believe we should set up here. My office is a bit, hmmm, how would you say it? There are many things all over the room."

"Cluttered? Messy?"

"Yes, that's the word. Cluttered," he looked a bit shy at that. "Sorry."

"You should see my office. This will work just fine. In fact, just give me a few minutes here and I will manage to clutter this up too," I replied with a smile. I had never met a messy German before; all of my family, my father, everyone I had ever met, had the uncanny ability to have clean, orderly houses. I was the exception, and my father was forever shaking his head at my "mess." He always said that my "mess gene" must have come from my mother's Italian/Irish side.

Johann gave me a broad smile. "My colleagues don't understand how I know where everything is, but I assure them that I am organized. It's just the way I am. You should see my flat. Why don't you settle in here, and I'll get the materials. Please remember that there's no smoking or drinking, and no use of pens."

"No problem. I know how to behave around rare books. I'm a librarian."

With that he left. I had found that we had a mutual understanding of messiness and had already fallen into a friendly, easy acquaintance that should make working with him a breeze. There is nothing as bad as an unfriendly or officious librarian. They can make your life a living hell.

I settled into my chair, took out my Dictaphone and inserted a new cassette. Then I took out my pencil case and two number two pencils that were beautifully sharpened, and placed an aluminum sharpener next to them. I was ready.

Johann returned a few minutes later with several large folders. These he spread out on the table and said, "We'll go through each folder together. Is that all right? I'll tell you what we've found out as we go."

"Great. I'll take notes on paper and Dictaphone, if that is okay with you?"

"Fine." He took out the first folder. "These are the love letters that we have. They are all originals, so we'll start here."

Johann gave me a pair of white cotton gloves so that I could handle each letter myself. He also put on a pair. I touched the first of the yellowed letters and felt a familiar thrill surge through me. I have always marveled at how close I feel to people in the past when I handle something they have touched or sit somewhere they have sat. I had the same feeling caressing Mozart's forte piano when I was in Salzburg. Knowing that Mozart had touched the very same keys that I was touching was a thrill beyond compare. Here was an actual letter that Dadi had read and kept. I was tremendously excited.

The letter was in French, dated January 23, 1907. My French was a bit rusty, and Johann helped me out in a few places. It read:

Enrique, My love —

Last night opened new vistas for me. Your love has changed me. I will never look at life the same way again. I am sorry we cannot announce our feelings to the world. You are the most important thing in the world to me. To be in your arms is beyond compare. I look forward to next Saturday.

—My love, F.   *23/1/07*

"Who is F?" I mumbled under my breath.

Johann shook his head. "No idea. Enrique Dadi's wife's name was Maria. Note the date."

"Yes, I saw. Dadi married Maria in 1910. So why couldn't he and 'F' get together? Very flowery handwriting, but I don't recognize it. It's very distinctive. He had an Italian friend named Francesca, but I know her writing. I don't think it was like this."

"There's more," Johann said as he picked up the next paper. It was another letter, much shorter this time.

E — I love you. Do what you must — F.

"Curiouser and curiouser," I said. "It's the same handwriting. Any date on that?"

"No, but it appears to be from the same paper stock. I would say that it is later than the letter of 1907, since the first one seems to have been the beginning of their love affair. This short one could be a few weeks, months later or even as much as five years. It is hard to tell. Here's the next. Just wait for this one."

My dear E—

My love to you as always. I haven't seen you or been with you in so long. I think of you every day, every minute. We must find time to be together. May I join you on your next trip? Let me know. I have never seen Vienna in October. It would be nice to walk in the woods together through the yellow and red leaves. I need to see you. I need to hold you. Write to me soon.

I love you—F.   8 Sept. 1915

"Wow!" I cried. I sounded like a ten-year old who had just gotten her first bicycle. "Wow!" I said again. "This is proof that Dadi was in Vienna in 1915. This is incredible."

Johann laughed at my enthusiasm. "Yes, that's what I thought. I almost jumped up and down when I saw it. I tried tracking him down, but couldn't find out anything. The records have all been lost or destroyed. But it seems like he was a visitor to Vienna more than once. The letter says 'next trip.' Interesting, isn't it? Notice the date? 1915. That is right in the middle of the war."

"Very interesting. I wonder if 'F' really did meet him there. What in the world was Dadi doing anyway?"

Johann then produced another letter from the folder. It was another love letter and from the same woman.

E—

I love you. Our trip to Berlin was magical. A lovely time, no? I wish we could be together all the time. I need you.

I'll bring you anything you want from Germany. I'd do anything for you— you know that. For just one moment, last night, I felt you needed me as I need you. I love you. I wish that our lives could be different. —F.

16/4/16

"April, 1916?" I asked.

"Yes."

"As I said before, curiouser and curiouser."

"Here's the last one," Johann said, producing the longest letter yet. "This one is the only one from Dadi himself."

I got excited as I held the letter. I don't really believe that inanimate objects can retain the feeling of the people who held them, but this letter seemed to embody the emotion that had flowed through the author as he penned it. This letter was in Spanish whereas all the rest had been in French. I never saw Dadi write more than a few lines in French, though he spoke it fluently. Maybe "F" was Spanish, but if so, why write all the other letters in French?

26/5/16   5:02 a.m.

My dear love, My All, My Everything—

We have been together almost ten years and I never tire of being with you. You say you would do anything for me, but would you really? I feel that I can do nothing about my life. Maria depends on me–you know that as well as I do. She is a fine woman, but my heart remains yours–always yours. When I am with her, I dream of you. That is the only way I can touch her–my eyes closed, heart and mind with you. You know that, no? And now, she is with child.

This is the first letter like this I have written in my life and it will probably be the last. Please destroy it as soon as you read it, please, for me. I am not accustomed to writing this way.

Thank you for always being with me, through everything. So many friends have died, so many more will die before this madness is ended. Such destruction, such sorrow. All I have done, I have done in the interest of peace. I think now that I will be misunderstood. People might judge me harshly, but you have not. When you were beside me the other night, I felt finally happy. I knew you understood and will help me. Our lives will change soon. We must still be together, sometime, somehow. You know I love you. I always will.

Your loving, Enrique

Enclosed is the music for General von Falkenhayn. He'll appreciate it. Please deliver it next Thursday evening at the restaurant where we had our first dinner in Berlin just a month ago in April. They will know you. Then return to Paris. We will meet then.

I read this many times before its meaning could sink in. Never, ever had I read anything like this from Dadi's hand. His letters to his family, friends, even his wife Maria were straightforward, somewhat dispassionate, written from an emotional distance. This was the first time I got a hint at the real Dadi and I was more than intrigued. Frankly, it made me like him all the more. I have always liked composers when I felt that I could at least glimpse a little bit of their personality, their humanity.

I finally looked up to see Johann gently nodding in agreement.

"I've checked every letter he ever wrote, at least the ones that we know about, and none are like this. It is definitely his handwriting, but what I'd love to know who is 'F'?" Johann said.

"Have you discovered what all this Vienna-Berlin back and forth was? What was 'F' doing for him? Who was she anyway? And the line about General von Falkenhayn. He must have been a mucky-muck during World War I, no? What was he in charge of?"

"A mucky-what?" asked Johann.

I laughed. "I'm sorry, I'm getting so excited I'm letting my New Yorker in. Just means someone of importance. General von Falkenhayn must have been high up in the German army, right?"

"Yes, yes, he was," Johann replied, "But, let me start from the beginning. These are the originals Elena Rodriguez sent us," he pointed to the love letters before us. "I think they came from outside the collection housed in Madrid. Elena wrote that they were on loan. There are a few other originals that came with these letters, all pieces of music. I'll show them to you later. As to the General, that is the most intriguing of all. Yes, he was a mucky-whatever. In fact, he was Chief of Staff for the Kaiser during the war. I've found out through some research that he was actually in Berlin during April of 1916. There was a conference going on here with the Kaiser to discuss some of the problems they were having in France."

At that moment, I wished I had paid more attention in European History class in college. "Give me a minute," I said as I thought through everything I could remember about the First World War. Luckily, I had read up on it when I began my dissertation. Since Dadi had lived through the war, I had needed to place him historically. I never thought that he would play any role at all in the whole conflict, though, and my memory of the period was still a bit sketchy.

"April of 1916," I mused out loud, "April of 1916 was during the battle of Verdun, right?" Johann nodded in agreement and so I continued, "Horrible time in the war–both sides literally bled the other to death. I know about this since my grandfather on my father's side was in the battle and wounded there. He had a limp for the rest of his life from it. So, I guess it was General von Falkenhayn who had master-minded this whole thing since he was Chief of Staff?"

"Yes, exactly," Johann replied. "I looked up Falkenhayn's biography the other day. The battle of Verdun was originally conceived to relieve pressure on the Austrian army fighting the Italians. Germany and Austria were allies, as you know, and Austria was doing badly. No one had expected the war to go on that long. Germany attacked at Verdun in February to help Austria, but it didn't work. The battle was drawn out for months and months, more than six hundred thousand killed for basically nothing, about three hundred thousand on each side, more or less. Verdun never surrendered. The Battle of the Somme started in April of 1916, to alleviate pressure on Verdun, but that didn't work either. There's your April date," he tapped on the love letter.

I was scribbling on my pad as fast as I possibly could. Johann paused to let me catch up and then continued, "Getting back to General von Falkenhayn, he was physically in Berlin in April and May. I have checked some sources here. The Kaiser was probably angry with him since nothing was working according to plan and the conference was to spell out some other strategies. I have no idea what Dadi had to do with all this, though. Don't forget Dadi was Spanish, but living in France. Both were sworn enemies of Germany and Austria."

I shook my head but couldn't figure it out either. "I don't really know either," I mumbled apologetically. "I'll transcribe these letters and while I do that I'll try to figure it all out." I was hoping that doing something by rote would allow my brain to come up with some ideas. I proceeded to copy each letter and then wrote out a translation. When I want to understand something or think something through I like to write things down instead of using the Dictaphone. Johann excused himself saying that he had to get something from his office. He came back a few minutes later holding a folder full of Xeroxes of the original letters for me. He was my kind of librarian.

"I'm not really supposed to do this, but here are some copies for you. I'll put the originals back in the folder and you can take that back to the family or to the archives in Madrid. I'm not sure to whom they belong, but they were on loan to us from Elena Rodriguez. They should go to her first. I've got everything that was in the folders copied for you, but I think we should work on the originals first. Are you ready for the next folder?"

My head was still swimming, but I said, "Fine, just a second." I needed to organize my thoughts, so, on a separate piece of paper, I wrote:

1. Who is "F"?

2. What was Dadi doing in Vienna, October 1915?

3. What was Dadi doing in Berlin, April 1916?

4. What did General von Falkenhayn have to do with Dadi?

5. What did Dadi mean, "The General will appreciate the music"? Was the General a musician?

6. What was the music and can I read it?

When I was finished, Johann glanced over my questions. "Yes, those are on my list too. I can answer only one question for you. The General was not a musician and could not even read music. I'm sorry but I have no other answers for you yet, but let's continue together. We may find out some answers when we look at the music. That seems to be the key to everything."

The next folder contained both originals and Xerox copies of music manuscripts. Johann picked up one original and said, "You see this one? This is the music that obviously went with the last letter. The crease marks exactly match and the two originally came together in the stack Elena sent me, so I think that we could start here."

The composition was a short piano piece. As soon as I saw it, I realized that it was in Dadi's hand. "Johann, this one was written by Dadi, I'm sure of it. I've looked through enough of his manuscripts to know. It is a bit sloppy, but still his handwriting. Looks like it may have been written on a train or something, but I know it is his."

"We weren't sure about this one. There are eight pieces here, and I think two of them may be his."

The composition looked unlike anything Dadi had written before. It was atonal; there was nothing melodic or elegant about it. There were no articulation markings, no tempo markings, nothing at all but the notes on the page. This was unusual in Dadi's pieces since he was always fastidious and marked more performance indications on the page than the actual notes. On the bottom of the page, and along the outside of the staves were some words written in Cyrillic script. I pointed to these lines and said, "Do we know what this says?"

"My friend Gertrude called me last night. It is in Serbian, believe it or not."

"Dadi's father was part Serbian. I think they spoke it at home."

Johann replied, opening his notebook, "I didn't know that. It makes more sense then. The writing says *From the Musician in France. Read as before. More on its way. Respond in kind.*' That's it."

I wrote that all down. "I'm not sure what that means. That went with the letter to 'F', right?"

"Correct. It's interesting that it was still in Dadi's possession. I'm not sure if it ever made it to the General, but let's continue." Johann then produced another manuscript. This composition appeared familiar, not the music, but the handwriting. The notes on the page seemed to call to me.

"Wait a minute," I said. Something was beginning to dawn. "I know this handwriting. It is very beautiful, the calligraphy just so, the way the noteheads are shaped. It is very familiar. Ummm…Erik Satie!" I cried, slapping my hand on the table and surprising Johann so much that he almost fell off his chair. "Yes, it must be his," I continued. "He was friendly with Dadi at this time, and he published a lot of music before the war. This is just a small piano piece, but I know them all. This one is new. It has never been published." I looked up, getting even more excited. "Is it possible that this is really a Satie composition that was never published? I'm absolutely sure it is his handwriting." I started to tap out the notes, using the top of the table as a makeshift piano. The piece translated from my hands to my ears and I began to get even more excited than I already was. There was a tempo marking at the beginning—*Modéré*—"moderately" in French. Thank goodness it wasn't marked *Presto*, since my piano skills would not have been up to the task. I played it slowly all the way through. Yes, this sounded like Satie. The piece had strangely dissonant harmonies that were pleasing to the ear nonetheless, and a circular melody that seemed to fall in on itself. Johann waited patiently for me to finish playing on my phantom piano.

"I've never heard this piece before," I said when I was finished. "I wrote my Master's Thesis on Satie's piano collection *Sports et Divertissments*, that's how I know the handwriting so well. Before I wrote anything, I played through all of Satie's works for piano. I'm sure this is unknown. What a find! What a terrific find!" My voice kept getting louder and higher as I explained the significance to Johann. I could barely contain myself. I wanted to dance around the room and actually found myself standing. I didn't remember when I'd stood up.

Johann nodded, "I knew it was French, but thought it might be by Dadi and then copied by someone else."

"No, no. It's Satie. Lots of his works were published in his own calligraphy. I know Dadi was friendly with most of the French composers in Paris, and was close to Satie in particular. They used to have drinks together every Thursday afternoon, if I remember correctly. But to have a piece that was never published, that's surprising. It wasn't dedicated to Dadi or anything. Well, let's start a chart to sort all this out and label this Piano Piece #2–That's Handwriting #2. Do you think that's fair?"

Johann nodded in agreement. I turned back to the composition that lay before me. My hands were trembling and all I could think was: "A new piece that I get to edit and publish. An article in *Musical Quarterly,* maybe even a small item in the *New York Times.* My work, my career, my job prospects are looking up."

Johann broke through my reverie, "I believe you about Satie. Now that you mention it, the handwriting does look like his. Well, that just may be our first mystery solved." He smiled at me.

"Not really, Johann. The question remains–what was Dadi doing with it? It's certainly good enough to publish. I'm surprised that Satie didn't."

We continued to look through the remaining group of compositions. There were eight pieces in all but there appeared to be six different handwriting styles. One looked suspiciously like Debussy to me, but I wasn't sure so I didn't say anything to Johann at first. At the end of several hours of work, I wrote a little chart for myself that looked like this:

Composition	Handwriting	Comments
Piano Piece #1	Dadi	Cyrillic on bottom, which says: "From the Musician in France. Read as before. More on its way. Respond in kind."
Piano Piece #2	Satie	
Piano/Flute	Unknown A	Looks neo-classical
Solo Violin (?)	Unknown B	Looks like there should be a piano part
Viola/Piano	(Debussy?)	1917 on bottom of page
Piano Piece #3	Dadi	Cyrillic on bottom, which says: "From the Friend in France. Read as before. Troubled times ahead. I will try to talk to them and ask for help."
Flute	Unknown C	atonal
Voice/Piano	Unknown D	Words in German/Johann says they are by Goethe

Johann looked over my chart and agreed with everything I had written. He specifically pointed to the "Debussy" and said, "If this is true, it is even more interesting. This chart looks similar to something I drew up a week ago with a few major exceptions: your discovery that the second piano piece is by Erik Satie and the possibility that the viola/piano piece could be a Debussy sonata. This means we should look to other composers for the answers. I hadn't thought in that direction. This changes our whole perspective on Dadi."

"You know, Johann, come to think of it, the Satie piece does look a little familiar. Not because it is definitely his style, but it looks like I may have seen it before somewhere. I just can't place it."

The whole morning had proved to be a little overwhelming. More and more questions kept popping into my head, and in some ways, I felt I was drowning in too much information and too much excitement. I wanted to tell Carlos everything and maybe even call my friends back home to tell them all that I had found.

At that moment, in the extreme quiet as we looked at the eight compositions laid out before us on the large, dark table, my stomach rumbled so loudly that it could have matched the sound of the jackhammers I had heard before.

"It's late," Johann said graciously, ignoring my body's siren, "It's almost two thirty and I'm hungry. Shall we go to lunch?"

I glanced at my watch. "Sure, that sounds like a wonderful idea. Can I leave my briefcase and computer here or should I take them with me?"

"Leave them here. I can lock the door."

As we wound through the construction maze again, Johann started talking about the renovations to the building and then his own work. Johann had a Master's degree in bassoon and had started a doctoral program in New York, but gave up after two years. He had been working at the library for three years as the music specialist and absolutely loved it. He was taking library courses at night and planned to finish his degree in library science in just three more months.

He then told me more about himself. He had grown up in East Berlin and had helped knock down the wall, but in some ways he still felt uncomfortable in West Berlin. He felt that the people in the West resented the Easterners. Judging from some offhand comments Steffi had made at lunch the day before, I thought he might be right, but I didn't want to say so. Although my cousin, along with almost everyone else in the area, wanted Germany to be reunited, the enormous cost associated with bringing East Germany up to the economic level of the West hadn't crossed many people's minds in the heady days after the wall came down in 1989. Someone was paying for all the renovation and it sure wasn't the East Germans. Johann thought that there was trouble brewing.

We went to a small restaurant near the library. It was dark and cozy and we talked as if we had been friends for a long time. His stories of living in East Berlin during the 1970s and 80s were fascinating. He felt lucky now to be part of a unified Germany, something no one had thought possible even fifteen years ago. His grandmother had cried with joy when she walked through the Brandenburg gates without fear.

When we were served, Johann ate as if he were starving and, after a few bites, actually ordered another main dish. I envied him his ability to eat anything and still not gain weight. I, on the other hand, just look at food and it miraculously appeared on my hips. Thank God Carlos doesn't like skinny women. My salad and mineral water were supplemented with heavy, dark bread and butter, the likes of which are just not made outside of Germany. The taste and texture are unlike all others I have ever had, and since bread and butter is my favorite food, I've had a lot of it. On my last trip, I even smuggled some of it back with me, but it only lasted a few days.

After a longer lunch than we had intended, we walked slowly back to the library, both of us still tired from the intense work of the morning. On the way, a large black Mercedes drove slowly by.

"Russian Mafia," Johann commented in an offhand way.

"What?"

"Russian Mafia."

I laughed out loud. "Are you serious?"

"Oh yes," he said with a straight face. "This is a large problem here. They all drive the same type of car–big black Mercedes. They are all the newest models. Notice how all the windows are black? It is special bullet-proof glass."

I smiled, not sure if I should believe him or not. He looked at me again with a very earnest expression.

"Oh, I'm serious, Leigh. There've been some arrests, but the police can't really do anything, and besides, one of the prosecutors involved in the whole affair was found dead in his apartment just last week. He was shot in the head. We're all quite frightened."

The car stopped and double-parked on the street. I looked at the big black Mercedes with all the black windows, and I must say that it did look quite menacing. A large, stocky man with dark brown hair got out from the passenger side to buy cigarettes at a nearby kiosk. Johann stopped and looked at me. "See? Russian," he said nodding toward the man.

And, I swear, if he had had white hair, the man at the kiosk would have looked just like Boris Yeltsin.

"Okay, I see your point. Let's get back to work–we have other mysteries to solve."

It was nearly four thirty when we got back to the rare book room. The door was still locked and my computer and briefcase untouched. We still had one more folder awaiting us.

CHAPTER 10

▼

Johann left me in the conference room as he went to get the last folder. I sorted through some of my charts and notes from the morning. With everything I had seen that day, the picture I previously had in my head of Dadi was changed forever. He was no longer the distant, quiet Spanish composer who experimented with his music. Now, he was a tormented lover, in love with a woman he could never have. He was a collector of other people's works–Satie definitely, maybe Debussy, too. He was a passionate and intriguing person, a multi-dimensional artist whom neither I nor anyone else had had a clue about before today.

Johann returned, but had a puzzled look on his face.

"Anything wrong?" I asked.

"One of the other librarians, Marina, said that I had another visitor while we were out. He told Marina that he would wait for me until I returned from lunch. There doesn't seem to be anyone around. That's strange. I wasn't expecting anyone. You see, everyone must have an appointment to see the materials we have here in the rare book section."

I grew immediately wary and looked quickly at the desk to see if anything had been touched while we were at lunch. It looked exactly as I had left it. "Johann, did Marina give you a description of the guy by any chance?"

"She said he was tall, with dark hair. I don't know who that could be."

It rang an alarm bell in my mind. I felt that I should tell him what had been going on for the past couple of weeks.

"Johann, I didn't want to bring this up, but some strange things have been happening recently–all surrounding my work with Dadi. I was being followed in Madrid by a tall man with dark hair."

As Johann looked at me, a strange expression crossed his face. He chuckled a bit and said "Now, you're joking, yes?" When I shook my head, he frowned and said, "You are serious about this, aren't you?"

"Yes, I am. And that's not the end. I'm sure someone searched my room last night at the Pension where I'm staying." I realized then that I hadn't told him about the photographs Elena had given me. I felt that I could trust him. He had, after all, given me copies of everything we had looked at so far. "Johann, I have some photographs of things that were in the collection at the archive in Madrid. Perhaps you'd like to look through them with me. Elena hadn't told anyone about photographing these pieces, and, in fact, had forgotten all about them until I showed up. I have a feeling that this is what they were searching for. I can't be sure. The photos are now in the hotel safe at the Pension."

"What is in the photos?"

"Lots of music. All types. I think there's even part of an opera. I started going through them on Saturday, but haven't gotten far. We can do it together, if you'd like, maybe tomorrow."

"I have some appointments tomorrow. I'd like to look them over tonight, if that is convenient for you. This all sounds very intriguing and we make a good team. We can look through them while everything is still fresh in our minds. Now, should we go through the last folder? It is the least interesting one, I think, just sketches."

"Okay, Johann, let's do it."

He opened the last folder. In it were just three original pages and one photocopy. He was right. It looked like Dadi had been working out the form or the structure of a piece, something definitely atonal.

"This is interesting," I murmured. I got out a piece of manuscript paper to try to recreate Dadi's thought process, but nothing worked. There were notes literally scattered all along the page, seemingly at random. Some of the notes were next to letters and numbers; a few sharps and flats were scattered here and there. Each page was similar. I tried playing some of it on my phantom piano, but there didn't seem to be any sensible pattern to it. Johann tried to break up each phrase to see if it matched any of the music we had seen, but to no avail. Finally, a pretty young woman opened the door to the conference room and reminded us that the library was closing; it was already six o'clock.

Johann introduced me to Marina, the fine arts librarian. As she was turning to leave, Johann asked, "Oh, Marina, did my visitor ever come back?"

"No, I'm sorry. I didn't ask for his name or card because he said he would wait."

I stopped her this time, "Marina, could you describe the man?"

She gave me an odd look, paused and glanced over at Johann to see if she should respond. He must have nodded because she said, "He was rather quiet and intense. Very soft spoken. He was tall, dark hair and eyes. He was carrying a briefcase. He was wearing a tan trenchcoat."

When she left, I turned to Johann. "I'm sure it's the same man who was following me. We should be careful when we leave."

Johann nodded, but I could tell he was still not convinced that we could possibly be in any danger. Maybe he thought I was being melodramatic. He helped me pack up and then left the room to put the three folders into a safe in his office. We were the last ones out of the section and Johann flicked off the lights and knelt down to lock the heavy glass doors. We walked through the maze as the other librarians and workers were calling it quits for the day. Johann waved good-bye to the security guards at the receptionist's desk and we went out the front. Once I hit the cold air, I shivered and realized I must have forgotten my black cardigan on the back of the chair. I couldn't possibly leave without it. It is my favorite piece of clothing and besides, Berlin was at least twenty degrees colder than Madrid.

"Johann, I'm so sorry. I think I left my sweater behind and I'm freezing. Can we go back and get it?"

"Sure, I can unlock the doors again. We'll just have to sign in at the front desk."

We signed in and wound our way through the now silent building. Without the sounds of renovation and the bustle of the work day, the silence was absolute. Our heels clicked on the worn marble floor and reverberated throughout the passageway. The shadows and darkened hallways gave off an evil and intimidating presence. I was just about to suggest we could get the sweater in the morning, when we finally got to the heavy glass doors. Johann stooped down to unlock them. As he was crouching down, I peered through the glass and thought I saw some movement in the corridor where the conference room was. It was so dark inside that I couldn't be sure.

"Is someone working late?" I asked.

"No, no. We were the last ones out," Johann replied while pushing the door open. He flipped on the lights and began walking down the hallway on the right toward the conference room. With the lights on, the offices took on a less threatening atmosphere, and I allowed myself to believe that no one could have been there but the two of us. We opened the door to the room and I retrieved my sweater. I put it on, feeling much more like myself, then Johann helped me with the raincoat and we were ready.

"I'm not that hungry since we ate so late. Would you like to come back with me to the Pension now? We could start there and then have a late dinner. How does that sound?"

"Sure," Johann said as he switched off the lights to the room and started back to the main door. As we neared the exit, from far away, we heard something fall. We looked at each other, and I was instantly paralyzed with fear.

"That sounded like it came from near my office," Johann said as he turned the opposite direction and started down another hallway.

I grabbed his arm to stop him and urgently whispered, "Call Security. Don't go down there. Call someone for help now. We've got to get out of here. You don't know who it might be."

He shook his head, patted my hand in a somewhat patronizing gesture and said, "Don't worry. It was probably nothing. We've had a terrible time with mice in the building," and started down the hall again.

"Mice, my ass," I whispered under my breath as he turned the corner.

I decided to take my own advice, so instead of following him, I looked around for a phone. My knees were shaking hard. I tried the first door next to the entrance. Thank goodness it was open. I went to the desk, picked up the phone and called Security. I'm not sure if they really understood my German since I was still whispering–don't ask me why–and was so nervous that I was probably speaking in English.

There was more noise coming from down the hall so I hung up the phone quickly and started through the door when I heard Johann yell, "Hey, what are you doing over there?" Then a second later, "Hey." It was followed by a heavy thud and dead silence. I gasped, but then held my breath, trying not to faint. Johann might need my help.

Shakily, I started toward the hallway Johann had taken, but as I neared it, someone turned out the lights. The entire area was plunged into a darkness so complete that I couldn't see anything at all. It didn't matter whether my eyes were open or closed. I waited a second, closed my eyes to try to acclimate them to the dark and strained to hear anything at all. They always say that if you lose one sense the others become more acute. But even without my eyes, there was still nothing to hear. After a few seconds, I tried opening my eyes again, but it made no difference at all. I was still absolutely blind. My breathing sounded loud to me and I could almost discern the beat of my heart hammering in my chest. I started inching down the hall, my feet shuffling over the carpeting. With my left hand on the wall for support and my right reaching out to see if there was anything in the way, I was hoping that I would find a light switch or something, but the wall was absolutely smooth. I made progress down the corridor, even if at a painfully slow pace. I had never gotten to see Johann's office and didn't really know where it was. Why did I have to meet up with the only messy German in the entire world?

Somewhere to my right, I heard a slight groan. "Johann, Johann, is that you?" I called, my voice sounding extra loud in the pitch darkness. There was no answer. My heart kept pumping wildly, and I held my breath for a moment to calm down. I heard the groaning sound again, and it seemed like I was getting closer or at least it was getting louder. I kept calling to Johann now and then, in case he was awake or, I shuddered to think, at least alive. Maybe it was the burglar who was groaning. I got to another hallway and turned toward the right. This building was truly a maze. Where were those security guards anyway? I touched the opposite wall and noticed that a doorway was open. I searched the inside and outside wall for a light switch, but couldn't find one. I started into the room, tripping over some things on the floor. I couldn't hear anything—no groans, no moans, no breathing—nothing. I continued my faltering baby steps into the room and bumped into the desk. My hands went out to see if there was a desk lamp or even a telephone, but I couldn't find either. In the process, I accidentally pushed something off the desk and heard a light bulb shatter when it hit the floor.

"God damn it. Shit. Oh God damn it. Jesus Christ," I said through clenched teeth, feeling every bit the frustration of being blind and helpless. Cursing like that in the dead silence made me feel stronger and more in control for some reason, but, frankly, it did nothing to help my predicament.

At that moment, the door to the office I was standing in slammed shut and I heard the footsteps of someone running down the hall. I started to turn toward them, but stopped when I heard Johann's voice.

"Leigh, are you there?" His voice sounded like he had a bad cold. I must have woken him up with my foul mouth.

"Yes, it's me. Where's your light switch? I can't see a thing."

"On the wall, next to the door."

"I can't find it. I'll try again."

I could heard him struggling to get up, but he obviously couldn't handle it. "Oww," was all I heard and then another soft groan. Just as my toe stubbed into what I believe was a wastepaper basket, the hall lights flickered on and we heard the security guards coming in. I was almost blinded by the light coming through the small window on the door to Johann's office. After the pitch darkness, it was all the light I needed. I glanced around. The office was a complete mess. Papers, files and books were strewn everywhere. The broken lamp lay next to Johann, who was sitting on the floor, shielding his eyes with his right hand, while his left was bloody, probably from the shards of glass from the light bulb. I ran over to him and knelt down.

"Johann, are you all right?" I helped him up and into his desk chair. I opened the door to his office and yelled for the security guards.

"Over here. We need help."

Two guards came jogging round the corner. They were big, tall and athletic looking. They completely ignored me and went straight to Johann, who was trying to stand up as they came in the door. His knees buckled under him, and he fell back down into the chair.

"Herr Spurber, do you wish us to call for a doctor?" one guard asked.

I turned from the doorway. "Yes, he needs an ambulance. Call for one immediately." I must have used my "teacher voice," as Carlos calls it, and sounded like someone in authority, because one of the guards immediately got on his walkie-talkie and called for the ambulance.

"It will be just a few minutes. Can you tell me what happened?" one of them said, immediately turning back to Johann and ignoring me again.

"Did you see anyone leave this section? The intruder might still be in here," I said with an edge of panic in my voice.

They glanced my way. "No one is here," the taller one said. I didn't know how they could be so sure, but let it pass. At least with them in the room, I felt a lot safer.

Johann cleared his throat and I turned my attention away from the guards and back to him. "There was someone in the office when we came back. He pushed me down and hit me with this," he pointed to one of those Beethoven busts they sell everywhere. It was speckled with blood and looked in fact to be marble instead of clay. I realized that it could have killed him. "I must have fainted right away. I don't remember anything else, except Leigh calling for me. I feel sick. I'm really very dizzy." He rubbed the back of his neck with his bloody left hand, leaving stains on his starched, white collar. I felt terrible about the broken light bulb and the resulting injury to Johann.

The guard wrote a few things down on a small notebook he had produced from his breast pocket. "Description?"

"Tall. Taller than me. Dark hair. I didn't get a good look."

The guard then turned toward me. "Did you see him?"

"No. I'm sorry. The door to this section was already locked and we opened it and came in. Then we heard something coming from this direction. Johann went to see what it was and I called Security. Then someone turned off the lights. That's it really."

"Has anything been stolen?" the guard asked, looking around the office, obviously disgusted by the mess.

Johann answered, "Someone has been through all my folders, files, everything and now look at this." Turning toward his desk, he continued, "They even broke the lock on my desk drawer where I keep my radio." He opened the drawer and continued, "The radio is still here, though."

The sensation of *déjà vu* hit me like a ton of bricks. This sounded exactly like my conversation with the police after my break-in. It was happening all over again, but this time it wasn't my things that had been touched.

Johann smiled wanly at me, "My office is cluttered, but not usually this bad. Oh, wait. He was over by the safe when I came in. We keep things we are working on in individual safes in our offices instead of returning everything to the main depository each night."

I hadn't noticed the safe at first, but I looked across the room to where Johann had gestured as he spoke. The safe was partially obscured by a filing cabinet whose four drawers were all open. I walked over and knelt down.

"Johann, it's empty."

"Oh, no!" he cried and stood up by sheer force of will. He looked a little wobbly on his feet. He made his way slowly to the safe, using the desk to support himself. He looked at the empty safe, and then at me. The look in his eyes was one of bewilderment and loss. "Why? Why take materials like that? We needed those pieces. They were on loan. How will I ever explain this?" His voice nearly cracked toward the end.

"Johann, Johann," I said as soothingly as I could. "It wasn't your fault. There's nothing you could have done. Don't worry about it. We'll find the materials. It wasn't your fault." I felt like adding "It's all *my* fault," but didn't out of cowardice.

He kept shaking his head, looking hurt, guilty and a bit scared at the same time. There was absolutely no color in his face and I was afraid he would faint.

At that moment, two paramedics bustled into the room with all their paraphernalia and went immediately to work on Johann. I wasn't sure exactly what they said, since I don't know many of the German medical words, but I was pretty sure he had a bad concussion, not to mention the bloody hand that I had accidentally given him. He must have been truly hurting because without the least resistance, he meekly laid on the stretcher they had brought. I started to follow as they wheeled him down the hallway, but the security guard with the notebook stopped me.

"I'm sorry, *Fräulein*, but we have to ask you some questions."

"But, I should be with him. It's my entire fault. I..." My voice trailed away and I started to cry. There was no way at all to stop crying once the floodgates had opened. I felt as if I had put Johann in harm's way. Up until this point, no one I knew had really gotten hurt, but now Johann was on his way to the hospital and I was sure the other "accidents" weren't accidents at all. He could have been killed.

I buried my face in my hands, trying to regain my composure, but sobs just kept welling up within me. The guards were patient; the quiet one brought me a glass of water, and I managed to choke it down. I took a few deep breaths, regained a semblance of control and began answering their questions. I didn't have much to tell them, and suggested they talk to Marina, the fine arts librarian, who had actually spoken to the man who more than likely had hit Johann and stolen the materials. After over an hour of grilling, I felt as if I had been the one who had been hit on the head. My temples were throbbing and my eyes were burning, partially from crying earlier and partially from trying not to. I finally asked if I could go and see if Johann was all right. They told me the hospital he had been taken to and let me go.

I gathered up my briefcase and computer. The guards retrieved the phone from the floor in Johann's office so that I could call Steffi. By then, it was about eight thirty, and thank heaven, she was home.

"Uebler."

"Steffi? It's Leigh."

"I was getting worried. Are you still at the library? I thought they closed early on Mondays."

"It's a long story, but could you pick me up here? There's been a robbery, and the music librarian got hurt. I'd like to check on him in the hospital. I'm upset and really need some company."

"Sure, I'll be there as soon as possible. Are you all right? My boyfriend, Conrad, is here. Is it okay if he comes too?"

"Of course. Just get here. I probably look like hell."

"Are you okay? Do you need to see a doctor?"

"No. Just get here quickly. I'm a bit shaken up, though. Thanks." I hung up the phone. In my mind's eye, I could see Steffi starting up the big old Mercedes and coming to get me. It was a comforting thought.

The guards said they would walk me out. As we passed the other offices, they opened each door that was closed, to check if anyone was there. They finally got to the last door near the front entrance, inside stood a large Xerox machine. I remembered that Johann had given me copies of everything that had been stolen. I asked the guards if I could copy something. Their initial response was hesitation, so I made up a white lie and said that the materials I needed to copy were things Johann probably would need in the hospital. Though reluctant, they let me use the copier. I must have used my teacher voice again.

I popped everything into the self feed drawer and made three complete copies. The large machine did the job in no time at all. On the wall opposite the machine, the librarians kept their office supplies on neatly arranged shelves with little tags indicating what was on each. Johann probably had nothing to do with it. I got three manila envelopes and put one copy in each. On the first, I put Johann Spurber's name. The other I addressed to Carlos, and placed it in the desk next to the entrance where I had used the phone to call Security, hoping that the librarian would just put it in the outgoing mail slot. The other copy I would give to Steffi when I saw her. I put the original ones Johann had given me back in my briefcase and snapped it shut. The guards were obviously confused by all of this, but they waited patiently. Maybe they were afraid I would start to cry again.

When we got to the front entrance, I could see Steffi's car waiting at the curb. The guards were turning away to go back to the office and file their reports. I knew I couldn't face the long stairs alone.

"Could one of you walk me to the car? I'm still a little shaky."

And they both did, one on either side of me. When I slid into the front seat of the Mercedes, Steffi leaned over and hugged me. That did it. I started to cry again, and this time I couldn't stop. From the rear seat, someone produced a beautiful, soft, monogrammed handkerchief, which I proceeded to use until it was soaked through and stained with the last vestiges of my mascara.

CHAPTER 11

▼

I finally stopped crying and sank back into the comfortable seat with a sigh of exhaustion. Then I started laughing at myself as I always do when I've been crying–it seems to be my defense mechanism kicking in. Steffi still held onto my hand and squeezed it to tell me she was still there. I smiled at her as I wiped my eyes one last time.

"Thanks for everything," I said, meaning every word of it.

"What's family for anyway? Do you feel like going to the hospital or home? You look pretty tired. Actually, you look like hell."

"No, I don't want to go home. I really should check to see how Johann is doing."

Steffi started up the car with no argument. She turned to me again and said, in an offhand way, "By the way Leigh, this is Conrad. Conrad, Leigh," and she then pulled into traffic.

I turned to the rear seat. Conrad smiled a bit shyly at me. I'm not exactly sure what his smile meant, but I had certainly made a first splash.

"So nice to meet you. I guess this is yours," I said holding up the wet handkerchief.

"Glad to meet you, too, and the handkerchief is yours now. Are you feeling better?"

"Yes, thank you." I turned toward the front and lapsed into silence. I was just too tired to try to be friendly. If Conrad were as nice as Steffi thought, then he would understand.

A few minutes later, Steffi pulled in front of an old, stately hospital building. She looked at it through the passenger door window, leaning toward me. "Not my choice of hospitals, but it's closest to the library. I'll park. You two go in and I'll meet you in a few minutes."

I agreed with Steffi as I looked at the dingy, dilapidated building. I love old, stately buildings, but prefer my hospitals state of the art. This one looked in need of restoration along with the rest of East Berlin. I had the feeling that 200-year-old germs could, and did, live in the walls.

I dutifully got out and so did Conrad, who, like a gentleman, offered me his arm. He was much taller than I and had a powerful body that seemed to glide over the pavement and up the stairs with the grace of a dancer. I felt safe holding onto him, and halfway up the stairs, noticed that I was clutching his arm tightly as if he were a life preserver and I was drowning at sea. I must have been cutting off the circulation in his arms, but he didn't say a word about it, and I just kept clinging. On our way in, he asked me the music librarian's name, and I gave him a little sketch of what had happened. Once inside the emergency room, Conrad took over, speaking to the receptionists and nurses for me and getting all the information on Johann. I was just not up to the task—in either English or German.

The emergency ward was crowded with crying children and worried adults, all waiting patiently in a large room lit by fluorescent lights. In the States, people would have been demanding to see the doctor. I had expected screaming and yelling, but other than the children's crying, there was a quiet pall over the whole place. Everyone spoke in hushed, urgent whispers. The longer I stood there waiting for Conrad to finish, the more panicked and uneasy I felt. I'm not normally claustrophobic, but I was beginning to sweat and felt as if I couldn't breathe. My eyes darted around trying to locate all the exit doors, while I tried to convince myself that there was plenty of oxygen in the building.

After my mother's death from lung cancer ten years ago, I often had a nightmare of being suffocated by Easter lilies and white mums. I would wake up gasping for breath and fighting my way out of the covers. Now, I felt as though I was in a waking version of the same dream. It didn't help that there were two floral arrangements on the receptionist's desk, and the sickly sweet smell of gardenias and roses fought with the odor of disinfectant and human waste. The combination was turning my stomach.

Just when I felt I was about to scream and run for one of the exit doors, Steffi put her arm around me and I leaned into her. After a few minutes a nurse came and led us to a semi-private room in another wing of the hospital. It was quieter here, and I relaxed a bit. Steffi walked with me, holding my hand while we followed Conrad and the nurse. The nurse was clad all in white, but her uniform looked like it needed a good washing. She stopped at a door and motioned us into the room where Johann was lying in the bed closest to us. Snoring sounds came from the other side of the room–a curtain hid its occupant. Johann had a white bandage on his left hand and on the back of his head. He was staring at the ceiling with a frown of concentration, as if counting the tiles was of utmost importance, and he had just forgotten his numbers.

He seemed puzzled when Conrad and the nurse walked in, but smiled when he saw me. He lifted up his right hand and I took it gently in mine.

"How are you feeling?" I asked in a hushed tone.

"I've felt better, but I'll be fine. Did Security catch the guy?"

"No, I don't think so, but I don't care about that now. I want to know how you're doing. What do the doctors say?"

"I'll be out tomorrow. They just want to observe me overnight. I'll be back at work by the end of the week. My hand hurts a lot, though." He opened and closed his left hand, wincing when he had completely unfurled his fist.

"I'm so sorry. Is there anything I can do?"

"My parents are on their way. I'll be going to stay with them for a few days. Maybe you could come by with those materials. I'll need something to do. I need a distraction."

"You should get some rest, Johann. You shouldn't think about this stuff yet."

"Have to keep my mind busy. You don't know my mother," he smiled. "Besides, it'll be fun. Take my parents' phone and address and call me tomorrow afternoon. We'll see how things are and we can make plans." He wrote the address on a little piece of paper Steffi gave me from her purse.

At that moment, an elderly couple bustled into the room, obviously Johann's parents. His father was tall with a full head of wavy, white hair combed back in a dramatic fashion and held there with a little bit of Brill Creem, giving it a pinkish sheen. His mother reminded me of an emaciated bird. She was elegant, precise, and all bones. She was wearing a floor-length fur coat, too warm for the season and completely out of place at the hospital. Her coat, hair and shoes (all I could see of her) had the look of money. She gave off an air of disapproval when she looked at me. As soon as I saw her, I knew I would dislike her intensely. The jury was still out on his father, but then again, he had married the emaciated bird.

I tried backing out of the room to give them time alone.

"My God," Johann's mother cried as she crossed the room and grabbed Johann's bandaged left hand. "Why aren't you in a private room? Why didn't they take you to a good hospital near us? Why were you wearing that old suit?"

she said holding up Johann's clothes that were neatly folded on the chair next to his bed. I had thought the suit looked just fine.

I continued my exit, but Johann called me back as I hit the threshold to the hallway. "Leigh, come meet my parents." Maybe he didn't like them either, I mused.

We exchanged pleasantries, his mother giving me the once over. I shook her hand; her skin felt as thick as leather but loose on her bones as if it had been placed there and not attached to anything. The diamonds on her fingers were as big as my watch and left a mark on my hand when she shook it. Her palm was warm and as dry as if she had just sprinkled hot talcum powder on it. Mine, however, was freezing cold and still slightly moist from my attack of claustrophobia. I waited to see if she would wipe her hand on the fur, but she just glanced at her fingers in distaste. I hate to say it, but I enjoyed her dilemma. Johann's father didn't even offer his hand. To be polite, I introduced my cousin and Conrad.

I turned to Johann, "We'll be going now, but I'll call and come by to see you tomorrow." I waved the paper and smiled at him. "Number twenty-four Berg Strasse. I'll find it," I said, reading from the paper.

"Why, Leigh, that's only two doors down from Barbara and Oskar's," Steffi said, stepping up and taking the paper from me.

Johann's mother's eyebrows disappeared into her stylish bangs. "You know Barbara and Oskar Niedermeyer?" she asked in an incredulous tone.

Steffi spoke up. "Oh, yes. We're cousins–distant, but cousins nonetheless. Lovely neighborhood. We were just there last night for dinner." She put her arm around me. "Leigh, we should go."

I looked at Frau Spurber and for the life of me couldn't tell whether I had gone up in her estimation or her neighborhood had been sullied by my presence there. She was one cold, hard, lady and I felt bad for Johann who was the epitome of warmth and kindness. Where did he get those qualities? Maybe apples really do fall from pear trees. I said goodnight to Johann again, wished him well and left.

Steffi drove me back to her house instead of to the Pension and this time, I didn't object. I needed company and didn't want to stay at the hotel alone. Heinz was pulling up in his little green Peugeot as we were getting out. He had a bag full of my clothes. I was so grateful that I gave him an extra big hug and thanked him for his thoughtfulness. I was close to tears again from all the kindness my family had shown me.

We went into the building and rode the elevator up to Steffi's top floor apartment. Once settled in the living room, she brought out a bottle of red wine and poured a glass for everyone. She listened patiently while I told her the whole story of what happened in the library. I showed her my photocopies and she took her set and put them away. I was finally through with my story about midnight. Conrad was still there, quietly sipping his wine, refilling my glass, and listening intently.

Our conversation turned to other things. I found out that Conrad was a pilot for British Airways and that he was often in Berlin. Steffi had met him at the airport while she was waiting for a flight. They had been seeing each other for six months now, and looked quite pleased with themselves. I was really happy to see it. The divorce twelve years ago had been hard on Steffi, and raising Heinz almost single-handedly had been both a joy and a burden. She had done a great job of dealing with her life—rising in the ranks at the Pension from cleaning woman to manager. She and Conrad seemed to be truly in love, and I was happy that she was so content. I started to relax, but when we finished the second bottle, I hit the wall. The combination of wine and exhaustion took over and I excused myself and padded into the bathroom to change into sleeping clothes. While I was changing and getting ready for bed, Conrad helped Steffi make up a bed for me on the couch and didn't look twice when I came back in my ripped sweat pants and Picard T-shirt.

I settled in, wishing them goodnight, and fell asleep instantly. I woke only about an hour later with my heart racing and the feeling that I had lost something. I walked around the apartment, making sure the doors were locked and the windows were closed. I peeked in on Heinz who was snoring softly, and then went back to the couch, assured that everything was all right.

I felt antsy and needed to speak to Carlos. It was just after three, so he would probably be at work already. I dialed the number but got only his voice mail. Maybe he was being lazy. I tried home, next, and the answering machine picked up. I left a message telling him an abbreviated version of the whole story, downplaying how much I had cried and how scared I had been. Carlos knows me well enough that he would probably know anyway. I then gave him Steffi's phone number and asked him to please call me, no matter what time he got in.

After I hung up the phone, I stayed on the couch, hugging my knees. I felt more alone than ever. Maybe it was time to give up the degree and become a full-time librarian. Maybe it was time for some big changes in my life. Maybe I should think about having children with Carlos.

About a half an hour into my reverie, the phone rang, and I answered it immediately, hoping it didn't wake anyone else in the house. It was Carlos. I told him the whole story again, though in greater detail, and at the end of it, all he said was, "Why don't you come home right now and forget about all of it, and I mean all of it–the degree, the dissertation, the questions you have. Just let it go."

His suggestion reflected exactly my thoughts of the previous half hour. But I was still curious about everything I had found out, and as soon as he said it, I realized I wanted to finish. For my own feelings of self-worth, I had to finish something that I had begun.

"I'll be honest," I replied. "I was really scared last night when the lights went out. I felt so alone, but I've decided to make one last stop to Puerto Rico and then forget about it, at least for a while. Do you want to meet me there?"

"I'm very busy at work, but I'll see what I can do. Maybe I can meet you on Friday. We could stay at a hotel in Condado and take a few days off. Sit on the beach and relax."

"That'll be great. I'll probably be getting in on Thursday and I can meet you at the airport on Friday."

"No need. I'll meet you at the hotel. I'll bring your bathing suit and we can be decadent for a few days. I think you can use some time off."

"Sounds wonderful. I can't wait. I'll make my plane reservations and let you know."

"You should get some sleep now. I can't wait to see you. I'll call the Condado Hilton in the morning and make a reservation under your name for Thursday. Take care of yourself. I love you." With that, he hung up, but I stayed there a long time holding the phone, willing it to be Friday so I could relax and feel safe in Carlos' arms.

CHAPTER 12

▼

After a little while, I put the phone down, but still couldn't sleep. I thought over all the things that had happened, and I was excited about seeing Carlos in a few days. When I thought of Puerto Rico, I realized I had never called the Cardinal back. I got out the number and dialed. This time, a woman answered at his office, and put me on hold right away.

"Yes?" a soft, low voice said.

"Cardinal Dadi?" I asked, utterly amazed that I had actually gotten through.

"Yes? This is he. May I ask who is calling?"

I then explained exactly who I was and what I wanted. In the middle of my explanation, the line was so quiet that I thought we might have been disconnected, but when I paused, he said, "Please continue," and I did. When I stopped, he took a deep breath.

"Miss Maxwell," he began. "I can not help you. I have nothing of my father's, and am, frankly, not interested in any music that is not liturgical."

"Oh, I'm sorry, but I had gotten the impression from the music librarian here in Berlin that you had been here to see some of their manuscripts relating to your father. The librarian even told me that you were thinking of starting an archive yourself in Puerto Rico."

There was a pause. "I am sorry, he must be mistaken. I have nothing to offer you here, and assure you it would be a waste of time and money for you to come to see me. I am very busy during this period."

"I understand. Maybe we could just talk about your father, even for fifteen minutes, maybe a half-hour. It would allow me get another perspective on him and his life."

"His life and music are not linked at all. Is it not a fact that Mozart wrote his most cheerful music while he was sick and dying?"

"Yes, that's true, but I have found some interesting documents and music manuscripts that I would like to show you."

"Documents?"

"Yes, letters and the like that have never been published."

Again, there was a pause on the phone. "Well, if you insist on continuing with your work, perhaps we should meet. When do you expect to be in Puerto Rico?"

"This coming Thursday."

"Then come to the residences on Friday evening at seven o'clock. I will see you then." And with that, he hung up.

The conversation was a strange one. Why did Johann tell me that the Cardinal was interested in his father's work, when the Cardinal himself stated that he clearly wasn't? And why the change of heart toward the end? He had been pleasant enough, but I felt something was amiss. I was excited to get to talk with him and couldn't wait to finish my trip and get down to work at home. Finally, I felt as though I was getting somewhere, and when I turned off the lights, I had no trouble falling asleep.

In the morning, I woke to the smell of freshly baked cake and coffee. Steffi had obviously been busy. I stretched and yawned as the blood started rushing to all my muscles. As soon as she heard me stir, Steffi came out with a steaming cup of coffee. She sat down on the edge of the sofa, took my hand and asked, "How are you feeling this morning?"

I sat up, took a sip of scalding coffee and nodded, "Better. I feel more like myself." I blew on the coffee, making little wakes on the surface and took a few tentative sips. Steffi patted my shoulder.

"Come in the kitchen when you feel up to breakfast."

I heard some dishes being loaded into the dishwasher from behind the kitchen door and sat for a few more minutes enjoying the warmth of the covers and the taste of the coffee. I went to the bathroom and then took my mug into the kitchen where Conrad was sitting, reading the paper. He pushed it aside and asked how I was doing. He then handed me a section of the paper and went back to his breakfast. Conrad was my kind of guy–very low key.

He was in his airline uniform, and I asked him where he was off to.

"Flight to London at one, then to New York. I'll be back in two days."

"Lucky you. New York."

Conrad shrugged. "I prefer Berlin," he said, smiling at Steffi. I could swear that she actually blushed.

I glanced at the clock. It was eleven already; I couldn't believe I had slept that long. I hadn't even heard Heinz leave for school. Conrad got up, kissed Steffi and waved good-bye to me.

"Gotta run. I'll give your regards to Broadway," he said with a smile. Steffi followed him to the front door and I heard them murmuring. She returned a few moments later, poured herself a cup of coffee and sat with me. I devoured half of her homemade coffeecake and enjoyed her company. She told me all about Conrad. He had an ex-wife and two children, fourteen and ten years old. She was going to meet the children next month and was nervous about it. We sat there about two hours discussing this and that. Steffi had taken the day off from work to be with me, and I really appreciated it. I didn't feel comfortable driving in Berlin by myself, and I was still emotionally shaky from the night before.

I needed to get the photos from the Pension and to gather up my other belongings. Steffi's couch was fine for a few days. I also needed to make plane reservations. But first, I had to check on Johann. I asked Steffi if she would call the hospital. I hate speaking another language over the phone to people I don't really know—it makes me nervous not to be able to see their gestures. She called right away and found that Johann had been released early that morning and that he was doing fine.

To save time, Steffi said she'd drive over to the Pension, check me out and get my things while I took a shower and made my phone calls. I reminded her to grab the photos from the safe also. Johann had wanted to see them.

I took a hot shower and stayed under the steamy water so long that my fingers looked like prunes when I got out and my skin was a shocking shade of pink, but it felt good nonetheless. There's nothing like a pot of coffee and a hot shower to get you going.

I called Johann's home first. His mother answered.

"Spurber."

"Yes, hello. This is Leigh Maxwell. How is Johann doing? May I speak with him?"

"One moment," she said curtly, ignoring my question and banging the phone down a little harder than necessary for me to get the point.

"Hi. How are you?" Johann asked.

"You sound much better. How are you feeling today?"

"My head is still hurting, but I am much better. I've even regained my appetite. My mother says I'm eating too much."

"I'm sure she's glad to have you home for a few days."

"I'm not so certain about that," he said, more seriously than I'm sure he had intended. To hide the somewhat awkward moment, I barreled right on.

"So, when can I come and visit?"

"How about this evening? Come for dinner. Gretchen always prepares enough food for an army when I'm home. I need only to ask her to add another plate. It will surprise her when I tell her you're a vegetarian, but I'm sure she can handle it. She's such a good cook. Maybe she'll make her special apple strudel for you. It's the best I've ever had."

"As long as your mother doesn't mind cooking for one more," I said hesitantly. Eating dinner with Johann's mother was far down on the list of things I'd most like to do. Frankly, on the list it came right above sticking needles in my eyes.

"Gretchen is our housekeeper. She loves company, and don't worry about my mother. She and Father are going out to the symphony tonight and they're meeting friends for dinner before. You probably won't even see them."

"Sure, that'll be great," I said hoping my relief didn't show, but it must have, since he laughed right away.

"Come over around at five, okay? I know it's a little early, but I may tire quickly. And don't forget to bring the photographs. I'm really intrigued about them. I've already been on the phone with the head of the library."

"Any news?"

"No. Security never caught the man. Since it was an attack, no one is blaming me for being careless."

"That's good."

"I still feel bad about it, though. The head librarian is calling Madrid now to explain what happened. I'm glad I don't have to do it. I told them to speak with Elena Rodriguez and not Rafael Gazza, that was right, no?"

"I guess so. Elena was the one who gave you the materials. And don't feel troubled about the burglary. It's not your fault, you know. The burglar probably would have stolen more if you hadn't interrupted him. You should feel good about that."

"Yeah, I guess," Johann said, his voice trailing off.

"Get some rest. I'll see you around five. Can I bring anything? Wine, beer?"

"Nothing at all. See you then."

I felt sorry that Johann blamed himself, when, in fact, he should be blaming me. If we hadn't gone back for my sweater, he wouldn't be hurt now. I knew the burglar was there for the material on Dadi and nothing else. Frankly, in my heart of hearts, I knew that it was entirely my fault. What was in those papers that no one wanted me to see? I hadn't seen anything more suspicious than some love letters that may have been embarrassing seventy years ago, but not today. There were manuscripts of unpublished music by some of France's greatest composers, but were they dangerous? So what if Dadi collected music? So what if he had extra-marital affairs? What was so threatening that someone would follow me around Europe and hit Johann over the head? Come to think of it, what about the other scholars whom I had tried to contact, the ones who ended up dead? Did they get too close to the situation also? I needed more information before I could answer those questions.

I made a few more phone calls and got a flight for Thursday morning to Puerto Rico. That meant I had the evening and the whole next day to work with Johann. I also called Carlos again and left a message about my plans. Again, I left Steffi's number.

I was really looking forward to seeing Carlos and relaxing for a few days. No work, no family, no friends, no Dadi. I was also looking forward to being in San Juan. I was really excited at the thought of dangling my feet in the pool while sipping a Piña Colada.

By the time I got off the phone, Steffi had returned with my clothes and briefcase. We stowed some of my things in the hall closet.

Steffi sat down next to me on the couch, and said, "Since I took the day off, I have to work the night shift. Heinz is staying at his father's house tonight, so I think it best if you don't stay here alone. Since you'll be at Johann's tonight, why don't you stay over at Barbara and Oskar's?"

"Maybe that's a good idea, but I feel funny asking them. We're not all that close. If it weren't for my father, I would lose touch with most of my family over here, Barbara and Oskar being at the top of the list."

"Barbara called the Pension already this morning and left a message to call her. It seems that Frau Spurber has already been on the phone to see if we were telling the truth about having dinner there the other night. Can you believe that?"

"I believe anything."

"Well, that's our perfect excuse. Why don't you call Barbara and tell her you're visiting Johann tonight. Besides, they have plenty of room, and I'm sure Barbara would love it if you stayed in her house and complimented her on her furniture some more," Steffi said, rolling her eyes again in an exaggerated gesture.

"Sure I'll call. Do you have the phone number?"

Steffi dutifully dialed the phone and handed it to me.

"Hello, Barbara? Yes, it's Leigh. Thank you again for such a lovely dinner the other night. I had a wonderful time…Yes, that's right. I'll be going over there this evening for dinner. I'm expected around five o'clock. Yes…Yes, they're lovely," now I was the one rolling my eyes. Steffi giggled. "Yes, I saw the coat. Well, frankly, I don't wear fur…No, I've never been to their house before…Well, Steffi and I were just discussing that. Would it be possible to stay the night at your house since Steffi has to work and the Spurber house is only two doors down from you?…Thank you, Barbara…. Yes, we'll arrive around four just so I can set-tle in. Thank you again for everything. See you in a little while."

I hung up. "There. That's done. Barbara is green with envy over Frau Spurber's new fur coat. Can you believe it? I think it's awful. When I think of all the poor little animals that gave up their lives for her. And, besides, wearing it in October, when it's not even that cold, is just so tacky. Oh, don't get me started."

Steffi, knowing how I can get going on these topics, expertly changed the sub-ject. "Leigh, you should pack an overnight bag. I don't suppose you have a robe or nightgown, do you?"

"You're lucky I even have a pair of sweat pants with me. I usually just sleep in a T-shirt."

She laughed. "Well, since you'll be going over to Barbara's take a robe of mine at least to cover those ripped pants and that awful T-shirt," she said gesturing toward my Picard shirt.

"I love this shirt," I said somewhat defensively, looking down at Picard's face. "I got it at a *Star Trek* convention in New York. Patrick Stewart and William Shatner were both there."

"You know, you're in your mid-thirties already," she said. I winced. "We, your father in particular, were all hoping you'd grow out of this *Star Trek* phase."

I smiled at her. My *Star Trek* "phase" had already lasted 30 years. "Not a chance. As soon as I'm done with my dissertation, the next bit of writing I'll be doing is a *Star Trek* novel. I already have the plot line down."

She looked at me, unsure whether or not she should believe me. I smiled somewhat enigmatically and let it lie. I really did want to write a *Star Trek* novel and had already outlined the chapters. I work on it when I don't want to read or write anything more about Dadi. I call it an advanced form of procrastination. You learn such things when you've got a dissertation hanging over your head.

We packed an overnight bag and put the photos and the Xerox copies in my briefcase. I left my computer at Steffi's, since I didn't think I would need it. Even though it's portable, it still weighs too much. I took all my notes and the Dicta-phone. I was really glad I had packed so many cassettes. I was going through them like crazy.

We put everything in the car and drove over to Barbara's. When we got there, Barbara was again waiting for us at the gate, and she seemed happy to have us back. She put her arm around me as we walked through the garden up to the front door.

"I talked to Diana Spurber again and she told me what happened last night. You poor thing. If there's anything I can do…"

"Barbara, thank you so much for everything already, I really appreciate it. It is so kind of you to let me stay here tonight."

"Not a problem. Oskar and I have plenty of room, and especially now that the children are gone, the house feels too big sometimes. You know Oskar travels a great deal, and I'm often alone here by myself. Right now, he's gone to Moscow again. He is finishing some big business deal there, so I am happy for the company."

"Well, thanks, Barbara. It really makes things easier."

Steffi interrupted and said, "Barbara, I'll speak to you tomorrow about picking up Leigh. She's off to Puerto Rico on Thursday, so she'll stay with me tomorrow night and I'll drive her to the airport. I've got to get to work now." We walked her to the front gate. She kissed us both and squeezed my hand. "I'll see you tomorrow. Have fun and give my regards to Johann."

I went back into the house with Barbara. She led me to an immaculate room with, I swear, starched sheets and pillowcases. The feather bed was at least two feet high.

"You will be comfortable in here, Leigh. I'm giving you this room since there's a bathroom attached and you can see out to the garden. Some of the flowers are still in bloom," she said pushing aside the white gauzy curtains and staring into the beautiful garden beyond. "I hate October because you know everything will die soon, and it makes me very sad to think that winter is coming."

"That's too bad, Barbara. I like October with all its colors. And I like winter, too. Snow can be so beautiful, sometimes. I think living in the tropics and having summer year round would be boring."

"I don't know," she said with a sigh. "The beginning of autumn always makes me depressed. I always have the feeling that you lose something when the leaves fall. Maybe it's a reminder that each year, you lose part of your youth."

As she spoke, I looked at her more closely than I ever had before. I noticed there were wrinkles around her eyes, which she had tried to hide with foundation and powder, and for the first time I saw that beneath the tasteful lipstick, her bottom lip looked as though she chewed at it constantly. There was a tiny streak of lipstick on one of her teeth, marring the perfectly white caps. She had always appeared perfect, and had seemed perfectly content. I'd never even thought that she would use the word "depressed" when talking of herself.

She noticed me looking at her and smiled broadly. "I put some coffee on just before you arrived and made a little cake for us," she said a bit too cheerfully. "Why don't you settle in and meet me in the kitchen and we can have something together before you go over to the Spurbers. Okay?" She was back to the old Barbara, but the glimpse of the pensive, thoughtful person I'd just seen made me like her more than I ever had before. I felt like saying, "Will the real Barbara Niedermeyer please come out and stay?" but didn't.

At the doorway, she turned around and said, "Oh, Leigh. You know we're about the same size, so if you need anything to wear, I have a big collection. We have the same hair color too. I had never noticed before. I guess we really do look like relatives."

"No thank you, Barbara, I have plenty of things here. I'm only staying overnight. I'll meet you in a few minutes." With that she left. I had wanted to add that her hair color had come out of a bottle whereas mine was natural, but, as Carlos would say, I get a little too catty and mean sometimes. She obviously spent a great deal of time and money on the way she looked, and frankly, for someone in her mid-fifties, she looked terrific. I know that when I hit that age, I'll probably be permanently overweight and wrinkled, but hey, what the hell. I couldn't worry about that now.

I went into the spotless bathroom and washed my face, dabbed on some lipstick and makeup and met Barbara in the kitchen. I realized that I had only eaten some cake with Steffi and I was quite hungry. We sat down to delicious apple cinnamon turnovers that were still warm from the oven.

"So, what's this big deal Oskar's working on?" I asked to get the conversation going.

"Oh, he doesn't really tell me things. He says that Moscow's the next big market for computers. I don't know. I went with him on one of his trips and didn't like it at all. It was so gray and dingy there. It was also too cold, and even in the hotel the food wasn't good at all. He says there's potential to make lots of money, but I'd rather he didn't go there so often. Frankly, I would like him to retire."

"He's a little young for that, isn't he Barbara?"

"Not really, Leigh. He's ten years older than I am and that makes him 65 already. We have plenty of money to retire. It's not as if he needs to work. I'd like to travel and relax. He is often so tense and nervous, especially the past several months with all this Russian business. He won't even talk about it sometimes. I think that work for him is more than just a job. I think it defines him."

"Work does that for all of us, Barbara. At least that's true for me. I don't say that I work as a musicologist, but that I *am* a musicologist. But, frankly, I wouldn't mind retiring now," I laughed. "I've got so many things I'd like to do. And I agree with you, traveling would be great."

"Well, you know, Leigh, Oskar and I bought a house close to your father in Florida. Your Dad looks after it for us when we're not there. But, we've only spent a month there so far–in two years. I'd like to stay longer, but Oskar can't leave work for that long."

"Maybe when this deal with Moscow is done you can take a vacation together. Go and visit my Dad."

"Perhaps," she said a bit wistfully, but then smiled and while pointing around the room said, "Oh, but I don't mean to complain. We have such a beautiful house and everything."

"Yes, you do, Barbara."

"So, what is it that you're working on with young Johann? He's very pleasant, isn't he? His parents were so disappointed that he didn't become a doctor like his father."

"Yes, Johann's very nice. We got along great right away. We're looking through some things that I brought with me from Madrid. I won't be very long this evening. He really does need his rest. He just got home from the hospital this morning."

"Well, it's almost five," she said glancing at her watch. "You shouldn't be late. Here's an extra set of keys for when you come in. I'll probably be up. I usually don't go to bed before midnight anyway."

"Thanks, Barbara." I went back to the room and picked up my black cardigan. It was chilly outside, but I left my raincoat. Johann's house was only two doors down.

I waved good-bye to Barbara and found number twenty two. Like Barbara's house, it had a beautifully manicured garden, but it was at least twice as big. The walkway up to the house curled through flowers and clipped bushes and everywhere there was something interesting to look at. There was also a fountain running in their front yard and the sound was quite soothing. I could have done without the white marble cupids, though. I rang the bell at the gate on the sidewalk, and when I heard the buzzing sound, I pushed it open and started up the front walk. The stairs up to the front door were the annoying type that were too shallow for normal steps but so far away from each other that you couldn't take them two at a time. I guess they made you go up the path more slowly so you could admire the grounds.

As I reached the front door, I was about to ring the bell again, but it was opened by Johann's mother, in her fur coat, and holding a small evening bag. "Oh, it's you," she said, "I thought it was the driver."

"I'm sorry," I said for no particular reason.

She looked at me again, and the thought crossed my mind that maybe I should have taken Barbara up on her offer for better clothes. Mine were beginning to look rumpled from being in and out of the suitcase so often.

"Is Johann in?" I asked, tired of standing at the threshold.

"Yes," she said, as she turned away from the door and left me standing in the foyer by myself. From my vantage point, I could tell that the house was tastefully but sparsely decorated with Italian furniture and muted colors all in varying shades of white, beige and taupe. It was the type of place that I had always wanted to have, but wasn't willing to spend the money on. If it's a choice between a $5,000 sofa or a trip and CDs and books, well, I guess you know the answer. Maybe that's why I still use my old futon from college as a sofa.

As I stood there, somewhat awkwardly, unsure whether I should call to anyone, an elderly woman with frizzy gray hair that framed her plump face came out with a big smile.

"Welcome. You must be Leigh Maxwell," she said in perfect English.

"Yes, I am." I said holding out my hand.

She took it and gave me a firm, but pleasant shake. "I'm Gretchen. How does mushroom paté and pasta with fresh vegetables and bread sound to you?"

"Delicious. Thank you for going to so much trouble."

"Well, instead of standing here in this foyer, why don't you come and join us in the kitchen. I was just putting the finishing touches on the salad I was making. Do you like almonds in your salad? I think it's a nice touch."

"Love them."

She led the way through the house, and my first impression had been correct. The place was stunningly beautiful. I especially liked the windows. They were tall, ending only about 6 inches from the floor, with soft white curtains that allowed in all the sun but gave the room a feeling of privacy and intimacy. The house had an air of ease and comfort and the feel of old money. The furniture looked modern and unique, but comfortable too. The art on the walls was real; there were no framed posters in this house. I wondered what the Spurbers thought of Barbara and Oskar's museum. I'm sure they would feel the same way I did about it–it was just too cluttered and dark.

We got to the kitchen, which was bigger than my entire apartment in Boston. The smells emanating from the oven were out of this world. The room was a wonderful mix of restaurant functionality and stainless steel combined with what some magazines would call country comfort. The decor actually worked better than it sounds. There were windows everywhere overlooking a vegetable and herb garden, and a more formal patio and garden area beyond. Johann was in jeans and a sweatshirt, seated at a large antique kitchen table, sipping some hot cocoa and reading a novel.

Gretchen went straight over to the huge stainless steel stove and began to stir something in a large pot. She said, "I've brought your friend. It wasn't the driver after all."

Johann looked up and smiled. "It's so good to see you. Come have a seat, I figured we'd eat and work in here. It's my favorite room in the house. It's all Gretchen's anyway. Even this table belonged to her great-great grandmother. Right?"

Gretchen came over with a plate of crackers and paté. "Yes," she said to Johann, and turning to me, "It was my great-great grandmother's wedding present from her family. It's now about two hundred years old. How about some paté to start? It's made with mushrooms, not meat. Johann told me you were a vegetarian. Would you like a beer or wine?" Turning to Johann she said, "You shouldn't have anything. It might hurt your head."

"Wine, please," I replied.

"Gretchen, I'll have a glass too," Johann smiled, "Just one. I'm not on any medication now," he said, holding up his index finger to emphasize his point when he saw the disapproval in her face.

"All right," she said shaking her head. "Red or white?"

We both said "red," at the same time and laughed. I spread some of the mushroom paté on a cracker and was amazed that anything could taste so good.

"Gretchen, this is fabulous," I said with my mouth full. She poured us two glasses of wine and took one for herself back to the stove.

"Have more. There's plenty of it. Just help yourself."

Johann and I chatted for a few minutes, reliving the night before. I think talking about an experience like that is healing in a way. The robbery and hospital visit made us feel as if we had been friends for a long time. Johann didn't have anything more to add and security still hadn't a clue as to who the burglar was. We drank wine, ate paté, and talked. If anything, we felt even more comfortable with each other than we had yesterday. About twenty minutes into our conversation, I heard the gate buzzer ring and Johann's mother called out that she was leaving.

"Bye, Johann, Gretchen. We'll be back about midnight," she called from the foyer. I noticed she hadn't included me.

"Don't worry about my mother. She takes a long time to warm up to people."

"I'll bet," I thought, but said, "It's all right, Johann. I think she blames me for what happened to you. It's okay. Frankly, I blame myself."

Gretchen took that as a cue to bring us some cream of tomato soup and dinner officially began. The three of us ate together, which made me feel much better. I don't feel comfortable around servants or maids. Gretchen was more like a member of the family, and that's the way I liked it.

In all my life, I had never had such a wonderful meal. I've eaten in some of the best restaurants in Europe and The States, but Gretchen had them all beat. It took us over two hours to eat dinner, and at the end, we were stuffed. I wished we could begin again, and I asked Gretchen for some of her recipes, thinking that I should try them.

"I'll make some coffee. You two should get to work and in an hour or so, the strudel should be ready."

"Thank you so much for everything, Gretchen. Dinner was fabulous. And I've already heard how wonderful your strudel is. I can't wait."

When all the dishes were off the table, I pulled out the photographs and my Dictaphone and Johann and I got to work.

CHAPTER 13

▼

I opened my briefcase and put the photos on the table.

"Wow!" Johann said. "I hadn't realized there were so many."

"There're about one hundred and fifty photographs here. The originals were probably burned in the fire at the archive in Madrid, so we're lucky to have these. I had them enlarged so they would be easier to read."

"I'd like to look through them quickly first. I notice you've already started sorting them."

I began showing him the clipped together bunches. "Here's the largest group. It seems to me that this is part of an opera." Then, handing him another stack, I said, "This group contains lots of songs, some piano pieces, and here are some sonatas. Finally, these last three pages look like those sketches we saw yesterday."

Johann picked up the sketches first. "This looks to me almost exactly the same as the pages that were taken from the library yesterday. There's no real score here, just random notes and more of that Cyrillic writing. From what my friend showed me, I can see that we have the name Falkenhayn again. This could be more music for Falkenhayn. I don't know. I could get my friend to look at the writing again; it will probably say something similar. Let's look at the piano works first; they're easiest to deal with."

I gave him the small stack of photos that contained the piano works. I hadn't really looked at them since the weekend and I stood behind him so that we could read through them together. After a few minutes, Johann looked up, "Since you play the piano, why don't we use the grand in the music room. That way we can really hear what they sound like."

"Sure. Just lead the way. Playing piano will be a treat. I haven't touched one in over two weeks."

Johann led the way to the opposite wing of the house. The music room was spacious and filled with instruments—not just a Steinway grand piano—but also a harpsichord and 18th-century forte piano. There were framed manuscripts on the walls and busts of composers on stands between the large windows. Several antique bookcases housed literally thousands of scores. Johann smiled a little apologetically, "I know it's a little over the top, but when I was beginning my studies in music, my mother hired an interior designer and he went a little crazy with the room. The only thing I took from here was the bust of Beethoven I had in my office. I don't think I'll ever feel quite the same about that bust again," he said rubbing his head a little.

I went over to the beautiful seven-foot grand and sat down. I played a few scales to get my fingers warmed up. The piano was gorgeous and actually in tune. I couldn't imagine having such a wonderful instrument at my disposal all the time. I had priced them many years ago when I first moved to Boston, but even a used one in bad shape was over $35,000. I would love to have this music room in my apartment building, even if the decor was a bit over the top. If I had a room like this one, I could have salon parties where friends would come and play, sing, and drink wine. It was a nice thought. As I was playing the scales I asked, "Don't you play, Johann?" My fingers began moving over the keyboard to my favorite movement from a Beethoven sonata that I always use to warm up.

"Not really. Just enough to get by. It's a shame no one plays this instrument. My mother paid a lot of money for it."

Once finished with the Beethoven movement, I was ready to play. "Okay, let's have some of those piano pieces. I'll try the ones in Dadi's handwriting first."

After playing through four movements, we both realized that there didn't seem to be one unifying style to this music. One movement was very modern and atonal, the next sounded like it was written in the 19th-century. Nothing tied these pieces together. When we got to the fifth one, however, it was as if a lightning bolt hit us. I played the first few measures and stopped. We looked at each other.

"Oh my God, Johann, this is the Satie piece we looked at yesterday. But now it's in Dadi's handwriting and even has his autograph on it!" I cried.

"Yes, it sounds like it is the same, but play it through all the way just to be sure."

And I did. I had played it several times on my phantom piano the day before, but that doesn't ever take the place of hearing music played aloud. The piece was short, lasting only about two minutes, but it was hauntingly beautiful. The gorgeous circular melody seemed to speak directly to me. When I hear music that truly moves me, I have the feeling that a door has opened somewhere and I can catch a glimpse of, and understand the concept of, infinity or God. Usually, it moves me to tears. It is the only way that I have found to express my awe and wonder. When I teach, I sometimes talk about how music sometimes gave you a feeling that you can't really put into words. I tell my students that it's been the thing philosophers have talked about over the ages. They have tried to figure out how and why music can be so powerful while at the same time conveying nothing definitive. Once, after I described the feeling that truly beautiful music gives me, one student told me that she had never experienced that feeling. I couldn't understand how that could be, so all semester I kept suggesting pieces for her to listen to including everything from Beethoven's ninth symphony to Jimi Hendrix's "Purple Haze." I never found out if any of my suggestions had given her the experience.

Maybe it's not the infinite that I see, or God, but it is a sensation of depth, awe, warmth, sadness, and joy all at once. That's the best way I can describe it. The piece I just played gave me that feeling. When I was through, Johann and I were silent for a few moments. It wasn't the time for words, so I just played it again, this time with more feeling and certainty. It was more beautiful each time I heard it.

I let the last chord die away before I whispered, "It's so beautiful," Johann nodded in agreement. I continued, "But, I swear it's not by Dadi. It has to be by Satie. Why would it be in Dadi's handwriting? And look, at the bottom, he's even signed and dated it. 'E. Dadi 1926.' That's the year after Satie died."

"What are you saying, Leigh?"

"I don't know. Let's look at the photocopy again, see if there were any changes. It sounds the same to me, but let's compare to be sure."

We got my briefcase and the rest of the photographs from the kitchen and spread them out on the top of the grand piano. We found the copy of the piano piece and compared the two. It was exactly the same, down to the dynamic markings. Not one note, not one accidental had been changed.

"What does this mean?" asked Johann. "Let's go through it one step at a time. We have a piece that is definitely in Satie's handwriting, right?" I nodded. "It sounds like Satie, so stylistically it belongs to him. He never published it. Then we have the same composition in Dadi's handwriting dated the year after Satie died."

"Right," I interrupted, "It wasn't dedicated to Dadi or anything. Why would Dadi have written it out again in his own handwriting? I guess that it's okay to write out a copy. After all, there were no Xerox copiers, but why did he sign and date it? It doesn't make sense unless he planned to palm it off and publish it as his own."

As soon as I said it, Johann and I looked at each other, not wanting to believe Dadi was a thief but realizing that it was an entirely feasible hypothesis.

"This might change everything we know about Dadi," he said slowly.

"I can't believe it," I said and we both sank into silence looking at the two pieces, one a Xerox copy and the other a glossy photograph, lying side by side on the piano.

"Let's say we're right," I continued after a minute or two. "This could explain why there are so many Dadi pieces out there in so many different styles. Some of those songs," I picked up a stack of photographs, "look, they're in German, French, Spanish. I know only a few composers who write songs in so many languages, and only the best can do it so well. Maybe these were stolen from other composers also."

"You're getting a little ahead of yourself, but it is quite damning that Dadi signed it after Satie's death. Satie would have known his own music if the composition had been published under Dadi's name. Maybe that's why Dadi hung on to all this music for so long, waiting for the original composers to be out of the picture before he could use their music."

"I just can't believe it. That would make him a thief of the worst kind. I never thought I'd find this out when I started my research," I said, and we both looked at each other again. We suspected, however, that we had stumbled upon the truth. Too much evidence pointed in that direction. It was like a word that you can't figure out in a crossword puzzle, but given the first letter it becomes all too obvious. Dadi's changing styles, his ease of setting languages we knew he didn't speak well—this all could be explained if he had, in fact, stolen music from his friends and colleagues and published it under his own name.

"You know, Johann, I think we should look at some more of these things to try to prove this hypothesis. This is only one piece of music, after all. Maybe he dictated it to Satie and then finally tried to publish it himself in 1927. If he did steal music, we'll have to have more proof than just this one composition. I'm reeling from everything I've learned so far. First those love letters, and then finding that Dadi was in Vienna and Berlin during World War I, and now this."

"Remember that piece you thought could have been by Debussy, you know the one that had viola and piano in it? Let's look for that in the photographs."

We flipped through the photographs again, but found nothing that was even remotely like the viola and piano movement.

"You know that doesn't mean anything, Johann. The grad student from Chicago, Carson Barry, told Elena that there were more pieces in Puerto Rico. And he seemed, at least, to indicate to her that there was a big find there. Maybe Barry discovered the same thing that we just did when he was working down there. Dadi's son is a Cardinal. Maybe he has more music, although he said to me on the phone today that there's nothing of interest for me down in Puerto Rico."

"You spoke with the Cardinal?"

"Yes. I'll be seeing him in a few days."

"Give him my regards, and tell him to let me know if there is anything I can do to help get the archive started."

"Johann, he told me he wasn't interested in any of his father's music, and he said he had nothing in Puerto Rico. He told me you were mistaken about his interest in the materials you had."

"Really? That's very strange. He even took some of our things on loan to have them microfilmed. Well, he was probably occupied when you talked with him. At least he's going to meet with you. That's nice of him. I'm sure he's a busy man."

"I'm looking forward to it. Maybe I can retrace Carson Barry's steps and see what he was all excited about. I just don't want to have a similar accident."

"What accident?" Johann asked me.

"Carson Barry was killed in a car accident while he was working in Puerto Rico."

Johann looked concerned. "I didn't know that! I was wondering where Barry was. He was supposed to see Elena Rodriguez a while ago, and she had written something to me about him when I first received the materials from her. She didn't tell me this though."

"It was just a car accident, Johann. Nothing to worry about. You should see how they drive down there—worse than Boston, believe me."

"After last night, I'm not so sure it was an accident. I think you had better be careful."

"I'm all right. Don't worry about me. I wasn't the one in the hospital last night, after all."

"Point taken, but just be careful," he said, shuffling through some of the photographs on the piano. "Let's go through some more of this music."

We played through the rest of the piano works, but found nothing that matched the ten pieces from the Xerox copies. Next, we went through the songs.

They were all incredibly different from one another. The first three were in French and sounded like bad Debussy. Then, we hit one in German.

"Aren't these the same words as that vocal piece in the Xeroxed materials?" I asked Johann.

"Yes, it's a poem by Goethe. That doesn't prove anything. Even Schubert set the same poem several times. Let's see the music."

And again, we found that the vocal line matched a song in Dadi's hand exactly. It was too much of a coincidence.

"Who could have written this song, Johann? I don't recognize the handwriting in the Xerox copy."

"I'm not sure. Why don't you play the piano part and I'll sing it."

"Sure."

And I played softly while Johann sang. He had a lovely voice, as pleasant as his speaking voice. With proper training, he could have been a wonderful lieder singer. This particular song bordered on atonality, strange chords led to even stranger, but more beautiful chords; there was nothing very traditional about it. The composer set the words very carefully, and the full impact of Goethe's original poem was enhanced by the music's beauty. It was a strange combination of modern music and classical German poetry, but it worked wonderfully. When we finished the song, we both shook our heads.

"I don't really know this song or the composer. It sounds to me like it could be early Schoenberg or Berg. Strange that they would set this text, though. Berg especially would have set more modern poetry. I'm just not sure," I said.

"I don't think it's by Schoenberg, but it could be very early Berg," Johann replied. "I have a few original sheets of music by Alban Berg here somewhere. I'll look and see if I can find them."

"You what?"

"I have some music by Berg here."

"I can't believe you have original Berg manuscripts. What else is in this music room?" I said looking around, wanting to open all the drawers and look at all the scores.

"I have a few sheets from Berg's *Altenberg Lieder*. My mother bought it at auction as an investment years ago. I wanted to donate it to the library, but unfortunately she wouldn't hear of it. I take good care of it, though, and have let some scholars in to see it."

He opened one of the lower drawers in the bookcase closest to the piano and produced a folder containing a few sheets of music.

"These are the originals, written in Berg's handwriting," he said.

By putting the original next to the Xerox copy, we could see instantly it was an exact match.

"Oh, no! Not again. I can't believe what we're finding. I just can't understand how someone could get away with this. It's robbery of the worst kind. Berg didn't write that much music, but what he wrote, I know," I said.

"Berg's one of my favorites. It's terrible that he died so young and from something as stupid as a bee sting. Dadi's German songs, or at least some of them, could have been Berg's. Dadi published a whole cycle of German songs in the 1930s, sometime. Do you remember when?"

"Dadi published his songs in 1937. This song was not in the group, though," I answered.

"Berg died in 1935. It seems we have a pattern here. Maybe some of those songs were not Dadi's, maybe some were. We may never really know. But, it seems clear to me that Dadi was a real thief."

"I know, I know. I just don't want to believe it. I'm positive that these pieces are by Satie and Berg. I'm not sure I can convince the musicological world of it. If I can prove it, then it's the major find of the decade! Maybe this is what Carson Barry was trying to tell Elena when he said he had found some significant compositions. We all assumed they were unpublished works by Dadi. Maybe Carson Barry discovered some of the pieces were really by other composers. This is absolutely unbelievable."

"Let's sing through all the songs and we can make some guesses. You know, try to figure out which ones really could be by Dadi."

So we did. After about an hour, we had gotten through all the songs and played the one we thought was by Alban Berg again. As soon as we were finished, someone startled us by applauding. Gretchen had stolen into the room, taken a seat by the door and had been listening to us play.

"Oh, it's so good to hear music in this room again. Leigh, you play beautifully."

"Thank you, Gretchen. It's called about twenty years of piano lessons."

"No, it's more than that. You have a wonderful feel for music. What was that you were playing? It's lovely. Strange, but lovely."

"It's a song with words by Goethe. We're not really sure who wrote it. We've found some other interesting things in this stack of photographs. Here, listen to this piece and see if you like it."

I played the Satie composition again and Gretchen shut her eyes and concentrated on the music. After the piece was over, she said, "That was haunting, wasn't it? Who wrote that?"

Johann said, "Well, that's the question, Gretchen. We're not really sure right now."

"It sounds French to me, but then again, what do I know? Johann, I came in to remind you that you need your rest."

I glanced at the clock and noticed it was just after eleven. "Yes, I should really be going. I'll be staying at Barbara and Oskar's, so I can come by in the early morning and we could continue. Is that okay, Johann?"

"Fine. Actually, now that you mention it, I do feel tired and my head is beginning to hurt again. Thanks, Gretchen," he said smiling lovingly at her. It seemed to me that Gretchen had really taken the role of Johann's mother, and I was glad that he had this warm, loving person in the house.

"Do you want us to walk you back to Barbara's?" Gretchen asked.

"Well, thank you. That would be really nice. You can just watch until I make it to Barbara's door."

I bundled up the photographs and papers and put them in my briefcase, got my black cardigan and left through the front door again. All three of us walked down the long front path to the street, and I thanked them both again.

"Why don't you call us in the morning, dear? Maybe you can join us for breakfast. You should invite Barbara, also. I know she's very lonely over there, by herself all the time," Gretchen said as she hugged me goodnight.

After the delicious dinner, I couldn't wait to try another meal. It was nice that she was concerned about Barbara too. "Sure, that sounds wonderful. I'll call you in the morning."

I walked to Barbara's house and waved back at Johann and Gretchen when I had made it to the gate. They turned and went back to the house. I opened the gate and was glad that Barbara had left all the lights on for me. I was used to living in the city, where there really is no such thing as absolute darkness. But here, there were no streetlights on the block, and the individual houses and their walkways provided the only illumination. Most of these were already dark since everyone went to bed early, I guessed. Barbara's house was brightly lit, but even with that generous amount of light spilling into the street, I could see literally hundreds of glittering stars. I wasn't used to the beautiful sight. The sky looked like black velvet and I lingered on the sidewalk a little longer. It was a clear night, but nippy, and the breeze had a hint of winter in it.

I started up the path. Barbara must have been waiting up for me again since she opened the door as I started up the walkway. I've never gotten to ring the doorbell at this house, I mused. She glided down the stairs and met me halfway with a smile.

"Did you have a nice evening?"

"Yes, it was wonderful. Gretchen is a terrific cook."

"I wouldn't know. I have never been there for dinner. Gretchen is their maid, right?"

I wondered how Barbara didn't seem to know Gretchen at all, but Gretchen seemed to have Barbara pegged.

"Yes, Gretchen's a lovely woman. Very genuine and sweet."

"Well, she's a maid, after all," said Barbara. I had no idea what she meant by that, but decided to let it go. Barbara and I would never travel in the same social circles, no matter how much money I had. I just didn't understand her.

"Why don't we have some tea and visit a little?" she continued once we had gotten into the house.

"Sure, that's sounds great." Gretchen was right. Barbara must be very lonely, I thought to myself. Frankly, all I wanted to do was brush my teeth and go to bed. I remembered how inviting that feather bed looked, and even the starched sheets seemed to call to me, but Barbara would have been disappointed if I begged off.

We went into the kitchen again, where tea was already steeping. I wondered if she had just kept it steeping all night, or had surveillance cameras outside on the street so that she knew when I would be there. In the corner of the kitchen was piled a large group of matching suitcases that looked brand new to me, and a few older black briefcases that were surprisingly alike and all looked like mine, only in better shape.

"Are you planning a trip, Barbara?"

"No. I just bought a new set of luggage, Gucci bags, you know, and decided to get rid of the old ones. Do you want them? I think they're out of style now, though."

I hadn't realized that there was such a thing as "out of style" in luggage. I just thought that you bought bags and used them until they fell apart or got lost. Barbara's out-of-style luggage was a dark green with big red roses all over every piece. They were not really my type, but I hesitated because they looked like good quality bags that had never been used. I have a mish-mash of leftovers from my father and my sister, some of which need to be held together by ropes and ties when I travel. On the other hand, I didn't want to take the bags from Barbara. Don't ask me why. Maybe it would have made me feel even more like the poor cousin. So, after a few heartbeats, I said, "No, Barbara, thanks. I have so much luggage at home already," but I still looked over at the stack longingly, thinking to myself that if they had been black American Tourister bags I probably would have taken them. I scolded myself for being so petty. What was wrong with red roses any-way? They would probably have been easy to spot at the baggage claim carousels.

We had tea and coffeecake and talked a little about Johann's music room, his furniture, and the art on the Spurber's walls. Barbara had never been in the house before and I could tell that she was jealous and intrigued all at once. I knew that people in the neighborhood were never really friendly with one another. I thought back to those rowdy block parties we always have in my neighborhood in Boston, with kids running in and out of everyone's houses and groups of parents hovering over barbecues, grilling hot dogs. Here, there would probably be a few people standing in front of each house, not talking to each other and mentally cataloguing what the other families were wearing. I told Barbara she was invited to breakfast, and initially she was excited. But, upon hearing that Gretchen, and not Diana Spurber, had extended the invitation, she declined. Barbara is very silly sometimes, I thought to myself. I wondered if her curiosity would win out by the morning.

When it was time to turn in, Barbara asked if I would help her carry the bags to the curb—tomorrow was trash day and she didn't want them cluttering up her kitchen any longer. She put on a black jacket hanging by the kitchen door and we each took a few suitcases. She took one of the briefcases under her arm also. We started out the side kitchen door and down the walk to the street. When I was about halfway down, the phone rang, startling me since it was quite late to call. Barbara, who was ahead of me, said, as she continued down the steps, "Leigh, could you please get it? Oskar was supposed to call when he got in from his din-ner meeting tonight. Sometimes these meetings last really late into the night."

Sure they do, I thought. I couldn't imagine meetings going on until one in the morning. I put the bags down on the walkway and went back inside the kitchen door and answered the phone. Luckily, it was a portable phone, so I figured I could give it to Barbara right away since I really had no desire to speak to Oskar, who was probably a bit tipsy anyway from his high level meetings. The caller did, in fact, turn out to be Oskar. I said hello to him and asked him to hold on so that I could get Barbara. I opened the door and started down the steps, waving the phone and saying loudly, "Yes Barbara, it's for you." She waved back as if to say that she would be there in a minute. I watched her at the curb. She had obviously taken my stack down with her also, and was carefully arranging the bags in order of size. I wondered why she bothered, since the next people to see them would be the garbage men who would just hoist them onto their truck, but then realized that this was precisely the reason why her house was neat and orderly, and mine was always such a mess. She cared about things like this.

She straightened up, finally satisfied with her pile, and patted her hair to make sure that it was still in place. At that moment, seemingly out of nowhere, a large black Mercedes came careening down the street. We both turned toward the sound of squealing tires and Barbara looked at it like she didn't know what it was. I wasn't sure if the driver was drunk or if the car was out of control, but I yelled, "Barbara, get out of the way."

She turned and looked at me with a strange expression on her face. Just at that minute the car literally ran into her. There was a sickening dull thud when her body was thrown on the top of the hood and stayed there until the black Mercedes finally stopped. When the car backed up, her body slid away from it and flopped onto the sidewalk, crumpling in such a way that I knew it was completely lifeless. The car screeched to a stop next to the pile of suitcases. The passenger door opened and the tall man in the tan raincoat got out and quickly grabbed the luggage and briefcase and started putting it in the back seat of the black car.

I must have started screaming from my spot near the kitchen door, because he looked up toward me and our eyes locked. He had an indefinable expression as he scanned my face, and then he slowly turned to look at Barbara's lifeless body. I realized in that instant that he had mistaken Barbara for me. On the dark street, we probably did look similar—same height, same hair color, and she was wearing a black jacket. When he turned toward me again, I knew he would come after me next. I ran up the few walkway stairs and slammed the kitchen door shut, locking it with shaking hands. Oskar was still on the phone and I could hear him yelling, "What's going on? What's going on? What has happened? Is anybody there? Barbara? Barbara!"

I looked at the phone as if I didn't know what it was and hung up on him. I looked around the table for a number to call the police. I was sure it wasn't 911. Fortunately, the number was programmed into the base of the portable phone and I hit auto dial. I told the police that someone had been hit by a car and gave them the address. Then, I started rummaging around the drawers in the kitchen and I found a meat cleaver that I could use to defend myself. I stood in the kitchen corner waiting for the police, praying that the man in the raincoat had left. In the distance, I heard a siren and realized with relief that it was headed my way.

CHAPTER 14

▼

I stood in the corner of the kitchen, listening to the sound of the sirens. I felt better that I had the cleaver in my hand, though, frankly, I wasn't sure how I would use it. My self-defense course only taught us how to kick or hit someone, not how to use a weapon. If that man had a gun, I was sunk. I kept thinking of Barbara, playing the few last few seconds of her life over and over in my mind. This was the first time I had absolute proof that the tall man was lethal. A shiver ran up my spine when I realized that there had to have been two people in the car since he had gotten out from the passenger side. The tall man had an accomplice; he wasn't alone. I knew that I had crossed some line and that the man in the raincoat was not just trying to scare me off anymore, he was now trying to kill me. It was too late to walk away from the dissertation. Even if I did, I'd still be in danger. I knew too much, though I wasn't quite sure what, exactly, I knew. Why hadn't I listened to Carlos and changed my thesis topic? Why was I so stubborn all the time? Now, I had witnessed the murder of my cousin and I was sure that I would be next.

I stood in the corner of the kitchen for what seemed like hours, but was probably just over a minute. The sirens were getting much closer, and I heard a car door slam and the peel of tires from right outside. I pushed open the curtains and looked toward the street. The black Mercedes was gone. No one from any house on the street had ventured outside and I felt entirely alone, but I didn't want to move. Two police cars screeched up a few seconds later, lights flashing. Four cops got out. Two went over to Barbara's body right away, and two rang the bell on the gate. I opened the kitchen door and ran down the walkway to speak to them. The two officers, standing on the sidewalk, had odd expressions on their faces, and seemed to back away from me a little when I reached the gate and tried to open it for them. I realized then, that I was still clutching the meat cleaver, and dropped it in the grass. They relaxed a bit when it hit the ground.

"A big, black Mercedes," I said, "A big, black Mercedes came around the corner and ran into my cousin. I saw the whole thing! It went right for her! Then a man got out of the car and picked up some luggage that she was putting on the street. The car just left a few minutes ago. You should go after them. You should chase them down. Do something."

I must have been speaking in English, because one of the cops said, in heavily accented German, "Please, a little slower."

I looked over at Barbara. One of two cops near her straightened up, put his jacket over her body and then went to his car. He called in something on the radio and came to stand next to the other two in a show of solidarity, or strength, I wasn't sure which. All I could think was, "Oh my God, Barbara's dead," over and over in my mind, as if trying to convince myself that this wasn't a nightmare. The cops patiently stood on the sidewalk and watched me stare at the body, her pale legs sticking out from beneath the dark jacket in an unnatural fashion. Then I glanced over at them again. I wanted to yell that they should go after the black car and catch the murderers but my eyes were continually drawn back to Barbara's body. I just couldn't get myself to believe it. Only moments before, we had been eating cake and drinking tea. Part of me wished that I had been the one on the sidewalk, and part of me was relieved that I wasn't. My emotions were running wild and my normally high guilt level had just hit the red line.

In the distance, I heard another siren, probably an ambulance. By this time, almost all the houses on the street were lit, and I could see people looking out of their windows, but no one ventured outside. They didn't care enough to find out who was lying in the street. Besides, I was sure they didn't want to get involved, and I began to get angry and annoyed. No one ever wanted to get involved. I started to cry out of frustration, anger and fear. "Look, you have to go after them," I choked out. "They left just a few minutes ago. It's late. There won't be many black Mercedes driving around now. Find them. Just find them!"

"They're probably long gone by now, Miss," one of them said.

The cop, who had put his jacket on Barbara, said quietly, in beautiful English, "I already called it in. The patrol officers are looking for the car. Please describe for us what happened."

I shook my head, "I already told you. A big, black Mercedes came around the corner and ran into my cousin. Her name is, well, was Barbara Niedermeyer." I looked up just as Gretchen was opening her gate and coming down the sidewalk toward us. She had on a pink, fuzzy robe and matching slippers and a hair net. Her ensemble made her look like a giant pink penguin, but she didn't seem concerned about her appearance. She marched right up to me, oblivious of the looks she was getting from the policemen.

When she reached my side, she immediately put her arm around me and asked the officers, "Is there anything I can do to help? This is Leigh Maxwell. She's a graduate student visiting from America. I am Gretchen Bergman; I live a few doors down. Can we go inside, please, so we don't have to stand on the sidewalk and cause a commotion on the street? It's cold out here."

The police nodded; they seemed happy to get off the street, too. Gretchen skillfully maneuvered us to the Spurber house just as the ambulance pulled up. Three of the four policemen followed us and we all went into the house and sat in the tastefully furnished living room. Diana Spurber came in as we were sitting down, and looked in distaste at the policemen as if they smelled like cow manure. Then she turned to me and I flinched. There was a palpable expression of utter hatred in her eyes. She didn't offer us anything, not a seat, not a drink, not even her name. She seemed annoyed that I just sat down on the sofa without being asked, but I wasn't sure I would be able to stand even if I had wanted to. Gretchen disappeared for a few seconds and brought out a glass of water for me. The cops just waited quietly, seemingly in awe of the huge, beautiful house and the well-put-together woman who oversaw the whole thing.

Johann came in just then, and sat next to me on the sofa and held my hand. He was also wearing his robe and looked as if he had just woken up. Diana Spurber, on the other hand, was impeccably dressed in a beige cashmere sweater that matched the beautifully upholstered sofa. I noticed she had pearls on. She crossed her arms in front of her when Johann sat down. Much to his credit, he didn't even look over at her.

"What happened?" Johann asked softly.

One of the officers took out his notebook and began writing as I told Johann the whole story. I described everything—the green luggage with the roses, Oskar on the phone, the car, and the awful thud. Then I described the tall man in the raincoat and how he had taken some of the luggage and briefcases. I started crying when I told him how guilty I felt, and how sorry I felt about Oskar.

"Oh my God! I hung up on Oskar!" I cried. I explained that I was holding the phone when the car had hit Barbara. "Oskar's in Moscow. I think he's working on a business deal. He was supposed to call after his meetings. Barbara and I were both heading down to put the trash on the curb when the phone rang. I was closest to the kitchen door, so I answered it. I asked him to hold on so that I could get Barbara. When the car hit her, I screamed and ran into the house. All I could think was that I had to call the police, so I just hung up on poor Oskar. He must be frantic."

One of the cops interrupted. "Miss, you said that he was in Moscow? What was he doing there?"

"Barbara told me that he has been working with the Russians on some sort of business deal. He sells computers. I don't even know the name of the company."

The cop looked at the other officers and they all almost imperceptibly nodded in agreement. He put his notebook away.

"We'll have to find out what company he's working for, but it seems clear to me what has happened. Thank you for your help, Miss. We'll file reports immediately and try to contact Mr. Niedermeyer. The patrol officers may have found the car by now."

"I don't know what you mean. The man who has been following me for days is responsible. He's the one you should be looking for. I know now that he has an accomplice and that he's deadly. I saw him kill Barbara. Look at Johann. He was hurt last night at the library. I'm sure it was the same man."

They turned to Johann, "Sir, what happened the other night at the library?"

Johann answered, "There was a burglary and I was hit over the head with a, um, a heavy object. I spent the night in the hospital. It could have something to do with our work, the work Leigh and I were doing. I'd certainly investigate it."

"Yes, we'll look into all the possibilities. We first must find out where Mr. Niedermeyer is."

"Yes, that might be best," Johann agreed.

"Wait a minute. I'm serious," I interrupted after a few heartbeats, "This is all about the work I'm doing on Enrique Dadi, an early twentieth-century composer. As soon as I started working on this topic, I realized something was wrong. All the scholars who have gotten as far as I have are now dead. I mean it. I'm the only one left. Johann, tell them."

Johann interrupted, "Yes, the man Leigh described getting out of the Mercedes does fit the description of the man who hit me last night at the library. I think it's an avenue worth exploring."

"Exploring? No, it's the *only* avenue to pursue, Johann. I know it now for certain. These people are deadly serious. They're ruthless. I don't know what it's all about, but maybe it's about some of our findings. They're not just stealing computers or your library materials. This is about murder now."

"Leigh, I understand, but in all seriousness, it *was* a black Mercedes and Oskar is in Moscow doing business. I told you about the Russian Mafia problem here.

You didn't quite believe me. Maybe something didn't go the way it should have in Oskar's business dealing, and this was a warning to him. It might have nothing to do with you at all."

"But, why would they start taking the luggage? They probably thought it was *my* luggage. The tall man went right for the briefcase. Come on, Johann. You of all people should believe me. You were attacked by the same guy. You've got to believe me." My voice cracked by the end of the sentence and I felt like screaming out of frustration.

"I think they should look into both. I agree it seems like it's the same man. I wish you had seen him last night so we could be absolutely sure."

One policeman interrupted us, "Yes, miss. We'll contact Oskar Niedermeyer and talk to him about the possibility. We'll also look into the Enrique Dadi connection. That's D-A-D-I, right?" I nodded. "Did you get the license plate number?" he continued, "Or part of it?"

"No, I'm sorry. I was standing by the kitchen door when it happened. I keep running the whole event over and over in my mind, but I never saw the plate. When I think of it, it seems like it's all going in slow motion. Barbara looked at me. She was looking at me when it hit her. She had an odd expression on her face, as if she knew something was wrong. Maybe she didn't move on purpose. She just stood there," I trailed off.

Johann put his arm around my shoulder. "It wasn't your fault. Look, you weren't driving the car. There was nothing you could do. If Oskar hadn't called, you would both probably be hurt or dead by now."

"I was just getting to know Barbara, really know her, Johann. She looked at me, even while the car hit her. She just looked at me. I was the last person she saw in her life, I…" Panic edged into my voice and I started to cry again.

The policeman said, "Well, that will be all for now, Miss. Where can we reach you tomorrow if we have more questions?"

"I was supposed to stay at Barbara and Oskar's tonight, but I can't bear to be in that house. Do you think you could drive me to the Pension Schwarzer Adler? My cousin, Steffi, is working there now."

"Nonsense," Gretchen said. "You should stay here–with us. We've got a first-rate alarm system, and plenty of room. Don't you worry about anything." Turning to the policeman, she said, "She'll be right here with us."

"Thank you, Frau Spurber," the policeman said, and the three of them filed out of the room following Gretchen. I looked over at Diana Spurber to see if she would correct them, saying that Gretchen was only a maid, but she hadn't moved a muscle for the entire time we had been in the room, although I could see her eyes darting around, taking everything in. She looked more like a skinny vulture than an emaciated bird.

When they were in the foyer, she turned to Johann and said in a voice that seemed to cut the air, "I'd like to speak with you in the kitchen. Now."

She turned on her heel and walked quickly out the door. Johann stood up and said, "I'll be right back. Don't go anywhere," and patted me on the shoulder.

I sat there alone, straining to hear anything from the kitchen. Gretchen came back in and said, "Okay, dear, let's get your things and close up Barbara's house." As we left the Spurber house, we saw all the police cars drive away. Most of the lights were still on in the neighborhood, but not a soul was on the street. The ambulance was gone, and there was a chalk mark on the sidewalk where Barbara's body had been. I started to cry again, but Gretchen distracted me by being all the more efficient.

"Come on. Let's get those things," she said in a voice that I could only describe as chipper.

We went in through the side kitchen door–I knew that I had left it open–then through the kitchen into the main part of the house. As we gathered up my belongings, Gretchen kept up a running commentary in an attempt to get my mind off what had just happened. She was like the Rock of Gibraltar, and I was grateful she was there with me. The house was enormous in its emptiness. I wondered how Barbara could have dealt with such loneliness. I hadn't brought much to Barbara's, so I was done packing in just a few minutes. As we were about to leave, the phone rang. I looked at the clock on the wall; it was about two in the morning.

Gretchen picked it up immediately. "Niedermeyer....Oh, Oskar, hello. This is Gretchen Bergman. I live a few doors down....Yes, there's been an accident. It's Barbara. A car went out of control and hit her in front of the house. I'm terribly sorry Oskar, but she died from the injuries. Yes, I'm so sorry....Yes. She's here with me. Well, hold on." Gretchen handed me the phone. "He wants to talk to you."

I didn't know what to say to Oskar, nor did I really want to talk to him. What do you say to someone whose wife you just saw murdered? I took the phone from her and took a deep breath. "Hello, Oskar. Yes, I'm terribly sorry. I...Yes. I...Well, the police are working on it right now. I'm so sorry about hanging up, I wasn't really thinking clearly. I was very upset...Yes, I'm sorry. I know you're upset, well,...yes. I'm sorry, I'm so, so sorry...Here she is." I felt terrible handing the phone back to Gretchen. There was nothing I could do or say to him, so I kept apologizing.

Gretchen took the phone and put her arm around me. "Oskar, the police are searching for the car right now. They'll be calling you, I'm sure. Could you tell me where you're staying? I'll tell the police…Ja, I've got a pen…Leigh will be staying with us at the Spurber house. I'll give you the number there, 522-7447. I'll see you tomorrow. Try to get some rest. I know it's difficult. There's nothing anyone can do right now. Good night."

"Thank you, Gretchen. I really couldn't have told him. He was very upset. It was all my fault anyway."

"Nonsense. Oskar will be all right, though I'm sure he was shocked by the news. They haven't gotten along for years. They hardly talk to each other. I'm sure it's more of a shock."

"Really? They always appeared to be the perfect couple."

"Well, now, isn't that always what people try to portray?" she said as she led me out of the house and closed the door behind her. "Everything here is appearances. You have to keep up a good face for the neighbors, but there are really no true feelings behind the beautiful doors, sometimes. That's the saddest thing of all, I think. Who really cares what the neighbors down the street think? My parents used to live for that. They were miserable, but they stayed together because they didn't want the shame of breaking up. 'What would the neighbors say?' they always asked themselves. They would have been so much happier apart. So many lives are lost that way here. People have to make their own way, live their own lives without hurting others, and if the neighbors don't like it, then, they just have to learn to live with it. Am I right, dear?" she said patting my arm.

"Yes, I guess so. I know that my father isn't happy with my choice of boyfriend, but he hasn't said anything to me about it. I'm happy with the situation. I've never really cared that much what people think of me. Just what I think of myself." I paused, "I think you would like Carlos, my boyfriend. He's very sweet. I'll be seeing him this weekend. We're meeting in Puerto Rico."

"That will be good for you. You need a little vacation."

I looked over at her. She didn't know that part of the reason I was going to Puerto Rico was to continue my work on Dadi, but in a way she was right. I needed to be in Carlos' arms. I needed to feel protected, and Carlos always did that for me. I thought about sitting on a beach in Condado with my eyes shut feeling the warmth from the tropical sun on my skin. Having witnessed a murder, I decided I was going to stop. I would see the Cardinal in Puerto Rico and give him my findings and explain that I was withdrawing from my degree program. I just couldn't take it anymore. I didn't say all this to Gretchen. A doctorate wasn't worth a life. I'd go to Puerto Rico and relax, and then apply to library school.

When we got to the house, Johann was waiting in the foyer and Diana Spurber was nowhere in sight.

"Would you like something to drink? Maybe you should call your cousin and tell her what happened."

"Sure, I'd love something alcoholic. I don't much care what."

Gretchen, Johann and I went into the kitchen. As I telephoned Steffi, Gretchen got out three glasses and a bottle of brandy. I told Steffi what had happened and where I was staying. She sounded much more upset than I would have expected her to be, and I could tell she started to cry. She told me that she would come over to the house as soon as she was done at work, which would be about nine the next morning. She also said that she would call my father and explain what had happened, and that I was safe and sound. She was glad that I wasn't at Barbara's house alone.

When I hung up, I sat down at the big kitchen table and sipped my brandy. I don't normally like brandy, but this was delicious, and the knots in my neck and shoulders seemed to loosen up with every sip I took. There was a companionable silence around the table, but I kept reliving those last few moments of Barbara's life. Gretchen picked up the phone and called the police, giving them the information about where and how to contact Oskar. When she was through, she said, "Well, I think I'll say goodnight. I'll set the alarm. You should be fine here tonight. Johann, give Leigh the bedroom next to yours, so if she needs anything she can just go next door and ask you." She opened a kitchen cabinet and took out a brown prescription bottle. She turned to me next and said,"I also think you should take two of these, so you can get some sleep." She handed me two pink pills.

"What is it?"

"It's nothing very strong, just a relaxant to help you get to sleep. You need to rest. What you've been through in the past few days would be hard for anyone."

I had never taken anything like this before. I've always shied away from taking any drug that would leave me out of control, even on a small scale–I guess I don't count liquor. But, on the other hand, I did need to stop playing the movie of Barbara's death over and over in my mind. I needed to sleep, so I downed the pills with a hefty gulp of brandy and thanked Gretchen for her thoughtfulness.

When Gretchen left, Johann took my hand and said that he would stay up with me as long as I wanted him to. We stayed there for maybe half an hour, talking about Barbara and Oskar, and drinking lots of brandy. I heard stories that I had never heard before. About Oskar's roving eye and all the affairs he had had. I heard about Barbara's nervous breakdown ten years ago. About how their eldest son was charged with embezzlement and may face time in prison, and how the middle daughter flunked out of college. I began to see a completely different side of the family than Barbara had shown anyone. It saddened me that she never let anyone in to see it. Maybe she wouldn't have been so lonely in her sadness. The thought depressed me utterly.

"It's all such a waste, Johann. It's all such a waste."

"I know. There wasn't anything you could do. You can't blame yourself for everything."

I looked at him, and he seemed very far away from me. Actually, his face seemed to be a bit wavy, as if I was looking at him in a funhouse mirror. I started giggling and couldn't stop. At first, Johann looked concerned and asked, "Are you okay?"

My laughter was contagious, and he started to laugh himself. When I finally calmed down, I managed to say, "Johann, you look funny. You have such a big nose, and you're so far away." I started laughing again, but somewhere in the recesses of my mind, I knew the pink pills had taken hold of me and I began to panic. I had assumed it was something like Valium, but maybe it was something much stronger. I managed to get more serious and said, "Johann, I think this is the brandy and pills talking. You know, I think everything in here is pretty funny looking," and started to laugh again.

He stood up, and said, "Well, time for bed." He took my arm and guided me up the stairs and into a beautiful bedroom with a canopy bed. It was the kind of frilly bedroom that every little girl would love to have. Mosquito netting was gracefully tied at the back of the headboard, and the antiques in the room were inviting. Johann went to a door that I thought was a closet, and said, "Here's the bathroom. I'm just next door on the right if you need anything." He clicked the light on in the bathroom and I looked in to see a gray marble vanity and tub. I threw myself on the bed, kicking my shoes off the side and giggled some more.

"What a nice room. I'm sure going to sleep well tonight," I said. I felt as if I wouldn't care if the man in the tan coat walked into the room right now, and part of me wished I hadn't taken the pills. I took one of the fluffy pillows and got on my side, into what I call my sleep position, and shut my eyes.

"Sleep well," Johann said as he covered me with a blanket. "I'll be right next door if you need anything. Don't worry about waking me up."

"Sure," I said sleepily. Part of me wanted to sleep, but in the deep recesses of my exhausted and now drugged mind, I was still nervous and wound up from the night's events. I knew that I was pretty much helpless now. I prayed that the burglar alarm was as good as Gretchen thought it was. I couldn't respond at all if something happened now. I needed my wits about me, but couldn't possibly muster the energy. I thought to myself that I would never again take any relaxant on top of brandy again, even aspirin.

I must have drifted off to sleep, but woke a short time later, completely nauseated. When I opened my eyes, the room was spinning out of control. I spent the rest of the night, as my mother would say, praying to the porcelain God.

CHAPTER 15

▼

When I had finally gotten all the poison out of my system, I lay down on the marble floor of the bathroom and closed my eyes. Getting sick was probably a good idea under the circumstances, but it takes a little time for your body and mind to realize it. After lying on the floor for about half an hour, I was completely chilled and started shivering. I got up, washed my face, brushed my teeth and went back to the frilly white bed. This time I put on my Picard T-shirt and got under the covers. When I laid down, I swear I could actually hear my bones creak into place. The sun was just coming up and the blue-orange hue of dawn trickled through the lace curtains. One ray of sunlight started creeping toward the bed. It was a beautiful sight but I needed darkness, so I put the pillow over my head and fell asleep for the next few hours.

Gretchen woke me a little after nine, telling me that Steffi was downstairs waiting for me. She had come directly from work. Gretchen told me to take my time and that she would give Steffi some coffee and breakfast. I should meet them downstairs in the kitchen when I was ready.

"Was the sleeping pill effective?" Gretchen asked as she was leaving.

"Oh yes, Gretchen, it certainly had an effect," I said, but the sarcasm was lost on her.

She smiled and said, "I thought it was a good idea. I'll see you in the kitchen, dear. Take your time." With that she left.

I slowly stretched out. I had muscle aches in places I didn't even know there were muscles and my stomach hurt, as if I had done five hundred sit-ups. I took a quick shower to rid myself of the sweat and a residual feeling of nausea and got dressed in the only other outfit that I had brought with me. I made my way downstairs feeling more human than I had just a half-hour before.

Steffi was sitting at the kitchen table with Gretchen and Johann when I came in. When I entered the room, she got up immediately and gave me a big hug.

"How are you feeling? Did you get any sleep?"

"I got some. What about you?"

"I'm so shocked by all of this. I can't tell you how upset I am about Barbara. I've been jealous of her all my life and now she's gone. I feel so sad and sorry that I didn't know her any better."

"I know how you feel. I was just getting to know her myself," I turned to Johann and Gretchen and said, "Did the police call this morning with any news?"

Gretchen got me a mug from a kitchen cabinet and we all sat down. "Yes, they did. They found the car. It was abandoned near the Ku-Damm, actually right around the block from the Pension where your cousin works. Barbara's blood was on the headlights and they could see where the body hit the car. It was an unregistered vehicle and the entire car had been wiped clean of fingerprints. The license plate had been stolen a few days ago from the airport. Barbara's luggage was still in the car, though it had been opened and, in some cases, ripped apart. Now, why would anyone want to rip up perfectly good luggage, I'd like to know? The briefcase was missing."

"I swear they were looking for my materials on Dadi. If they knew that I had made photocopies of everything I've seen so far, I can't imagine what they would do."

"Maybe we should let them know that," Johann said. "You know, let them know that they can't stop the flow of information any more. Too many people have seen it all."

"Well, after what we found out last night..."

Steffi interrupted. "What did you find out?"

"Johann and I think that Enrique Dadi stole a lot of the music he published. This is still a hypothesis, but we think that he took other composers' music and published it under his own name. We found two pieces that point in that direction, an Erik Satie piano work and also an Alban Berg song. The problem is that I can't imagine why anyone would kill for that."

"That happened, what, sixty, seventy years ago? Why would anyone care that much *now*?" Steffi asked incredulously.

"I don't know. I have no idea why anyone would resort to burglary, much less murder, over something like this."

"Well, is there any family left? Would they care about black marks on their family honor, or anything?" Gretchen asked.

"I'm sure Dadi's family would be upset if they knew their father was a liar and a cheat, but Dadi had only two children. The elder is a woman—she must be in her late-eighties by now. He also had a son who is a Cardinal in the Catholic Church. I can't imagine either of them doing any harm to anyone. So, if it wasn't a member of the family, then who else would care so much that they would murder for it?"

"Somebody cares. That much is certain," Johann said and we all nodded in agreement. "We should just let the police handle it," he murmured as an afterthought.

Silence descended on the kitchen table. I was thinking that the police didn't really believe me and that they would waste lots of time investigating the Russian connection, but I didn't want to bring it up again. We sat and picked at the delicious coffeecake Gretchen had put in front of us. I could only manage a little bite with my coffee, but felt better having eaten something.

While I was on my second cup of coffee, Diana Spurber came into the room. She went up to Johann and put her hand on his shoulder and asked how he was feeling. It was the first time I had actually seen a gesture of warmth from her, and it surprised me a little. It seemed to have surprised Johann too, because he jumped when she touched him, as if she had static electricity in her hand.

"I feel fine today, Mother," he replied in a courteous, but guarded manner.

"Good. You need your rest. You are just a few days out of the hospital and need to take care of yourself more." She looked over at Steffi, "Oh, Good morning," but said nothing at all when she glanced at me.

Gretchen had gotten up from the table and poured Diana Spurber some coffee into a beautiful antique cup and saucer. The cup was made of such fine china that when the morning sun hit it, the hand painted flowers adorning the rim seemed almost translucent. I noticed that Gretchen put a packet of Equal into the delicious brew along with a splash of evaporated milk, a sure way, at least in my opinion, to ruin it.

"Is there anything else you would like?" Gretchen asked somewhat deferentially, while handing her the cup.

"You know I never eat breakfast," Frau Spurber answered, and then took her first sip of coffee. She grimaced, "Not quite as good as normal, is it? I guess we've all had a long night." She looked over at me after hurtling her last barb and left the room.

Gretchen seemed unfazed by the whole conversation. She sat down and looked at Johann with a sigh and said, "Ah, your mother," while shaking her head. Johann stared sullenly into his coffee cup, and Steffi and I sat there feeling uncomfortable.

Steffi was the first to break the silence, "Leigh, maybe you should come home with me and we can have a quiet day together."

"Johann and I were going to do some work today, but I really think I should just give up on all this now and forget about it. If I knew who to give all my work to, I would. Then, I'd just walk away. Maybe give up the whole degree thing. There're no jobs anyway. Maybe I should just go to law school, everyone else does." I was just blabbing on and on.

Steffi stopped me by taking hold of my hand. "I think you've been through hell for the last few days and you still need some rest. Why not forget about it all now and get some sleep. You can make up your mind about everything else when you are rested and back in Boston."

Johann nodded. "Don't make any rash decisions. We've come this far. Let's play through some of the pieces like we did last night. I still need some more sleep, but maybe later this afternoon we can get together. How about that? We could work for a few hours later, just don't tell my mother."

"I wouldn't dare. Besides, I don't think she has even acknowledged my presence."

"Well," said Steffi, "I'd like to go home and take a nap or something. I've been up all night and we had a house full of surgeons from a convention last night at the pension. They had me working all night. Every three minutes the phone would ring, 'could we get this?' 'could we have more towels?' 'where can we get beer at three in the morning?' I swear it was non-stop. I think Leigh and I should go over to my apartment and then come back here in the afternoon. While you're working, I'll look in on Oskar and see if there is anything I can do for him. I'm sure he'll take the first flight out of Moscow and he'll be here by noon or so. Maybe I can make him dinner or something. I don't know. I should be there for him."

"Sounds wonderful, Steffi."

Johann nodded. "I'll see you mid-afternoon. How about three o'clock?"

Steffi and I packed up my clothes from the previous night and got in her Mercedes.

"Isn't it funny," I said as I got into the car, "that last night, that big, black Mercedes looked positively evil but this one has always been so inviting."

"Things aren't evil in themselves, though a big Mercedes does tend to look intimidating. I feel so sorry for Oskar. When I get back to the apartment, I'll call and leave a message for him."

We talked about the previous night as we drove to Steffi's apartment and I filled her in on everything that had happened, including the sleeping pills and brandy combination.

"That was stupid. You should know better."

"Well, I learned my lesson. I don't even like brandy. I hope that my stomach settles down a little bit. I still feel queasy. I also feel guilty about Barbara. You see, I know it was me they were after."

"Well, you can't blame yourself. You should just thank God you're alive. And I wouldn't discount the Russians, either. We've had a real problem here."

The Russian connection thing was driving me nuts, but if Steffi thought that it was worthwhile looking into, then maybe I wasn't to blame after all. I let a few moments pass. Finally, I said, "Well, it sure feels like it's my fault. Before I arrived, no one had been followed, hurt, or killed. I feel like a jinx. Johann, Barbara, it's all like a bad dream. Thank God nothing has happened to you or Heinz. When we get back to your house, I'd like to try calling Carlos. I haven't talked to him about all this yet."

We pulled up in front of her building. We got into the elevator and went up to the apartment. Heinz was still in school, and Steffi told me he was spending another night with his father. The apartment was dead quiet. Steffi checked messages on her answering machine. There was one from Carlos, telling me that he had booked a room at the Caribe Hilton in San Juan, and that he'd probably be out of touch until we saw each other Friday evening.

Next, Steffi gave Oskar a quick call and then went straight to bed. I tried calling Carlos back, though, true to his word, he wasn't at home or at his desk at the office. I left a brief message about what had happened and said that I'd still be going to Puerto Rico tomorrow morning, and would call him from the Hilton if I didn't get another chance to call today. I also called my father to say that I was fine.

After, I settled in on the sofa, but couldn't sleep. I tried reading my murder mystery, but I'd just seen the real thing. Barbara's death had taken less than twenty seconds, but it would probably take me twenty years to get over it. I'm sure I'll never forget the sound of that dull thud.

I felt a bit antsy, and wanted to do some work. I was angry with myself for leaving my briefcase at Johann's house, but I did find Steffi's copies from a few nights before and sat down at the kitchen table with some coffee and a blank pad.

I tried to figure things out as best as I could. I tackled the few pages of sketches first, trying to connect them with pieces I knew, or the pieces that Johann and I had played through the day before but, again, to no avail. It was bugging me more and more that I couldn't figure out what they all meant. Unfortunately, I'm not one of those people who are good with puzzles. If I don't figure them out right away, I lose patience and get frustrated. I gave up on the pages only about an hour after beginning. I've seen Carlos trouble-shoot problems at work for hours. His job is all about puzzles; it would drive me crazy.

Making myself some more toast, I read a German magazine Steffi had on the coffee table to clear my mind. My German was getting more and more fluent, but I still didn't much care which German movie star was sleeping with which German politician. I gave up on that and went back to the sketches. I kept musing about Dadi's mysterious lover and the lines: "Falkenhayn will appreciate the music." I kept looking at the page, but there really was no music to appreciate. What was Dadi doing anyway? I started counting the notes, to see if there was a pattern. Maybe there was a hidden message somewhere—nothing. Then I counted all the a's, then the b's then the c's, but again nothing.

By this time, Steffi was up, having slept only a few hours. She didn't look that great, and had purplish circles under her eyes. She joined me in the kitchen and drank some of the coffee I had made.

"I just can't figure this out," I said to her. "The thought occurred to me about an hour ago, that maybe this weird music isn't a sketch for a piece, or even an avant-garde composition, but rather a message of some kind. It's probably a message for Falkenhayn."

"Who?"

"Falkenhayn was the Chief of Staff for the German army during World War I. Johann looked it up. I hadn't remembered."

"Well, what does it say?"

"No idea. I've tried counting notes, rests, accidentals, frequency, all to no avail. I just don't know what else to try."

"Let me see." Steffi studied the pages. "I'm not a musicologist, but I can read music, all those piano lessons as a kid, you know." After a few minutes of looking at the pages she said, "This does look weird. Maybe it's not a message, but rather he was trying to figure out how to put one into a piece. Take this little bit here. It has an 'F-Db-A-G#-E##-Ab-Eb-E-G#.' So is anything repeated?"

"I've tried all that. I just can't figure it out. That phrase has nine notes, the next four notes, the next eight. It doesn't make that much sense."

She looked at the page some more, but gave up quickly. She glanced at the kitchen clock and said, "Since it's two thirty already, I think you should get ready to go to Johann's. Even though Oskar hasn't called me back, I'll drop in anyway."

Just then, the phone rang and Steffi answered. It was the police. They wanted to talk to me and I got immediately nervous. They were polite and said that they had my statement but they needed to get my address and phone number where I'd be, for the next week or so, in case they had any more questions. I don't know why, but I didn't trust them. So, I lied to them and said that I would be staying in Berlin with my cousin for the next two weeks. They already had the information. Steffi didn't say a thing.

We drove back to Johann's and Gretchen let me in again. Steffi told us that she was going over to Oskar's and would be back in a few hours. Johann was already in the music room and I joined him there.

"Hi, Johann. How are you feeling? Did you get any sleep?"

"Yes, thanks. I did. I feel a little better, but I am still very tired."

"Well, let's just do some work for a few hours and then I'll go home early with Steffi. She still looks pretty bad herself. She's over at Oskar's house right now."

Johann and I looked at the Satie piano piece and the Berg song again. We were hoping that by looking at it with fresh eyes we would see something we hadn't the day before. After sleeping on it, we still had the feeling that these were stolen pieces and not by Dadi at all. Then I told Johann about my new theory that the sketches were messages for Falkenhayn. He seemed intrigued by that, and we both started to try to figure it out but we couldn't do it. We looked at each group of notes on the page and started writing down how many were in each series. It looked like this: "9/4/8/2/5/9/6/2/3/5/9/2/4/2/8/7/3/6/11."

"Doesn't look like much," I said after a while.

"No, it doesn't. But, there are lots of sixes and twos. I don't know if that means anything."

"I think this is a good avenue to pursue, but I just can't crack the code, if, indeed, there is one."

"Not only are there lots of sixes and twos but lots of e's and f's. I wonder what that means."

At that moment, Gretchen came into the room with Steffi. She looked exhausted and I could tell she had been crying.

"Hey, are you all right?" I asked her.

"I'm fine. It's just that Oskar is all broken up about Barbara. He's really upset. The kids haven't even come home yet. The middle daughter, Helga, said she couldn't leave work during the day. Can you believe that? Her mother died, for God's sake. At least Oskar's secretary is there with him. I don't think he wants to be alone."

"Well, I've heard they aren't the closest of families."

"Yeah, but it's her own mother. God, I hope that Heinz cares if I live or die."

"You know he does. He loves you. You're a great mom."

Steffi started to sniffle a little. I went over to hug her, but she waved me away and said, "I don't know why I'm crying like this. I just feel so bad that I never liked Barbara and never really got to know her."

"Hey, why are *you* feeling so guilty? There's nothing you could have done."

"I guess not. It's fine. I'll be fine. I just think I need to go home now. I'm very tired."

I glanced at my watch and realized that it was already about six o'clock.

"Yeah, I think that would be a good idea."

I said my good-byes to Johann and Gretchen. I felt sorry leaving them, knowing I was off the next day to Puerto Rico. In just a few days, Johann and I had become close–there's nothing like trauma to cement a friendship. We exchanged e-mail addresses and I promised that I would keep him up to date with everything I found. Of course, I invited them both to Boston any time and with that, Steffi and I left, waving good-bye from the car as it pulled away from the curb.

When we got back to her apartment, she took out a bottle of red wine and some cheese and crackers. We drank, and talked, and tried to make ourselves feel better. I knew I would miss Steffi, too. The time I had spent in Berlin had been productive on many fronts. I found out that Dadi had a lover, that he had been in touch with a German General during World War I, and that he had stolen music from at least two composers. I had plenty to write about, but I was still leaning toward giving up the doctorate altogether. I decided to just go home and think over what I should do.

I had also gotten to know my cousin better, and I had made a new friend. When Steffi finally trundled off to bed at about nine that evening, I finished packing and got ready for the next day of travel. I was looking forward to my trip. I would be one step closer to Carlos, and I would finally get to relax. I was also looking forward to meeting Dadi's son, the Cardinal. I resolved to hand over the materials to him and be done with it. I had accomplished a lot on my trip, but I still had one stop to go.

CHAPTER 16

▼

Steffi drove me to the airport in the morning. We said our good-byes quickly, since we were both sad that it might be another five years before we saw each other again. I had spoken to Heinz on the phone, and he said he'd try to visit me in Boston soon. Steffi promised the same thing. While I stood at the curb waving good-bye to her, the thought crossed my mind that someone might still be following me. The tall man must know that he had killed the wrong person—he had looked directly into my eyes. I scanned the area to see if I could catch a glimpse of anyone who looked familiar but they all seemed to be tourists or businessmen, very innocently going about their own business. After my cursory glance, I quickly left the curbside, checked in, and went immediately to the gate. I got myself some coffee and sat in a corner, watching as the people went by.

I was excited that I was going to Puerto Rico and couldn't wait to get on the plane. I wanted to get started as soon as possible since it was going to be a long day. My flight had originated in Madrid, so I first had to get back there and then make a connection to San Juan. Exhausted wouldn't begin to describe how I'd feel by the time I got there.

Sitting in a corner with my back against the wall, I kept looking around expecting to see the man who had been following me. No one looked familiar. When we boarded, I sighed with relief.

The flight was bumpy but mercifully short. The airport in Madrid was in utter chaos and I had to fight my way to the gate. There had been unexpected thunderstorms, and every flight into or out of the city had been delayed. People were everywhere, children were crying and cranky, but I didn't really blame them—I'm sure we all felt like crying. From a harried airline attendant, I found out that my flight was delayed by two hours. I was irritated to be sitting there, just waiting. I wanted to keep moving to put more and more distance between Barbara's murderer and me. I kept scanning the gate area certain that someone was watching me but didn't recognize a soul. I hoped the killer thought I was still in Berlin.

After waiting for an hour and not being able to get into my mystery book, I bought a few Spanish magazines, the newspaper *El Pais,* two Bounty bars, and a strong Spanish coffee. While I waited at the gate, I started reading and eating and tried not to appear too anxious. When our flight was finally called–three hours late, not two–I had downed four Spanish coffees and both Bounty bars and was feeling jittery and queasy. I looked around the gate area for the thousandth time and then boarded the plane. I began to relax when I got into my seat–an aisle, thank heaven–and buckled my seat belt. No one was next to me and I was hopeful that once the plane took off, I could spread out a little. Maybe, for once, I had lucked out. Just moments before the plane left, though, I got up to go to the bathroom, partly so I could see if anyone looked suspicious, and partly because the four coffees hit my bladder all at once. Things on the flight seemed fine.

When I got back, an elderly lady in a yellow polyester pantsuit was occupying the window seat next to me. I guess I wasn't going to be able to spread out after all. She was busily stowing her bags under the seat in front and behind her, and settling herself in for the long flight. She smiled at me and I gave her a small nod. After takeoff, I relaxed and took out my magazines. Unfortunately, the lady, who was sitting next to me, started talking. I tried my best to give her the hint that I really wanted to be left alone, but to no avail. By the time we were over the Canary Islands, I had heard about her seven grandchildren, all unbelievably bright, her daughter-in-law, with whom she had constant fights (surprise, surprise) and the three husbands she had already buried–God rest their souls. I am the kind of person who doesn't enjoy idle chatter on planes. The reason why I bring so many things to read is that I prefer to sit by myself and read, not talk to someone I have no intention of ever hearing from again. A friend of mine met her future husband on a plane, and another always collects business cards. She actually gets together with the people she meets. I just don't like it. I either feel that it's intrusive or an utter waste of time. Maybe that's me just being ornery, but I still didn't like it.

When I was younger, in order to remain anonymous and actually have a little bit of fun, I used to make up stories when people would talk to me on planes or buses. Once, when I was a freshman in college, on the Amtrak run from Providence to New York, I told someone that I was a Ph.D. student in Physics at Yale.

It turned out the man I was talking with was the head of the department—oops. I've never done that again.

So now I usually carry a Walkman, sit down quickly, put headphones on sometimes without actually turning up the volume, and then begin reading. Although this usually works, it obviously doesn't with little old ladies who had seven grandchildren. Edna, as she had informed me she was called, just didn't get hints. When I got up to go to the bathroom again, I looked around for another seat, but the flight was absolutely full. It seemed everyone was on his way to vacation in sunny Puerto Rico. By the time we had gotten dinner and the movie began, Edna was still at it. Her first husband sold pianos, which is how they met, since she played and wanted to buy one but couldn't afford it—aren't they just so expensive? Her second husband sold shoes—you know those old-time shoe stores where the salesmen actually knew their inventory, and got you the correct sizes right away, and always had everything in stock? Her third husband sold insurance, and so on and so forth. I had been listening to over two hours of this, so when the movie started, something that starred Sylvester Stallone, I asked the flight attendant for headphones, figuring this would give Edna even more of a hint. I hated to pay the five dollars, but it would be worth it to have her off my back.

Once I had paid for the headphones, I politely but firmly excused myself, told Edna that I wanted to watch the movie, and put them on. I wasn't even sure what was playing, but at that point I would have watched just about anything. As soon as I plugged the headphones in, I heard the first song in the *Altenberg Lieder* by Alban Berg. I stopped dead and listened. Two nights ago I had seen the original manuscript for the piece in Johann's music room. Edna glanced over at the channel number displayed on my seat rest and said loudly, while she tapped on my forearm, "Oh, no dear, to watch the movie it's channel one for English and two for Spanish."

"I'm listening to a beautiful song, Edna. It's by one of my favorite composers."

"Oh, well, then I'll listen to it, too. You're obviously so knowledgeable about music." With that, she took out her own set of headphones—where she got them I don't know, since I hadn't seen her buy one from the stewardess—and turned to channel six, where the second Berg song was just beginning. After about a minute of listening, she scrunched up her nose, and said, "Oh dear, oh dear." I thought she might lose interest in me because of my "bad" taste in music, but to give her her due, she kept listening until all five songs in the set were over.

At the end of the cycle, I smiled at her benignly and said, "Wasn't that beautiful?"

"Well, I don't think I'd use that word for it, dear. Interesting, maybe."

I asked myself why "interesting" is always used as a negative when talking about "modern" music. Those songs are almost one hundred years old now. Haven't we had enough time to "get used" to all this modern music? Right after the Berg songs, Schoenberg's *Variations for Orchestra* began. I was completely surprised that this music was programmed at all, since these pieces were not usually considered Top 40. I'd bet they aren't even played once a year by WCRB, the classical station in Boston. I assumed that the music on an airplane would probably have been Pachelbel's Canon or maybe Beethoven's Moonlight Sonata for the thousandth time, but I was pleasantly surprised and smiled when the Schoenberg began. I was sure Schoenberg would be pleased to hear his music at thirty five thousand feet.

"Oh dear," she said over the music again. "You don't actually like this, do you, dear?"

I nodded, and again, she continued to listen. I must say that I was impressed that she didn't put down the headphones, or turn to the movie, or to the other music stations. Most people would have, I think, but she listened attentively all the way through, and because of her willingness to try new things, I decided that I would play musicologist for a while and talk to her about the music we were listening to. Actually, it's one of my favorite things to do, introduce people to music that I love. Not just Berg and Schoenberg, but Medieval, Renaissance, Romantic, Rock, Jazz, it doesn't much matter. I guess that's why I am such a good music appreciation teacher. I never tire of introducing people to Beethoven's Ninth Symphony because it's such wonderful music. I've listened to it countless times and it never ever gets boring. Neither does teaching it.

At the end of the piece, I took my headphones off and said, "Well, Edna, let me tell you a little bit about Schoenberg's *Variations for Orchestra*. A lot of people say that he's the reason why 20th-century music sounds so strange, you know, all the atonal music that he wrote. We call it Serialism. But the music that he wrote at the beginning of his career sounds very romantic. Some of it sounds a little like Mahler to me but he then started experimenting and writing other kinds of music. The compositional distance he traveled in a short time was astounding. You see, Schoenberg himself considered his compositions as just another step in a long German musical tradition. He studied all the big composers inside and out, composers like Bach, Mozart, Beethoven, Brahms, and loved and respected them. But Schoenberg asked himself why he should compose in their style, when it wasn't really what he wanted to do, or how he wanted to express himself. He felt that music should reflect the age in which it is written. So, his music really does take the next logical step in a process of development. I don't mean to say that his is better, but it is part of a tradition and should be listened to with that in mind."

Edna nodded. I could tell she was a bit out of her depth, but she seemed genuinely interested. "So," she said slowly, "What does Bach have to do with this piece? I mean it's downright ugly, don't you think? It's not really pretty and Bach is so pretty sometimes. I love playing Bach."

"Music doesn't always have to be pretty, Edna. Some of the best music is not pretty at all. Think of the first chord in the last movement of Beethoven's Ninth Symphony. It's downright ugly, dissonant, and disturbing. But to get back to Schoenberg's *Variations for Orchestra*, the people who programmed this music for the airline have actually picked a fascinating piece here. You see, it's based on an acrostic."

"A what?"

"You know, in poetry, when each line begins with a certain letter, and if you look down the whole poem the first letters all spell something–like the beginning poem in *Alice in Wonderland*. Take the first word in each sentence and you get Alice Pleasance Liddel, the little girl for whom the book was written. Well, you can do basically the same thing in a composition. But in music, it's a little different. You know that there are really only seven notes if you don't count sharps and flats, right?" She nodded and I continued. "Think of a piano. Well, let's start with 'a', okay? So, there's a, b, c, d, e, f, g. If I wanted to translate Bach's name into music, for instance, I would use a 'b', 'a', 'c' and then what? There's no 'h' because once we've hit 'g,' it's the end of the scale and we just start over at the beginning. So, we keep wrapping the alphabet around until we use up all twenty six letters. Here, let me show you."

I took out my black flair pen and wrote the following diagram on the cocktail napkin that had been under my Coke:

Notes:	Alphabet			
a	a	h	o	v
b	b	i	p	w
c	c	j	q	x
d	d	k	r	y
e	e	l	s	z
f	f	m	t	
g	g	n	u	

"Okay?" I asked in my teacher voice. She nodded vigorously, very interested in what I had to say. "So, let's say you wanted to put my name in music, Leigh, which is spelled L-E-I-G-H, then the notes you would use would be...."

She interrupted me, "E-E-B-G-A, right?"

"Yes, that's right. That's an acrostic in music. When Schoenberg uses Bach's name in this piece it's an act of homage. I can't tell you how much time and energy musicologists spend looking for these things. They're not usually there, but it's exciting when you find these acrostics. Lots of composers from the Middle Ages on have put secret messages, lover's names, anything they want into their music." I paused, and looked down at the cocktail napkin. I noticed that the flair pen I had used was beginning to run where the napkin was slightly wet, making black veins on the white surface. I stared at it, practically in a trance. Light was beginning to dawn, and as I thought about Schoenberg's use of B-A-C-H, my pulse quickened.

Edna was also excited but for different reasons, and said, "Now my name would be E-D-..."

I interrupted her and said, "Oh my God! It's that simple." She stopped and I paused again.

"Are you all right, dear?" she asked.

I looked over at Edna and grabbed her arm, "Thank you. Thank you. That's why there are so many e's. Oh my God, the whole thing is an acrostic. Oh my God. I can figure it out now."

I jumped out of my seat, upsetting my pull-down tray and spilling my leftover drink on Edna's right foot as I grabbed my briefcase from the overhead compartment (whose contents had indeed shifted during takeoff), and sat down with the pages of sketches.

Edna was puzzled by my behavior but was interested in what I was doing, so I had to explain why I was so excited.

"Edna, I've been working on a dissertation on the life and works of a Spanish composer. He's not a really big name but big enough to be interesting. While I was poking around a library in Berlin, I came across these pages of music that seemed to make no sense. They didn't appear to be sketches or even an avant-garde composition. Then I got the idea that they were messages for someone. I just never thought of something as easy as an acrostic. I was looking for frequency of certain notes or the number of sharps, flats, and the like, but now I see that all I tried was too complicated. I have a feeling this is the answer to the whole thing."

"Let me help you figure it out, if I can," she said sounding as if nothing this exciting had happened to her since her last grandchild was born. "I read music. You know, I play piano. Not very well, but my parents insisted that we all learn how to play."

"Sure thing, I could use some help, and talking this through with someone would probably put things in focus for me. I'm not very good with puzzles, you see. Anyone else would probably have figured this out a long time ago."

I took out all the sketch pages, and turned first to the ones that I had photocopied from Johann–they were easier to read than the glossy photographs. I sat down with the one we had tried to solve just the night before. There were sharps and flats all over the place and I decided that Dadi had probably done something unusual with the acrostic, but now that I knew what the method was, I felt certain I could crack the code. So, I wrote down the first section in notes.

"Okay, Edna, the first group of notes is F-Db-A-G#-E##-Ab-Eb-E-G#. I think to keep it simple, he would have kept the first seven letters just like the notes, so the F is an F, the A is an A, and the E an E."

"Oh, this is just like Wheel of Fortune!" cried Edna. "It's my favorite show! I never miss a night." I swear she even clapped her hands in anticipation. Did that make me Vanna White?

"Well, let's write down what we know, or at least what we think we know. Nine notes means that we have a nine-letter word that begins with 'f' and has an 'e' and a 'c'. Here, let's write it down."

F	Db	A	G#	E##	Ab	Eb	E	G#
F		A					E	

"Now what would come after an F and between an A?" I mused aloud.

"Dear, don't you play Wheel of Fortune? It's so easy. The letter has got to be an R, of course. I just hope this is in English."

"Oh God, Edna, I never even thought about that. How stupid of me. Of course Dadi wouldn't be writing messages in English. But what language? Spanish? Serbian? German? Russian?"

"Well, I guess you would have to ask yourself who the message was intended for, no?"

"It was intended for a German General, so let's try German first. But some of the pages have Cyrillic writing on them. If it's Serbian or Russian, then I'm sunk."

There was silence for a bit.

Edna interrupted, "I'm sorry, dear, but I don't speak German or Serbian for that matter. If it were English or French, I could help, seeing that I'm so good at the Wheel, you know. But, why don't you look at some of the other words–the little ones. Like this one with two notes, or this one with three. You see? This one has a D-E-Db. That must be easy."

She was right. D-E-Db–if it was in German, then D and E would be the first two letters of the word, which would most probably be "*der*" the German word for "the." Of course it could also be "*dem*" or "*den*," other forms of "*der*" in German, too. "Okay, Edna, I think that word is *"Der."* So, now that I know that 'r' is Db, maybe I can figure out how he came up with it in the first place."

"Well, since there are all the sharps and flats, maybe he used flats first and then sharps, in order to fill out the rest of the alphabet. Here, let me see." She wrenched the flair pen out of my hand and started writing quickly. At some point, she frowned, crossed out what she had written, and turned the napkin over again. Then, she quickly made another chart, growing more excited as she wrote. Maybe she really was great at Wheel of Fortune, because her second chart made a great deal of sense.

a	a		o	ab
b	b		p	bb
c	c		q	cb
d	d		r	db
e	e		s	eb
f	f		t	fb
g	g		u	gb
h	a#		v	a##
i	b#		w	b##
j	c#		x	c##
k	d#		y	d##
l	e#		z	e##
m	f#			
n	g#			

"See?" she said, pointing with pride at the napkin. "See? The Db makes sense."

I looked at the page and nodded. "It does, Edna. So, let's use your chart now to see if the first word means anything." Then I translated the notes F-Db-A-G#-E##-Ab-Eb-E-G# into *FRANZOSEN*.

"Well, that's not helpful," she said in a disappointed tone.

"Oh yes it is, Edna, Franzosen means Frenchmen in German. We're on the right track!" My hand was shaking with excitement, and I quickly filled in the rest of the letters. At the end, I came up with the following message:

Franzosen festgefahren in Verdun. Englander werden an der Somme im Juni angreifen. Um deutsche Truppen von Verdun wegzunehmen.

She looked at the German words on the page and said, "Well, what does that all mean?"

"Let's see," I said. I was having trouble with the word *wegzunehmen* and then fished out my handy little German-English dictionary I always carry when I travel. I looked it up, and after thinking the whole message through, I wrote down:

French entrenched in Verdun. English will attack at the Somme in June. Move the German troops away from Verdun.

"Wow!" I said. "Verdun again."

"You know what that was all about, don't you dear? Verdun and the Somme, I mean."

"Well, I know about Verdun, but I'm not sure about the Somme."

Edna shook her head and said, "I don't either. I wish we had an encyclopedia here or something we could use to look up what the Somme was."

"My father is a World War I buff. He knows everything. I could ask him when we land, I guess."

"Why don't you do it now? There's a phone right in front of you, dear."

I looked longingly at the AT&T phone in the cradle of the back of the seat in front of me. I knew it was supposed to be very expensive, maybe as high as seven dollars a minute, but I grabbed it anyway. If spending this money would get me a job or maybe even tenure, then what the hell, I'd make the call a short one. I took out my well-used American Express card, inserted it into the slot, and dialed my father. I now know how people felt when they were calling overseas not so many years ago. I could feel myself getting nervous. When my Dad answered, I told him where I was calling from, and that I had to keep it quick.

"You're calling from where?"

"Daddy, I'm calling from the plane," I practically shouted. "Can you hear me okay?"

"Yes, it sounds a bit noisy, but I can hear you just fine. You don't have to shout. You're my first call from a plane. What's wrong?" he asked, concern creeping into his voice, when he realized how unusual it was for me to call him like this.

"Everything is fine. I'm on my way to Puerto Rico."

"How is Steffi? She was very upset about Barbara when we spoke last."

"Steffi is fine, just shaken up. I really don't want to talk about Barbara right now. I'll call when I get to Puerto Rico and we can talk then. But, I had a few questions about something related to my work. I need to know what the Battle of the Somme was all about. You know, during World War I."

"Oh, well, that was an important battle. I can't believe you don't know about it, being an historian and all."

"Yes, well, I don't, so could you tell me but really quickly? Then you can give me the whole story once I've landed," I glanced at my watch, getting a little antsy that the call was costing me so much money.

"I should really refresh my memory and look it up. I want to be right about it all."

"Daddy, please, just the basics."

"It was the battle the English troops started so that they could help out the French who were entrenched and bleeding to death at Verdun."

"Yes, I know about Verdun, but what about the Somme?"

"The Somme is a river and that's where the English, under General Haig, tried to put pressure on the Germans to pull them away from Verdun. Basically, Haig's troops attacked to alleviate the pressure on the French. Verdun was a massacre on both sides and the British tried to stop the stalemate."

"I have a message here from Dadi to a German general that says: *French entrenched in Verdun. English will attack at the Somme in June. Move the German troops away from Verdun.*"

"Well, that was obviously to inform the German troops where the attack from the British would take place–the river Somme. Maybe this is why the British were so surprised at the resistance they got from the Germans. They had expected the battle to be much easier. Falkenhayn, the Commander in Chief of the Kaiser's army, had troops there waiting, perhaps because of this communication. Historians, and I mean not just music historians like you, but general historians, are going to find this all very interesting. It sounds very intriguing."

"So, Dadi really was a spy. I can't believe it."

"Well, from my perspective, he was definitely in the thick of things if he knew von Falkenhayn."

I looked down at the paper and couldn't believe what I was looking at. The fact that he had helped the Kaiser and the Austro-Hungarian Empire seemed in character, though. I knew that Dadi had gone back to Madrid after the war and supported the Franco regime during the Spanish Civil War there. Most artists and musicians left or were killed supporting the Republicans. Dadi had fascist leanings. I shook my head, and glanced at my watch, and realized I had probably used up about fifty dollars already.

"Daddy, I'll call you when I get to the Caribe Hilton, but thanks for your help."

"Any time. This was fun. I'll look up some of the exact dates and things in my books and see if I can get more detailed information on von Falkenhayn for you. You know, shortly after the battle of the Somme, he was fired for being incompetent. I'm not sure if he really was or if he found himself in a war that no one could win."

"Well, thanks for your help, Daddy." I interrupted, "I'll call you soon."

"Have a good flight. Bye."

I got off the phone and told Edna what I had learned from my Dad. It definitely looked like we had deciphered some important messages from World War I. We took out the next page, and we got down to figuring out the German words. We spent the next hour translating all the music into the messages that, had they been discovered seventy years ago, would have put Dadi in jail for spying. The Dreyfus affair would now probably be a footnote compared to what historians would have called the "Dadi Affair." And anyway, poor Dreyfus was innocent, whereas Dadi certainly looked guilty to me. At the end of an hour, we had about eight messages and all of them in reference to the war, and all of them helpful to the German and Austrian side. Not only was he a spy, but he was a spy for the wrong side. He sure was a slick character.

"Edna, I can't believe all that I've learned about this man. Before I started really delving into his music, I just thought he'd make a good dissertation topic. His compositional style was so erratic, his songs compelling, and some of his music was so beautiful. But now I've learned he was a spy for the Kaiser during the First World War, and that he probably stole quite a bit of the music he published, and that he was having an affair with a woman before and during his marriage. I certainly hadn't expected to find out all this."

"It makes it all the more interesting. Don't you think?"

"Yes, I guess it does. But to be honest, musicological circles don't like to be shaken up like this. All the hoopla when the Bach chronology was changed in the 1950s, you would have thought someone had tried to kill the President. Musicologists are an odd lot. In some ways, I think, they don't really like change."

"You have enough evidence, though, to prove all these allegations. And you have a compelling topic. I think you'll do just fine," she said patting my hand in a maternal manner.

I nodded slowly and began composing the first sentence of my dissertation in my head: "Enrique Dadi, though he appeared to the music world as a supportive friend, an intriguing composer and a patriot, was in fact…"

The flight attendant came by to collect headphones. I hadn't noticed that the movie was over. In fact, we were already starting our descent. People were sleeping all around us, and the airplane was dark except for our two lights overhead. Edna and I hadn't slept a wink. We were still on the edge of our seats. I put away the briefcase and thanked her. For once, I gave her my address and phone number and knew that we would keep in touch. Maybe I should talk to people on planes. I guess you never know who you might meet. The flight attendant came around, and made everyone buckle up for landing, and put their seats in the upright position. People were stretching and yawning all around us. One by one, they opened the shades on the windows and the cabin was bathed in tropical light.

When we finally touched down, the airplane erupted into applause. Don't ask me why, but this happens every time I've landed in Puerto Rico. It doesn't seem to have anything to do with where the flight originated. People always clap. I guess they feel strongly about this beautiful, little island; I know Carlos does. I joined right in, clapping and whooping. I felt invigorated, alive, and excited. I couldn't wait to tell Carlos my news.

CHAPTER 17

▼

A friend of mine once said that stepping out of the airport in Puerto Rico and into the baggage claim area feels like being slapped in the face with a warm, moist, and slightly used dishrag. He is absolutely right. From the air-conditioned comfort of the plane, you are hit with a wave of warm, sticky, humid air–air that feels like it has already been breathed.

When we got off the plane, I said goodbye to Edna. She was on her way to St. Thomas, so she went directly to her gate for her connecting flight. I tried calling Carlos, to tell him I was safely in, and also that I had found the key to the messages imbedded in Dadi's music but his voice mail picked up, and I didn't want to speak into the machine. I hung up and followed everyone else to the baggage claim area downstairs. In Puerto Rico, baggage claim is open only to the passengers; they had a horrible time years ago with stolen luggage and over-crowding and closed the whole place off. An entire side of the area is a glass wall. Just outside, hundreds of people were pressed against it, waving and knocking on the windows, hoping to attract the attention of the person they were picking up. It seemed as if half the people on the island were there.

I knew it would be a little while before I could collect my bags, so I stood off in a corner and looked outside watching the people wave, feeling alone, and wishing that at least one person out there was waiting for me. Children in sandals and shorts were running underneath the green palms, giggling and playing games. Police were waving their arms wildly while blowing their whistles in an attempt to keep traffic moving. Tour guides for the various cruise ships stood at the curb in the distance next to vans with names like, "Royal Majesty" or "Princess Cruises," and the like, emblazoned on the sides. I've never taken a cruise nor am I likely to. The last time I was in Puerto Rico, my friend and I got a tour of one of the ships while it was in dock. I got seasick just from the tour; the damn thing wasn't even moving.

A buzzer sounded and the carousel started up. We all stood around waiting for our bags. After about an hour of watching while all the Pampers boxes, garment bags, and fine luggage sets went round and round, the carousel stopped. An attendant took the remaining few bags off the conveyer belt and put them in a corner next to the office. Mine hadn't arrived. I shut my eyes out of frustration and then dutifully trooped off to the baggage services department. The thought crossed my mind that someone may have taken my luggage in order to look for my work on Dadi, but I was pretty sure that no one, except the people I trusted, knew when I was coming to Puerto Rico. I hadn't even told the police in Berlin where I would be. I hadn't seen anyone I recognized and I certainly hadn't seen the tall man. Besides, the airline had lost my bags the last time I had come, and that time they hadn't shown up until two days later.

The airline representative I spoke with was sympathetic, but thoroughly unhelpful. I explained that I had a black garment bag and another smaller green bag with a red, white, and blue belt that my Dad had given me to make sure that it held together. She wrote down all the information, took my name and the number of the Caribe Hilton Hotel, and told me they would call as soon as they found the bags. I didn't have much hope of having my Picard T-shirt in time for bed, though luckily, I still had all the manuscripts and photocopies with me in the briefcase. I had wanted to keep them with me just so I knew they were safe, and was glad I had.

It was late afternoon by the time I got out of the airport and I was thoroughly unprepared for the heat. Even though the baggage claim area was humid and sticky, outside was even worse. I hadn't realized that they had valiantly tried to air condition the large room. I had shed my black cardigan when I got off the plane, but now I rolled up the sleeves of Carlos' white shirt and went to get a taxi at the curb. In five steps, I was covered with sweat.

For the past six years, there has been construction at the airport. I have no idea what they're doing or why. American Airlines has gotten a new terminal, but the rest of the construction site just seems to feed on itself. Taxis were everywhere, but they were either in the process of being loaded or were standing empty as if abandoned. I toyed with the idea of taking off with one, but didn't really feel like spending the evening in a Puerto Rican jail.

I finally found a lone taxi down near the TWA counters. The driver was an elderly man in a starched guavera–the dressy cotton shirts that are a staple on the island. He was listening to a small AM transistor radio that seemed to be stuck on the highest volume setting and tuned to a talk program. He was somewhat displeased when I opened the car door and asked to be taken to the Caribe Hilton.

He grudgingly put the car in drive and pulled into traffic. Actually, he pulled into a traffic jam. Police were attempting to get people to move, but there were too many baby carriages to be loaded into mini-vans, too many grandmothers waving at or kissing grandchildren, and, in general just too many stubborn and slow people not paying attention to anyone. Only the far-left lane showed any signs of movement at all. I glanced at my watch, but then realized I had no idea what time it was. Was it only six hours difference between Berlin and San Juan? And how much time had I been in the air and delayed in Madrid? I couldn't tell anymore. I listened to the AM radio, hoping there would be a newsbreak so that they'd give the time. I didn't want to bother the driver again, especially since he seemed to be making headway along the left-hand side of the road around the airport, and I didn't dare distract him.

Listening to the AM radio, I smiled at hearing the Spanish accent in Puerto Rico again. I am much more comfortable with it than with the accent in Spain, and a part of me felt like I had already come home. The subject under discussion was the increasing murder rate in Puerto Rico—it was worse than New York, New Orleans and Atlanta combined. The host kept talking about how random the crimes were and how no one was really safe. I started to get nervous and stopped listening to him after a little while. I didn't need to think about murder any more; it had already struck close to home.

We finally got out of the airport and took the two-lane highway that connects the Muñoz Marin Airport with the rest of San Juan. On the right hand side, you could tell where the ocean was because huge high-rises stood in a row, pointing outward. Right next to the roadway and in front of the large buildings, every type of fast food you could ever want to eat—and lots that you wouldn't—was available. Next to the Kentucky Fried Chicken, now known as "KFC' in an attempt to keep "fried" out of the name, was Burger King, Dunkin' Donuts, McDonald's and then Pizza Hut. I stopped noticing after Church's Fried Chicken, Baskin Robbins and Wendy's went by.

Puerto Rico is an interesting mix of Hispanic and American culture. While seemingly American on the outside, with fast food restaurants, and Sears, and JC Penny stores in abundance, there really is a difference in culture. Sometimes I think it's as if the window dressing is American, but the heart and soul of the place is Hispanic. Some of my old friends from college are from Puerto Rico, and I had visited them several times during summer breaks. One of my friends wants

Puerto Rico to become the fifty-first state but another is all for maintaining the status quo as a commonwealth. If Puerto Rico becomes a state, he argues, American culture will just wipe out the remaining Hispanic culture. He once asked me, "How many people in Hawaii really still speak Hawaiian?" That really struck me, but as I looked at the fast food chains go by, the Chevrolet dealerships and Sam's Clubs, I wondered if indeed it was a losing battle.

Once we left the area, I saw the lagoon and the hotels of the tourist section of Condado spring up. The city of Old San Juan is actually on the tip of a small island. The island is only about three miles long and is cut off by a small inlet, which leads to a large lagoon. On the other side of the lagoon is the San Juan harbor where the cruise ships are docked. There are beautiful, low white bridges connecting the various roads leading from the mainland to Old San Juan. They are only about one hundred yards wide where the ocean feeds the large lagoon, and you can walk across the bridge, watching the waves from the ocean crash into the rocks on either side. I have done this many times after drinking and eating in the tourist section. It is unbelievably beautiful.

The colors of the ocean range from a pale sea green to a dark midnight blue, with every color in between popping up here and there. At any given time, there are wind surfers in the lagoon and cruise ships on the horizon, and the clean, vibrant smell of salt hangs in the air.

The Caribe Hilton is just on the tip of the San Juan side; the Holiday Inn is on the Condado side. Once over the bridge, heading toward Old San Juan, the road curves to the right, past an old Coast Guard barracks, now abandoned and waiting for a developer, and then curves to the left. At the second curve, the driver skillfully maneuvered into the Hilton driveway and curled through the lush vegetation to the front entrance which is set back from the street. The reception area was right there, completely open to the breezes from the outside. When I was first in Puerto Rico, I once commented that the louvered metal windows on many of the houses would be bad for insulation. "Insulation from what?" my friend had asked. I realized then that I had lived all my life in a cold climate. I had no idea what it was like to live, actually live, in the tropics, not just vacation there for a week now and then.

I got to the reception desk and checked in, fortunately with no hitches. I told the woman behind the desk about my lost luggage, and asked where she thought I would be able to purchase a few items like a T-shirt, a pair of dress pants, and some underwear. There was a gift shop and a small clothing store in the hotel for my convenience. They would be closing at eight o'clock, and since it was only a little after six now, I could settle in and purchase some things with plenty of time to spare. I could also charge them to the room. Taking the computer out of my briefcase, I asked her to put it in the hotel safe. I wondered if I should put all my papers in, too, but decided that I might get down to some work later, and that I should have them with me.

I went to the sixth floor, and was pleasantly surprised that Carlos had managed to get a room with a view toward Condado and the ocean. The sun was going down, and the lights from the hotels were sparkling on the water. It was a magical sight. I stood out on the balcony, watching the sun set and breathing in the fresh, salty air. In the distance, I could hear the ocean crash against the rocks leading to the lagoon, and I shut my eyes and concentrated on the sound, and felt better than I had for a long time. The sound of crashing surf has always had a soothing effect on me.

After a few moments, I sat on the bed and called Carlos. Still no answer but I left a message giving him my room number so he could call me back. Then, I phoned my father. I hadn't spoken to him about Barbara's death at all, and frankly, I didn't want to.

"Hi, there, Daddy."

"I was getting worried about you."

"The plane ride took a long time, so did the taxi. The traffic here is just murder." Bad choice of words, I thought, but continued, "I got in a few minutes ago. I'm at the Caribe Hilton, room 633."

"I spoke to Steffi a little while ago. She's okay, but Oskar is still broken up. I think I may try to go over for the funeral."

"I'm sorry about all of it, Daddy."

"It wasn't your fault."

"It feels like it sometimes."

"How are you doing? Do you need anything?"

"No, thanks, I'm fine."

"Do you want to go to the funeral with me? I'll pay for the flight."

"No, I don't really want to go. I'm very tired and I still feel very guilty about Barbara. You can represent our family at the funeral."

"Well, you can't blame yourself. Steffi told me it probably had to do with Oskar's dealings with Russia, and that maybe the Russian mafia has gotten involved."

"Everybody says that, but I'm not sure. In some ways, I'd love to believe it."

"Well, you should. Steffi said they were having a real problem over there. I called Oskar last night. He says he'll probably take some time off after the funeral, maybe even come here for a while."

"I think maybe he should retire. Daddy, I also wanted to thank you for all the information about the Somme and all."

"I've been reading up on it since our conversation, but I'll talk to you in detail when I have it all together, probably tomorrow. You really should safeguard everything you've gathered so far. This is very interesting."

"Thanks Daddy, I will. I'll talk to you tomorrow," I said.

"How long will you be in Puerto Rico?"

"Well, I think I'll just see Dadi's son, the Cardinal, tomorrow. He told me on the phone to come to his residences. I don't think he's got much to show me, so I'll probably have a short meeting with him. Then, I'll take the weekend off and leave by Monday. Carlos is coming down tomorrow and we're just going to relax together."

"I didn't realize your boyfriend was meeting you there," my father added—his dislike of Carlos was palpable. I decided to change the subject.

"Well, I've got to run. The airline lost my bags and I have to buy a few things, like some underwear."

"I love you. Take care of yourself and be careful."

"Thanks, Daddy. I'll talk to you tomorrow. I love you, too." We hung up then, and I glanced at the clock. It was just about seven thirty, so I only had a half-hour to shop for an outfit that I could wear tomorrow for the Cardinal. Carlos' white shirt was so dirty by now that it could probably walk around on its own. I grabbed my purse and hurried downstairs, but before I did, I grabbed the things out of my briefcase and decided that they, too, should be placed in the hotel safe. My father was right. I should really make sure everything I had was locked up. I was probably too tired to work anyway.

I rushed downstairs with all my papers, and put them in a few large envelopes that the hotel provided. Then I placed them in the safe alongside my computer. I wanted to keep the briefcase with me, since I should look professional during my interview with the Cardinal. All that was left in it were some blank pads and empty Dictaphone cassettes. Then I hurried to the little store in the hotel.

The small clothing store at the Hilton was surprisingly well stocked. I also needed some shoes since I was wearing my old Reeboks, and while extremely comfortable, wearing sneakers just wasn't done in Puerto Rico—especially if you wanted to meet a Cardinal. Unfortunately, the only shoes they had were a bin of plastic flip flops with big daisies on top. Since I had to wear my Reeboks, I settled on a nice pair of dressy tan linen pants that seemed to hide my sneakers (and the extra ten pounds around my hips, probably from the Bounty bars I had eaten in Madrid). I also bought a dark blue, short-sleeve rayon shirt that would look good with both jeans and linen. Luckily, both items were in the sale bin and weren't that expensive, considering where I was buying them. I also picked up a tooth brush, some underwear, a pair of shorts and an extra large T-shirt with the Puerto Rican flag all over it to sleep in. In my new outfit, I looked professional and, at least, clean. The Cardinal hadn't seemed that anxious to talk with me, so the interview would probably be a short one anyway.

I went upstairs with my booty, shut the air conditioning off in the room, and opened the sliding glass doors, not only because I like the heat, but because I didn't want to mask the sound of the ocean. Besides, once the sun went down, the temperature would drop at least ten degrees. I took a quick shower, washed my hair with their shampoo-and-conditioner-in-one, brushed my teeth and put on my new clothes. Afterwards, I felt human again and, surprisingly, didn't feel jet-lagged. I needed some dinner and a drink or two. I made my way downstairs and went to the outside bar area. The breeze had picked up and the ocean was cooling everyone off. I sat at the bar and ordered a daiquiri, and was pleased to see that the bartender made it with fresh squeezed lime juice and good, dark Puerto Rican rum. It was absolutely delicious, tangy but not too tart, and the pulp from the limes floated on top of the foam. I sipped it at the bar while watching the last few tourists play around in the pool, the underwater lights making their legs appear smaller than they should have been, and even whiter than they were. Laughter reverberated off the water and echoed into the bar. The piped-in music wasn't even annoying, and I found myself more relaxed than I had been in what felt like weeks.

Carlos had once talked about moving down here permanently and had wanted me to come with him, but there wasn't much for me to do, musicology-wise, so I had vetoed the plan. Maybe the next time the subject came up, I wouldn't be so quick to say no. But then again, the island might be very different if you were living here, as opposed to merely visiting and sipping daiquiris while watching the tourists play. The talk show I had listened to in the cab about the murder rate still had me a little on edge.

After my drink, I got up and went in search of food. There are several restaurants in the Hilton, ranging in price from merely over-priced to ridiculously over-priced. I chose the former. I had a plate of pasta and some salad and garlic bread. I also had a wonderful glass of Chianti with the meal and was feeling quite pleased with myself.

At the end of dinner, while I sipped a second glass of wine, I looked out into the bar area and thought I recognized someone. It took me a second to realize that a man at the bar looked just like Rafael Gazza from the archive in Madrid. I signaled for my check, gulped the last of my wine, and kept my eye on the back of the man. It seemed like too much of a coincidence, and I didn't want to miss him.

I signed the check, added a good tip, and got up to go across the hall and into the bar again. Just then the man, or should I say Rafael, turned and walked down the corridor, past the reception area, and into the disco named Juliana. I followed about one hundred feet behind, trying to catch up but not wanting to run, and said loudly before he turned, "Rafael, Rafael, it's Leigh." He didn't even hesitate when I called his name and seemed to speed up when he heard my voice.

When I got to the door of the disco, there was a bouncer and a cashier waiting. When I tried to run in after Rafael, the bouncer stood in the doorway and barred my entry.

"Fifteen dollars cover charge," the cashier said in heavily accented English.

"What?"

"Fifteen dollars. The cover charge includes two free drinks," she said putting two red tickets on the counter.

"But I just saw someone I know go inside. Could I just look around for a minute? I'm afraid I'll miss him. I'll be back in a few seconds, I swear," I said, turning toward the entrance again.

There was a slight pause. The bouncer shifted his weight so that he looked even more imposing and I could see less of the door.

The cashier said, "Fifteen dollars. No exceptions."

I was getting frustrated, but needed to see if Rafael Gazza was really in Puerto Rico. "Can I charge it to the room?"

"Sure," she said, getting out a form. I quickly signed it and ran past the bouncer, without picking up my coupons for the drinks. Once inside the doors, disco music blared. I lived through the disco era as a teenager and I must say that Juliana had the decor, the music and the setting down pat. It was like being thrown into a time warp. Girls in slinky rayon dresses and spiky high heels stood at the bar, waiting for a chance to dance on the already crowded floor. The twirling mirrored ball slowly dropped dots of lights on everyone in the place, and strobes kept flicking on and off. Off the dance floor, the room was dim and dark, full of red velvet, red wallpaper, and small candles on the café-size tables. I could barely see anyone at all. I started looking around at the bar and then around the little tables that surrounded the dance floor, but to no avail. I had lost him. No one even looked vaguely like Rafael Gazza, and everyone was at least ten years younger than I was. I began to wonder if I had been imagining the whole thing. I checked out the restroom area, wondering briefly if I should check the men's room, but decided against it after a couple of guys came out looking like John Travolta in *Saturday Night Fever*, only not nearly as alluring, and gave me the once over. Donna Summer was singing "She Works Hard for the Money." I couldn't believe it, but I knew every word of the song by heart even though I had never liked disco all that much.

I went back out to the bouncer and cashier, and asked if there was another way in or out of the club. They shook their heads, while handing me the coupons that I hadn't picked up in my haste. I then asked them if anyone had come out while I was inside. Again, they shook their heads. They wanted to get rid of me, I was sure.

I took the coupons and figured I might as well check out the bar to see if Gazza might reappear any time soon. I went back into the noise as Gloria Gaynor began to sing. I ordered another daiquiri and stood and watched. No one asked me to dance.

I kept looking around and took a tour of the place every ten minutes or so, hoping to find Gazza. The thought struck me during my second "free" drink that if Gazza were really here, then who else knew where I was? How did they find out at which hotel I was staying? I was sure I had only told my father and Steffi. The pounding music and the smoke were beginning to get to me and I began to feel a bit claustrophobic. I decided my best course of action was just to turn in for the night.

I rushed out of the club, bumping into the bouncer on my way out. He really must have hated me. Once I opened the door to my room, I was struck with the breeze coming through the open sliding glass door that led out to the balcony. My adrenaline kicked in before I realized that I myself had left it like that. I looked on top of the bed where I had put my briefcase but saw absolutely nothing. I began to panic and I could feel my blood literally drain into my stomach. I looked around the room, even in the bathroom, but didn't find anything. Someone had been in the room while I was away and had taken my empty briefcase. All I had left was what was in my pocketbook—my wallet, passport, tickets, a few pens, an old Clinique lipstick or two, my address book, my Dictaphone and a few sheets of paper with the message translations on it. I mentally thanked my father for suggesting that I take care of the things in the briefcase by putting them downstairs in the safe.

I went to the phone, called the receptionist, and told her there had been a robbery. Two security guards from the Hilton came right away, took my statement, and left. They would look into the situation, they said, though their attitude suggested that the theft of an empty briefcase wasn't such a big deal to them. I was happy that at least my papers and computer were secure downstairs.

I was upset but it wasn't a total disaster. My materials were still safe. However, I now knew that someone was, indeed, following me, and I was absolutely convinced that it must have been Rafael Gazza in the bar earlier. Maybe he was the man's accomplice in Barbara's murder. Then again, hadn't Elena told me that he was religious? How could a truly religious person ever justify murder? Then I thought back to the Crusades, the recent terrorist bombings, and almost every other war I could think of, and realized what an incredibly stupid question that was. I tried to remember everything I could about what Elena had told me about Rafael. Maybe I should call her and see if he was still in Spain. I thought back to the looks he had given me while I was visiting the archive, the suspicion (could it have been fear?) in his eyes.

I put the safety lock in place on the inside of the door and put a chair in front of it as I had in Spain. I went onto the balcony, taking a mini bottle of red wine I had retrieved from the bar in the room. Then I sat looking out at the lights of Condado and listening to the ocean. I sat there for a long time before I came up with some type of plan. What had Gloria Gaynor said? "I will survive."

CHAPTER 18

▼

The next morning, I was up bright and early. I had coffee and juice in my room, and got dressed in my new clothes. They still smelled a little smoky from the half-hour or so that I had spent at the disco. I am always very appreciative that Boston has a no-smoking ban in restaurants and bars. I don't have to wash my hair at two in the morning to get rid of the smoke smell any longer. I went downstairs to the concierge, got a good map of Old San Juan, and found out where the Cardinal's residence and offices were. I was in luck. On Fridays the library there opens to the public at ten in the morning, and closes at four, plenty of time to see what they had in their collection before my appointment with the Cardinal in the evening. Since it was only about eight o'clock, I decided I'd go to Old San Juan, walk around, and get my bearings. I went into the convenience shop at the hotel, bought a thick pad, a few more cassettes for my Dictaphone, and another set of batteries. Then I got a taxi right outside the hotel and headed to Old San Juan.

From the Caribe Hilton, it is a straight shot to Old San Juan. On the right hand side of the narrow island is a one-way road heading toward the old city; on the left-hand side, the road is one way the other way. At times, the two roads are close enough so that only a gas station lies between them. As you drive toward Old San Juan, the road gradually rises, and in about a mile, you are high above the ocean, with almost sheer cliffs plummeting to the water. San Juan is an old walled city located at the highest point on the island. The city itself is hilly, and from various streets you can see the ocean on your right side and the harbor on your left.

As soon as we reached the outskirts of the city proper, we passed one of the old Spanish forts called San Cristobal, and headed toward the largest fort, named El

Morro. There are several forts positioned throughout the city, and each has a different atmosphere. I like El Morro best. It is on the furthest tip of the island. There is about a half mile of green grass in front of the actual fortress; it is one of the most imposing structures that I have ever seen. There is no good way to describe it except to say that, if I were part of an invading force and the Spanish were entrenched in that fort, I would probably have given up before even trying. It is built right into the rocky cliff and overlooks the entire harbor and ocean. Nothing would get by the diligent soldiers in the sentry boxes that dot the outer rim of the fort. Right in front of this magnificent structure with its sweeping grounds, are a small ancient graveyard and a string of buildings that line the periphery. The Cardinal lived in one of those buildings. He certainly had a view.

The taxi driver let me out in front of a building that was painted canary yellow. The doors looked to be antique mahogany and the trim on the windows was painted a dark brown to match. It was a typical, old Spanish style mansion, one that looks large and imposing from the outside but even more impressive inside. Everything looked locked up tight.

I checked the map to make sure that I knew exactly where I was and how to get back. After making sure the library would be open at ten o'clock, I decided to tour the city. I went down the block and around to the most touristy section of the old city. Businesses were just waking up. Someone from the pharmacy in the plaza across the street was washing down the sidewalk with a hose. A few stray cats lounged around underneath the cars parked on the street. I tried to pet a few, but they all skulked away from me. I passed store after store, the Polo outlet, Boveda, a jewelry store, a few T-shirt shops and more outlets. After about twenty minutes of walking, I came across the cathedral located at the top of one of my favorite streets. There was a large black Mercedes limousine waiting at the curb in front. After my experience in Berlin, I gave it a wide berth.

The doors to the cathedral were open and from inside I could hear chanting. I decided to sneak in the back as quietly as I could. There were only about twenty people at the service. Most were nuns. I looked around and sat in a pew toward the back. The priest at the main altar was joined by a man dressed in red with a small red beanie on his head. I wondered why there were two people performing mass, one in black and the other in red. I am never sure who wears what colors in the Catholic Church. I thought back to the movie, *The Three Musketeers,* and tried to remember what Cardinal Richelieu wore, but could only see Charlton Heston's face.

The service was in Latin and chanted throughout. I sat back, shut my eyes and concentrated on the music. There is really nothing like the beauty of a single melodic line, especially echoing in a church. I remained in the back throughout the entire service, enjoying the peace and reassurance of ritual. At the end of the service, the priest, waving incense, and the man in red filed out with all the nuns. The few elderly people who had been scattered in the large church trailed slowly behind. After a few minutes, I looked around again at the austere but beautiful interior of the church, and headed outdoors. The priest was talking with a few nuns and shaking their hands. I waited my turn to file past and then thanked him for the service. The man in red stood next to him, smiling as the people walked by.

The priest thanked me for attending and said, "Oh, you were in luck. We were graced by having Cardinal Dadi celebrate Mass for us today."

"Cardinal Dadi?" I said, turning to the man in red.

"Yes, my child. I am glad you could come to Mass this morning," he said in a melodious, soothing voice. He was quite a bit taller than I was and moved with the grace of someone much younger than I knew him to be. He was handsome with deep black eyes, wavy, salt-and-pepper hair and a small goatee. He first appeared to be in his mid-sixties, but on closer observation, I would place him in his early-to-mid eighties.

"I've wanted to meet you for so long," I said, shaking his hand. "It is a great honor. My name is Leigh Maxwell. I spoke with you on the phone the other day. I was going to the library at your residences today to see if there was any material I could use for my research. I was going to wait for you there. I can't believe my luck that I would meet you here."

As I spoke, the smile seemed to become frozen on his face and he let go of my hand while saying, "Miss Maxwell. It is a pleasure to meet you. I'm terribly sorry, but I have a retreat to attend today and I must leave right after morning mass. That's why I suggested that we should talk in the evening."

"Yes, I know, but I wanted to explore the library first."

"The library is only for theological research and exploration. Raoul Perez is the librarian there. If you're interested in the doctrine of the church, then he'll be able to help you. Some of my own writings are there."

"That's wonderful. I am interested in theology and would like to see the library anyway. I'm interested in your writings as well. I will see you at your offices in the evening then?"

"Yes," he said quietly, leaving the word hanging as if there was something more he wished to say. He looked down the street toward the harbor and did not speak for a moment or so. I wasn't sure what was going through his mind, or if I should just leave. He finally turned his attention back to me and added, "I was very young when my father died, and I did not know him very well. I have devoted my life to the service of God, not the arts. I am terribly sorry, but I probably have nothing to tell you of any interest."

"I'd still appreciate meeting with you. I'll at least explain what I've discovered." I didn't want to appear too pushy, but this was as close as I had ever been to a member of Dadi's family. Again, he looked down the street toward the harbor and paused. As I waited for his answer, the thought crossed my mind that the Cardinal must have been in his early twenties when his father died. Why would he have said he was so young and didn't really know his father? Of course, early twenties is young, but he had made it sound as if he hardly knew his father.

The Cardinal turned back to me and smiled. He asked in a cordial way, "What have you discovered?"

"Well, Cardinal Dadi, I've found some interesting messages in the music that I've unearthed–messages that were intended for a German general during World War I."

"That *is* most interesting. I was only an infant at that time, but I know my father traveled widely during those years. Perhaps we should talk now for just a few minutes." He turned and walked down the steps of the church toward a bench on the sidewalk. I immediately followed, happy that he was willing to speak with me, but I wondered why we were talking now instead of this evening at his leisure.

He sat down and turned toward me. "So, what do these messages say? Do you have any of them with you? I've never heard of this before," he said in a hushed voice, very quietly as if afraid someone might overhear us.

"I'm terribly sorry, I don't have them with me, but the messages were embedded in some of your father's music itself. They were all short messages to a German general during the war."

"How clever. I would not have thought of that," he said slowly, seeming to contemplate the idea. "What do they say?"

"Well, they appear to deal directly with battles and armies during World War I. They speak of the Somme, Verdun and other famous battlefields. They were written to a General von Falkenhayn."

"Ah, yes. I know that Falkenhayn and my father knew each other. You see, my cousin married Falkenhayn's sister. So we're related through marriage. I believe my cousin is from my father's Serbian side. I am not exactly sure. We've lost touch with that branch of the family. I wonder how all the messages were sent back and forth."

"Well, I believe they used an intermediary, with the first initial 'F,'" I said, in what I hoped was a neutral way. I didn't want to offend the Cardinal by speaking to him directly of his father's extramarital affair. I was sure that the Cardinal would have denied it, or possibly have ended the interview if I had mentioned it.

"That must have been my cousin's wife, Franny. Her maiden name was Falkenhayn. You see, Falkenhayn was a very well respected family then, and my father's cousin came from a wealthy Serbian family. When you have the opportunity, you may want to look more closely into Falkenhayn's background. You'll find the two sides of the family were somewhat close for a time. 'F' must have been Franny."

I was writing all this down as quickly as I could. It made more sense now, that Dadi would have helped Falkenhayn out of family loyalty. I knew that as soon as I got home, I would have to do quite a bit of reading on World War I and probably get my hands on a few biographies on Falkenhayn. I prayed they were not all in German.

"Thank you very much, Cardinal. Those are wonderful leads. I'll certainly look into them."

He stood up then. "Who else knows of these findings?"

"No one. I've just discovered this and wanted to talk to you before telling anyone."

He stood up. "Very good. Well, Miss Maxwell, I really must be going."

"I look forward to seeing you this evening, then."

"Thank you for coming to Mass. I hope you found it, well, inspiring."

"Yes, it was very beautiful. I think Latin is such a powerful language."

"Yes, I agree. Mass should always be in Latin. It is God's language. I have never said it in any other language, and I never will. Now, I must say goodbye."

"Thank you, Cardinal."

He walked back to the front of the church where some of the people were still waiting for him. He spoke with them briefly, and then stepped away, his red robes billowing in breeze from the harbor. The little group watched him go, as if entranced. He entered the large black Mercedes limousine in one fluid movement. I would not have thought that the expensive car had been waiting for him.

I walked slowly back to the Cardinal's residence thinking over all that he had told me. Dadi's life was coming into focus now. I really wanted to know about Franny von Falkenhayn. I couldn't believe that Dadi had an affair with his own cousin's wife. As I walked through the streets, I noticed a pay phone at the corner. I still had a little time before the library opened, so I decided to call my Dad and ask about Falkenhayn's sister. Since he had told me that he would be doing the research today, I figured I would probably catch him at home. I dialed quickly and got him on the second ring.

"Daddy?"

"Hi, Leigh. Is everything okay?"

"Yes, everything's fine. I just got to talk to Cardinal Dadi for a few minutes. He told me that Falkenhayn had a sister named Franny and that she was probably the mysterious 'F' in all the Dadi correspondence I uncovered. The Cardinal said that she was the one who gave Falkenhayn all the messages. I didn't tell him they were lovers, of course. Could you see if there's anything in your books about her? You know, when she lived, died, anything interesting. Especially look for connections between Dadi and Falkenhayn."

"Sure, Leigh. Falkenhayn's sister. I've never heard of her. Well, well, well. Dadi certainly played around. Having an affair with the sister of the Chief of Staff in the German army during World War I sure was risky. The plot certainly thickens."

"I can't believe everything I'm finding. Well, I'm about to go to the library now, so leave a message at the Caribe Hilton Hotel. You already have the number. Thanks, Daddy."

"Anytime. This is better than running around doing errands. I'll let you know what I find. Bye."

I hung up the phone and continued to walk through the city. I got to the canary yellow building at exactly ten minutes to ten and stepped through the carriage-style doors into a huge courtyard, complete with two running fountains and a few full grown trees that towered over the roof of the three-story building. There were pots of red and white flowers in between the columns that lined the courtyard. The hallway that circled the entire periphery of the building was full of hanging pictures and frescoes on the walls, all of which had a religious theme. One large painting in the entryway was of a Father Escriva. I hadn't heard of him, but I stopped to look at the painting. It was an imposing piece, and the face of the man in the picture was downright fearsome. It was definitely not the face of someone that I would turn to for help or comfort.

I left the entryway and stepped further into the courtyard; a security guard stood near a lectern to my right, reading a newspaper, *El Nuevo Dia*. The atmosphere inside the courtyard was one of quiet serenity. I asked the guard where the library was. He told me that it was located at the top of the staircase, all the way on the other side of the residence.

I walked around the outside hall of the large building, hesitant to leave the calm of the place, and looked at the art on the walls a little more closely. I passed one set of windows and looked in. I noticed that the room was a small private chapel, probably used for small masses said by the Cardinal himself. There were only about four pews on either side, made of antique wood that matched the mahogany doors. The altar was simple, yet held a type of solemnity that some of the most ornate ones in Europe sometimes lack. As I stood there with my nose pressed against the window glass, I saw an elderly lady, stooped over and thin, enter the chapel from a hidden door in the back. Completely unaware of me, she quietly closed the door behind her and shuffled slowly into the room. She went over to a small painting of Jesus, and stared at it for a long time. The picture was only of Jesus' face, and his crown of thorns had caused great rivulets of blood to run down his cheeks. His expression was one of sorrow, rather than comfort, and I wondered what she sought in his eyes. After about five minutes, she lit a candle underneath the painting and bowed her head. She stayed there in quiet prayer for quite some time. I felt uncomfortable that I was being such a voyeur and moved on. I didn't want to disturb her prayers, and besides, I had work to do.

I found the staircase and went to the top. There was a small sign indicating the way to the library. I opened a tall, eight-foot antique door that groaned as I pushed on it. The library was a large room with bookcases housing many leather bound volumes. A frail, old man sat at a long table and appeared to be reading one of the heftier tomes. Luckily, for both the books and me, the room was air-conditioned. I shut the door quietly and went over to the librarian.

"May I help you?" he asked in a hushed, polite voice, though we were the only two people in the room.

"Yes, my name is Leigh Maxwell and I'm a graduate student in music history from Boston. I was hoping that I would find some materials on Cardinal Dadi's father here. You see, I'm writing a dissertation on Enrique Dadi. I met the Cardinal earlier this morning, and he said you may be able to help me."

He frowned. "We have only theological texts here, Miss. If you were looking for a volume on something having to do with the Catholic religion, then I'm sure we'd be able to help you. I'm sorry we have nothing at all on music, except of course, the standard hymnals used for religious services."

I had felt sure that the library would have had something even though the Cardinal had been discouraging. I figured there would be some personal memorabilia, letters, or photographs. "I assumed that the Cardinal's father, being such an important composer, would have something here. He wrote a bit of religious music also. You don't have any personal letters, any books about the Cardinal's upbringing or childhood? The Cardinal mentioned that there were some of his writings here. Is there anything of a personal nature?"

"No, I'm sorry. We do have some of the Cardinal's writings, but nothing pertaining to his family. And the Cardinal will not be in at all today."

"Yes, I know. I have an appointment to see him this evening."

Silence filled the space while I tried to think of what else I could ask him about, but my brain was tired, jet lag had hit, and I just couldn't think of anything at all.

"You may be able to see Doña Maria, the Cardinal's sister," he continued after a long pause. "She lives here with the Cardinal, but doesn't normally entertain visitors. I could ask if she'd be willing to see you. I know she was very fond of her father."

"Oh, please, that would be wonderful." I could have kicked myself for not thinking of it earlier.

The old man rose from his chair and shuffled out of the room through a small door behind the desk. I stood there and waited, and waited, and waited. He was gone so long that I began to worry if he had had a heart attack or something. I went behind the desk and opened the door to see if he had fallen, but there was just an empty corridor and a small staircase behind the door. I thought of following him down the hallway but I didn't want to appear too pushy. I quietly shut the door, tiptoed around the desk, and started to peruse the shelves.

The books were all beautifully bound and looked well-thumbed. There were many older collections, gorgeous editions of Thomas Aquinas, Augustine, Boethius, and many others. I saw one section on Isadore of Seville, a bishop who once wrote that music could never be put to paper. He believed that once gone from memory, music was lost forever. For him, there was no way to preserve music on paper. I was so interested in this idea, so foreign to our understanding and experience of music, that I started to read about it. I didn't hear the librarian come back.

"You see," he said, making me jump, "we have some beautiful editions here. You're welcome to look through them. We have some of the rarer editions and manuscripts in the back. I could show those to you also, if you're interested."

"Yes, I'd like to," I said replacing the book where I had found it. "Did you get to speak to Cardinal Dadi's sister?"

"Yes, Doña Maria will see you, but not until two o'clock this afternoon. She's saying prayers right now and does not wish to be disturbed. If you don't mind waiting, she'll see you then."

"Oh, that will be fine. Thank you so much," I said. "And in the interim, could you show me some of your manuscripts? I've been teaching medieval music to undergraduates for a few years, though it really isn't my specialty, and I've begun getting interested in some of the Spanish artists. Do you have anything that old?"

The man grinned, and when he did, he appeared twenty years younger and maybe an inch or two taller. "I certainly do. It is not often visitors are interested in the liturgy. I have many volumes that no one has seen in years and years. I'll bring a few of the most interesting codices out for you," and with that, he disappeared again. I didn't have the heart to tell him that I wasn't really interested in the liturgy either, but only in the music itself.

He came out several moments later carrying a few ancient volumes. He put them down on a piece of red velvet and handed me white cotton gloves. We sat down and for the next few hours together, and were entirely engrossed in looking at 9th-and 10th-century collections from Spain. I kept thinking that there was enough material for about five other dissertation topics just waiting for diligent graduate students to stumble upon. The two of us happily whiled away the morning talking about some of the more interesting aspects of the manuscripts. He was quite knowledgeable about the collection and the liturgy and, in return, I taught him a few things about medieval neumatic notation. On the dot of twelve, he got up and said that the library would be closing for siesta and would re-open at two o'clock, just before I could see Doña Maria. He told me I should come back to the library about ten minutes earlier and he would escort me to her private rooms in the residence and introduce us. I thanked him for the wonderful morning and all his help, and then left to find something to eat.

When I went into the courtyard, I was again struck by the fearsome heat. I wasn't sure I could deal with this all year long. It was nice while on vacation, but getting up every morning, dressing for work, and being covered in sweat by the time you got to the car would be a bit much.

I went out and into the main part of the old city. All the buildings are right on top of each other and the cobblestone streets are narrow. I walked into the first plaza I found and around the Pablo Casals museum. I looked into a few restaurants lining the square. The third one, named Amadeus, had an appealing menu, and I decided to try it. Plus, being a musicologist, I couldn't resist Mozart's first name. Once inside the restaurant, I walked to the back patio area where a few tables were set out around a small fountain. I turned around and decided to eat at the bar instead, since the air conditioning seemed to work better there. I ordered a salad, iced coffee and a Spanish tortilla from a friendly and talkative bartender. The food was so good that I ate quickly and was finished with plenty of time to spare. It was only a little before one.

After lunch I went for a walk, to the end of Calle del Sol and around the small plaza next to the Governor's mansion. The plaza overlooked the harbor and there were shady trees and benches on the side. I sat down and looked at a bronze statue of a several women holding candles. I remembered my friend telling me the story behind that particular statue. Sometime in the 17th century, the British—or was it the Dutch—had taken control of El Morro. The next day they were going to invade the city and take over the rest of the island. The Spanish were tremendously outnumbered and were about to surrender. That night, the women in town lit candles and walked through the streets in a final farewell and prayer meeting. The invaders saw the people and the candles from afar. They thought it was an army massing, so they vacated El Morro, drew up anchors, and left. I've always loved that story; it seemed a perfect way to resolve conflict.

As I sat there, I started to wonder what I would ask Doña Maria when I finally got to see her, and took out my pad and jotted some notes. "How well did you know your father?" was on top of the list. Maybe I would just let her talk and see where that took me. After writing down a few more questions, I glanced at my watch. It was already one-thirty. I headed back to the library and waited for the old man.

A few minutes before two, he returned and led me through the back corridor and up another flight of stairs. He stopped before a large door and knocked quietly. The door opened without a creak, and before me stood the old lady who was in the chapel earlier that morning. She had intense blue eyes and shocking white hair. She was a woman who had a kind of magnetic power about her and was stunningly beautiful in a timeless fashion.

She smiled softly and said, "Hello, child, come on in and have a cup of coffee with me," and motioned me into a large, severe-looking sitting room, filled with dark, Spanish antique furniture, straight-back red velvet chairs, and wrought iron candlesticks. She turned to the librarian, "Thank you, Raoul. It is not often I have visitors. You have always been good to me." I turned and also thanked the librarian, who smiled at both of us and softly closed the door.

Doña Maria walked slowly to a red velvet chair and sat down with some difficulty. She indicated a chair for me in front of her, and then rang a small bell on the table. A moment later, a nun in full habit walked into the room and brought us a pot of coffee and antique cups and saucers on a polished silver tray. I wondered how she wasn't dying of the heat. After she left the room, Doña Maria asked me to pour for both of us. As I did so, she began to talk.

"I'm very pleased to meet you, my dear. I spoke to a young man, not very long ago also, though I'm afraid I don't remember his name."

"Carson Barry?"

She frowned, "Yes, that could be it. I don't remember things too well recently. I'm terribly sorry. You are writing about my father?"

"Well, yes. My name is Leigh Maxwell and I am a graduate student in Boston. I have been working on my dissertation for over a year now and have just come back from a trip to Europe where I saw many of your father's letters and manuscripts."

"Really? I thought that we had all his personal belongings here. I'd like to see what you have, dear."

"I'm terribly sorry, I deposited all the materials I have in the hotel safe and didn't bring them with me. I don't have anything here to show you."

"I'm sorry to hear that."

"I could certainly get you copies of the originals and send them to you later. You see, I'm attempting to write a biography of your father. I was hoping you could shed some light on aspects of his life that we know nothing about. I find your father's music quite interesting."

"Yes, he was a very interesting person. He lived in a special time and he was a special person. I've never met anyone else like him in my life," she paused.

I could have added that we probably all feel the same about our own fathers, but I didn't. I reached into my pocketbook and took out my Dictaphone.

"Do you mind if I turn this on, Doña Maria?"

"Certainly not. I am pleased you are working on a dissertation about my father's compositions. He was a great artist and a great man. He surrounded himself with beauty, not just music but art, too. My mother was beautiful, as well. I was born during the Great War. My father was a serious man. The War had a profound impact on him, you know. After the War, he became very religious. It is from him that both my younger brother and I have been so involved in the church. Are you Catholic, my dear?"

"No, I'm sorry, I'm not."

She looked at me and nodded sadly. "It has been a great source of inspiration in my life. My parents were both very religious. It is important to our whole family." She was beginning to repeat herself, so when she paused I interrupted.

"Were your mother and father very close?"

She seemed surprised at the question, but considered it carefully. "Close? I'm not sure I would use that word. They were not passionate about each other in the modern day sense of the word, but I'm not sure that passion is an important part of any lasting relationship. My parents were never openly affectionate, but then again, my father was a stern man at times. He believed in discipline, in doing the right thing."

"I'll bet," I thought, but let her continue. I kept thinking about the love letters to the wife of his cousin that he had written before and during his marriage, and the spying he had done. How did doing the right thing fit in with all of that?

"My father traveled all his life, playing concerts, giving lectures and so on," she continued. "My mother was often left alone with the two of us, my brother and me, and our nannies, of course. My father was very well known and respected, but you know that already. They were the talk of the town, so the saying goes. When my mother and father were out together, they were such a beautiful couple. 'The beautiful Maria,' they would call my mother. I think they were content with each other."

"So when you were growing up, you didn't see your father that much?"

"Unfortunately, no. He was often performing or away composing. He needed solitude, you know. Children underfoot are not good for concentration."

"How did your father compose? Did he compose at the piano or at a specific time during the day? I've never read anything about his working habits."

"I rarely saw my father actively compose. I think he must have been like Mozart; he composed in his head, and wrote the whole thing down whenever he got the chance."

Not likely, I thought. After all, there was only one Mozart. Even Beethoven sat for hours at the piano to get one measure, one note, right. Dadi was certainly not in their category.

She continued, "When he did have to work something out, he would take it to the piano. That was his piano," she said indicating a small upright in the corner of the room. "It was given to him by my Uncle Fernando."

"I didn't know your father had a brother."

She laughed a bit at that, "Oh, no he didn't, but he did have a best friend who used to visit us often and we called him Uncle out of respect. He was considered part of our family. Such a lovely man. His name was Fernando Garcia de Paredes. My father used to laugh so when he would visit us. We both, my brother and I, loved him. He was so kind and loving."

"Do you have any letters between the two? Are there any pictures of your father and mother, and possibly your Uncle Fernando? Are there any pictures or letters, between your Serbian cousins and that side of the family?"

"Oh, yes, my dear. When I knew I would see you after lunch, I got these photographs out for you to see. I have no photographs of our cousins, we had only a few anyway, but many of the immediate family."

She indicated a small album on the table in front of us. I pushed my chair next to hers and we started looking through it. There were plenty of photographs of her mother, Maria, and the two children. The only photograph with the entire family seemed somewhat forced; no one in the picture was smiling and Dadi seemed to be standing off to one side by himself. But Doña Maria was right about one thing, her mother was gorgeous. About midway through the album, there were several pictures of Dadi and his children, the most intimate I've ever seen. He was smiling and laughing, something I had never seen in any photograph of him. In the pictures that were readily available in all the biographies, you could not even tell if he had teeth. I'd often wondered if he had wooden ones like George Washington.

On the page opposite the pictures of Dadi laughing, there was an intriguing photo of a young man with dark, wavy hair and a bushy mustache with a baby in his arms. Even in the faded photograph, you could tell he was incredibly handsome.

"Is this your Uncle Fernando?" I asked.

"Oh yes," she said sighing, "He was so good looking, don't you think? And that's me as a little girl. I remember once, when I was about five, I told everyone in the family that I'd grow up and marry my Uncle Fernando. Isn't that silly? I remember as a joke that he even gave me the ring on his hand! Wasn't that sweet? You know, the older I get, the more my youth comes into focus. I may not remember what I did yesterday, but the days spent with my father are very vivid, still." She stared at the picture long and hard, looking back on herself as a young child. I didn't want to disturb her reverie and waited a few moments.

I finally said softly, "Yes, it was very sweet of your Uncle Fernando to give you his ring. Did you know him when you were older?"

"Oh, no. He died terribly young," she said tears welling in her eyes. She had a faraway look, as if the tragedy had happened yesterday instead of a lifetime ago. She finally drew in a deep breath and continued, "It was so tragic. He was killed in 1921, just when things were being rebuilt after the war. He was somewhere in Germany, I think, when he died. I can't remember it, but my father, I know, was devastated by the loss. You see, they were best friends. My mother always said that after Fernando's death, my father became even more religious. One curious thing was that Mother once said, under her breath, that God must have punished father by killing Fernando. Now, why would she have said that? My father was always such a good man." She then turned the page and pointed to the next photograph. "See, here was the day that Fernando gave me his ring. We were having a picnic and were all laughing and playing."

The photograph was of Fernando and Maria again, only taken several years later. It was loose in the book, and she took it out and handed it to me. There was writing on the back of the photo, and I turned it over and looked. The inscription read, "To my favorite niece. I can't wait to see you soon. Your loving, Uncle Fernando." I stopped short. "Doña Maria, is this your uncle's handwriting?" I asked slowly.

"Yes, yes it is. That was written to me."

The handwriting was distinctive–there was no mistake! It was exactly the same as in the love letters addressed to Dadi. "F" was not Franny, Frederica, Felicia or Faith, but Fernando. Dadi had a male lover! That was why he had the affair before and during his marriage. Now that I knew the truth, the letters made more sense.

I was about to ask Doña Maria about it, but decided not to. She might be offended, especially since she seemed to idealize both her father and Uncle Fernando. But *I* knew. Dadi was homosexual in a time and a place where it wasn't acceptable. His wife had to have known but was powerless to do anything. I'm sure both of them kept it quiet for the sake of their reputations and the children.

I finished looking at the last few pages of the photograph album in a daze. The photos stopped in the early 1920s and Doña Maria closed the book.

"These are all the photographs I have, dear. My brother took all the others away from me. He says we shouldn't live in the past. He doesn't know where I keep this album and it was saved."

"What did he do with all the other pictures?" I asked.

"I'm not sure. Knowing my brother, he probably burned them. You see, my brother is very much like our father. He has very strong beliefs. He thinks that by living with the past, you sacrifice the present, and that is an affront to God."

"As a historian, I couldn't disagree more. I believe that by looking at the past, we understand more about the present, Doña Maria. Things become clearer and more in focus. We look to the past to understand ourselves."

"Very interesting, but my brother would disagree with you. He is very sure of his beliefs. I'm glad you came today. He's away on a retreat and usually doesn't like visitors disturbing me." She patted my hand. "This is a welcome change for me, you know."

"What is the nature of the retreat, Doña Maria? Is it for the church?"

She looked around the room and then leaned toward me. "Well, I thought you knew all about my brother. He is a very important person in Opus Dei. They go away for one day each month. My brother always comes back energized by the meetings."

"Opus Dei?" I asked blankly.

"Yes, dear. Don't you know about them? The founder was Father Escriva. You may have seen his picture in the entry way to the residence. He was beatified a few years ago by the Pope for performing a miracle, I'm not sure what. But he's really important for starting the Opus Dei branch of the church."

"Beatified?"

She looked at me, "Well, I see you really aren't Catholic, my dear. That is the first step to becoming a saint. Pope John Paul II beatified Escriva in 1989."

"So, I guess Opus Dei is very important. Why have I never even heard of it, then?"

She lowered her voice a bit and leaned toward me. "Well," she said in almost a whisper, "it's a somewhat secretive organization, but still officially part of the church. They are trying to get people to return to the faith. You see, one of the hardest things to do in our lives is to follow a faith, really follow it, do you know what I mean?"

"I'm not sure, Doña Maria."

"Catholics today pick and choose what they believe in the church. For instance, you consider yourself Catholic, yet you believe in abortion, or divorce. Or you want to use birth control, or have female priests. If you believe in those things, then you really aren't part of the Catholic faith. Do you see what I mean?"

"Yes, I do, but shouldn't the church change and grow with the times? Didn't Vatican II change some of the rules of the church to try to get more people involved?"

"Yes, dear, it did. But there are absolutes, like the Ten Commandments. You know they can't change with the times. Murder is still murder. Abortion still abortion. Divorce still divorce. Do you see what I mean? Pope John Paul thinks that we should get back to a more moral way of living. I think he views Opus Dei as one way to help to achieve that goal. And once more, there are many aspects of Vatican II that are disturbing to us Catholics."

"So, Opus Dei is very fundamentalist."

"My brother is very serious about the Church's mission, and Opus Dei is very important to him. He believes, as do I, that he will be the next Pope, not that Cardinal in Italy, whatever his name is. Eduardo will be next, I'm sure. He's so good, so moral," she said proudly, smiling broadly. "Father would be so proud."

"Yes, I met your brother earlier today," I said non-committally.

"You met my brother?" she asked, concern edging into her voice.

"Yes, I went to Mass at the cathedral this morning. It was a lovely service."

She seemed a bit nervous and glanced down at her hands folded in her lap.

I continued, "He was very nice to me and wished me luck with my research. He told me that the librarian, Raoul, would help me."

"Oh, good," she said, seemingly relieved.

I noticed the Dictaphone tape had stopped recording. I took out one of my new tapes and inserted it into the machine. The new tape lasted twice as long as the old, so I wouldn't have to worry about when it would run out.

We talked for just a little while longer. I hadn't intended to have a theological discussion with her. We eventually got back to the subject of her father. She told me that her brother had all the letters and manuscripts left from her father and that he would be the one to ask some of the questions I had posed to her. Unfortunately, she didn't know where everything was in the residence and never entered her brother's quarters. Cardinal Dadi was sounding more and more like a dictator to me, but she seemed happy enough to accept it.

The nun returned several hours later and took away our coffee cups and then addressed the elderly woman, "Doña Maria, you should get some rest. It's nearly six thirty and your brother will be returning shortly."

Doña Maria nodded when the nun told her that, and immediately got up. Turning to me, she said, "Well, I should be going. Thank you for this visit. If you could send me those letters and things you told me about I would appreciate it."

I took her hand and shook it. "I'll send you the updates on whatever I find. Thank you so much for everything. You've been so helpful."

I watched her leave the room. The nun turned at the door and said, "You may leave through that door," indicating the door I had entered from. "Follow it down the corridor to the right and then down the stairs to the front."

"Thank you." I put my things away, tossing the Dictaphone into my bag and then the pad. It had been a fascinating day and I was famished. I looked around again. Since our conversation, the room appeared more like a jail than a sitting room, and as I watched her shuffling away, I realized she was more a prisoner than a resident.

Before I left, I looked out the window toward the harbor. I have never gotten used to how quickly the sun sets in the tropics. In the north it is a long, protracted occurrence, but here, it's as if someone switched out the lights. I could see the street lamps twinkling all through the city, and the sky was already a dark blue. The moon was large and orange, hovering just above the water.

I opened the door to the hallway and shut it quietly. As I turned around, I noticed two men in the courtyard, two stories below. I wondered if one of them was the Cardinal, and if he had time for me now. I looked over the banister rail, and my heart stopped. Rafael Gazza was talking softly to the tall man in the tan coat, the one who had killed Barbara.

CHAPTER 19

▼

I stepped away from the rail slowly and quietly until my back was against the door. I tried to open it again, but it had automatically locked. No one came to the door when I knocked on it softly. There were a few courtyard lights down below, but on the third floor, everything had been turned off; there was a soft glow from a few windows next to the library on the second floor, but they did really nothing to light the hallway below. All the doors were shut, probably locked like this one. The only way down that I could see was the staircase, and it emptied right next to where Rafael and the tall man were standing.

I strained to hear what they were saying, but couldn't distinguish the words. They spoke in a soft tone that didn't carry well, but they seemed to be having an argument about something; there was a palpable edge to their voices.

Honestly, I had no idea what I should do, so I started inching around the periphery of the hallway, trying each door and window as I went past, but as I had suspected, each was bolted. There was no way in.

Luckily, they still hadn't noticed me. Thank God I had bought a dark blue shirt yesterday. When I finally reached the last door, I stopped and scanned the area for another way out. I couldn't just stay there all night. I thought back to the corridor that the librarian had used. There had to be another set of stairs and an inside corridor somewhere. How else had Doña Maria gotten into the chapel this morning without walking through the courtyard? The only problem was that it seemed that you could only get to it from inside one of the rooms. Spying the outside staircase again, I wondered if I could possibly get down to the second story without attracting attention. I slowly inched my way around to the top of the stairs, careful not to make any sudden movement or noise that might attract their attention.

When I got to the top of the staircase, the large carriage house doors to the street opened, and Rafael and the tall man walked over to greet whoever was coming in. I flew down the stairs in just a few seconds, glad to be at least on the second floor, figuring that the closer to the exit, the better off I'd be. The library windows were all dark but I went to the door anyway–it refused to budge. Then I heard a few doors shut on the first floor followed by silence. The only sound came from the fountains in the courtyard. Waiting a few heartbeats, I decided to try to get downstairs and out the front door. Once outside, the plaza across the street was filled with people and I would be able to get help.

I started toward the stairs, but right behind me a door opened. Before I could turn around, a man grabbed my arm. I gasped very loudly. Luckily, there was no one in the downstairs courtyard to hear. I turned around ready to try to twist my way out of his grasp, only to see Carlos' face. I heaved a sigh of relief, "Oh my God, Carlos, Thank God you're here." I whispered frantically. "We have to get out of here. I'll explain later. Let's go down the stairs over there. They're all gone for now."

Carlos was holding onto my arm so tightly that it hurt. "Leigh," he said in a harsh whisper. "Listen. You get out of here. How many times did I just tell you to forget all this about Dadi. I can't help you any longer. You have to go. Just get on the first flight out of here."

"What are you talking about? Let's go. Come on," I said as I tried to get him to let go of my arm. "You're hurting me. What's going on?"

"Look, just leave. I can't explain right now, but hurry," he hissed.

He pulled me out of the doorway and over to the staircase. I was sure that he was giving me bruises on my upper arm, and I said, "You're hurting me, let go. What are you doing? What is all this?"

Just a moment ago I had wanted only to get down the stairs and out into the city, but now I wanted some answers from Carlos too. He kept his grip on my upper arm and forced me down the stairs. No one was there; the security guard must have gone home too. There was only a thin shaft of light trickling through the window and muffled voices coming from a room opposite the front door and the chapel. When we got to the bottom of the stairs, a door opened to my right and light flooded the area. Rafael Gazza cried out to someone inside, "Carlos has her."

Carlos turned toward Rafaels' voice at the same time as he let go of my upper arm. As soon as I was free of him, I ran toward the front door, but in the shadows of the hallway someone was already moving to intercept me. I turned to my left and headed toward the chapel door. Luckily it was open, and I scooted in, shutting the door behind me. There were a few candles still burning so I could see where I was going, but the door had no bolt or lock on it–I guess this church was open twenty-four hours a day. I dragged one of the pews toward the door and wedged it between a support column and the entrance. It could open a little bit, but not enough to let someone in. Rafael started to push on the door. I could see his fingers curl around the outside and push. When he couldn't budge the door open at all, he began banging on it. He kept yelling, "Leigh, we can work all this out. There's no need to be afraid of me."

Did he really think I was that stupid? He kept trying to push on the door while knocking, but he wasn't making much headway. I knew I couldn't hide in the chapel forever–eventually they would get to me. I went to the area where I had seen Doña Maria come in and tried to find the secret door that led out of the room. I pushed on everything I could and finally found a small indentation. When I pressed it, a door opened and I stepped into a dimly lit corridor. I started down to my right, hoping I was going in the direction of the entrance, when I heard someone from around the corner say, "She's probably heading this way, let's go."

I turned away from the sound of the voice and started running. I wasn't making too much noise since I was still wearing my Reeboks, but my pocketbook kept banging against my hip and I could hear my keys tinkling inside. Why was I still carrying my house keys, anyway? I was a long way from home.

The corridor ended at the base of a staircase. I ran up, taking them two at a time, and opened the first door at the top, finding myself back in the library. Making my way over to the large entrance door, I quickly unbolted it and was back in the hallway around the periphery of the courtyard again. I headed toward the stairs, hoping everyone was still in the interior corridors trying to find me. I got to the top of the stairs, just in time to see Rafael crossing the courtyard, heading in my direction. Just then, the lights flicked on in the library.

My only option was the door between the two lighted windows next to the library. I shoved as hard as I could and to my surprise, it opened easily and I practically fell into the room.

I slammed the door behind me and leaned against it, breathing loudly. Cardinal Dadi was sitting at a large, antique desk; he got up and crossed the room in just a few paces. When he reached my side, he said in a soothing voice, "How may I help you, Miss Maxwell?" with an exaggerated emphasis on the "how."

"Oh, Cardinal Dadi, I'm so glad to see you," I gasped, grateful that he was there and seemed willing to help me.

"You seem upset."

A bit of an understatement, I thought. I took a deep breath and said, trying not to sound too hysterical, "There are some men out there that I can't face. Could you please call the police? I need help. I need help now. Please." My voice began to crack toward the end and I was still breathing raggedly.

"No need to worry about them here. Sit down," he said indicating a chair in a sitting area in the room.

When I made no move away from the door, he came over to me and took my arm. He was obviously someone who was used to people doing as they were told. He put his hand on my shoulder and guided me into a seat. His touch made it clear that there was no room for argument. I noticed he had an ornate cross dangling from his neck, and the large ring on his right hand sparkled as it caught the light in the room. From just outside the windows, I heard the sound of people running up and down the hall. I was grateful that I had found a haven.

I glanced around the room. Like Doña Maria's apartment, it was uninviting, dominated by a large, dark desk and an antique trunk directly in front of it. A few paintings of the crucifixion adorned the walls. The thought crossed my mind that all the paintings in the building involved the crucifixion in some way—death and pain were everywhere. There were no paintings of Jesus' birth, his miracles, or anything else of comfort. Not even the resurrection was in evidence, and from what I knew about Christianity, that was the whole point, wasn't it? Scattered about the room were candles in antique, massive, wrought iron holders. The rest of the furniture consisted of a few straight-backed chairs in cracked, dark brown leather, on one of which I now sat.

The Cardinal stood opposite me, clasping his hands together. He stared intently into my eyes as if trying to decide something. I wanted to say something, but his stare was so intense that I couldn't begin to form the words. After a few seconds, he said in a flat voice, "So, Miss Maxwell, you have not answered my question. What is it you want?"

"Cardinal Dadi. I fear I'm in trouble of some sort, and I really don't know what it is all about. Right now I need to get away from some men outside."

"You are in no danger here."

"Thank you. Thank you so much for your help. Could I call a taxi or someone to come get me? Do you have a phone here?" I asked as I looked around the room to see where the phone was kept.

"Yes, Miss Maxwell. I have a telephone, but it is unavailable."

I looked over at the Cardinal who was now still sitting rigidly on his straight-back chair. His eyes had a steely look and seemed to pierce the distance between us. In that second, I knew that he was responsible for everything. I was in deep trouble.

Just at that moment, there was a soft knocking from the outside hallway. It startled me. The Cardinal got up, crossed the room and opened the door. "Ah," he said in a silky voice, "Do I have to do everything? She's in here," gesturing toward me. Carlos, Rafael and the tall man came into the room. The Cardinal looked at them and held out his right hand. They each knelt on the floor and kissed the large ring that must have reached from one knuckle to the other. He seemed to enjoy the moment, a small smile played at the corners of his mouth. I had never seen anything like this and wondered if everyone was supposed to kiss the ring of a Cardinal. Did the President kiss the Pope's ring? I wasn't sure.

Most surprising, though, was the expression on the men's faces. Carlos refused to look at me or even in my direction. Rafael, in particular, looked like he was kissing the hand of his lover, slowly closing his eyes and savoring the moment. Rafael then said in a low voice laden with emotion, "Your Eminence, we are terribly sorry. We should have taken care of the situation a long time ago. We thought Carlos had the situation under control."

With that the Cardinal drew his lips apart in what I assumed was supposed to be a smile. He revealed startling white teeth that looked more like fangs to me in the dim light. He drew back his right hand and slapped Rafael so hard on the face that his nose began to bleed and his cheek was gashed by the impact with the ring. I gasped with surprise but Rafael seemed to have expected it. He lowered himself even more on the floor until he was almost prostrate.

"Yes, you should have," the Cardinal said in an almost whisper, and then bending a little lower toward Carlos, "This has been most inconvenient. I have other matters more urgent awaiting my attention. You were supposed to take care of this situation months ago." Turning to the tall man, he said, "And you, Juan. What shall I do with you? I have always depended on you, but you have failed in this case. What good have you done me recently?" He took the man's chin in his hand treating him like a little child. He looked directly into the tall man's eyes, then let go with a jerk—a gesture indicating his disgust with what he found there.

"Your Eminence. We're terribly sorry about…"

"I have not asked for an explanation," the Cardinal interrupted. "I have asked for only one thing, but all of you seem to be unable to do it." He crossed his arms and said something in Latin. The tall man, Juan, put his head to the floor, muttering something that I couldn't understand, and began to cry. Huge, heaving sobs wracked his frame and I almost felt sorry for him. The Cardinal quietly walked to his desk and opened a drawer. He took out several chains that looked to me like dog collars.

"You shall all wear these around your right thighs until you understand how to obey my commands. Tighten them well, the cilice will be your companion from this day forth until I tell you otherwise."

Cilice? I asked myself. Without looking up, all three men raised their hands and took the chains.

"Thank you, your Eminence for this pain. It will remind us to worship you and always do right by you. You are God's son," they all three chanted together.

Cilice? I kept asking myself. Was the Cardinal really into self-flagellation? Why were these men being punished by physical pain? I felt like I was watching a warped *Twilight Zone* episode. Then I thought back on their response, "You are God's son." They thought the Cardinal was God's son? What did *that* mean?

I knew I had better try to get out of there. I looked to the door on the opposite side of the room, wondering if I could make the distance before they caught up with me, but realized I had no chance against the four of them. I looked at my boyfriend as he knelt on the floor; I couldn't believe what I was seeing. I realized that I had never really known him. Our entire relationship had all been a lie. I wondered if I could ever trust my own judgment again. In the last few moments, my life had irrevocably changed. I knew I would never be the same person again.

The Cardinal turned to me next and seemed to look right through me with eyes that glistened in the soft light.

"And you..."

I interrupted him, "Cardinal Dadi, I am only a graduate student from Boston. I'm interested in your father's life and works. I mean no disrespect. I just wanted to write my dissertation and get a job. I can stop now if you ask me to. I really can. I wouldn't mind, I'll just leave everything with you and go to library school, or even law school. I swear I could just..." I stopped babbling when I saw the look in his eyes. They were utterly flat, though they had opened slightly wider as I had blathered on. He was not a man used to being interrupted.

"You have been sent to destroy me," he said in a voice that cracked with emotion. "But, I shall not be destroyed. Do you hear me? Not by you or anyone else."

"I don't want to hurt you or your family. I don't know what you mean. I..."

He held up his hand to silence me and then smiled the same predatory smile he had before. "Young woman, let us be honest with one another. You are gathering material in an attempt to discredit my father. We are a holy family. I *will* be the next Pope and everyone will then know that God speaks directly to me. Do you hear? To *me*. He has already told me his plans. We shall purge this world of our shame. We shall change the sinful ways of man, either by love or by fear. I care not how." He paused then and crossed his arms. He looked at one particularly graphic painting of a gray and beaten Jesus, walking through the streets of Jerusalem, weighed down by the cross. He continued, "It has been my experience that people are more loyal if they fear you than if they love you. People do not love Jesus so much as they fear everlasting hell. Don't you agree?"

I didn't want to get into another theological debate, though I wanted to point out that Jesus' message was all about love—one of the things that I thought made Christianity appealing. But I needed to keep him talking while I tried to figure out how to get myself out of this. I knew I would surely lose a theological debate with the Cardinal, so I shifted the conversation back to Dadi. "Your father was a great artist," I began slowly. "I found many beautiful compositions in Europe that have never been published" (no need to tell him they were stolen) "and you should feel pride over what your father accomplished" (no need to tell him his father was a spy).

"Pride? Pride? I should be *proud* of my father?" He then drew in a deep breath as if to steady himself and walked toward me. He sat in the chair right next to mine. His body seemed to exude cold, and I involuntarily pulled away from him. He put a frigid hand on mine. My hand twitched, but I didn't dare move it. He continued in an almost whisper, "I have collected everything of my father's for over three decades. Juan has just given me the papers he had collected from the Berlin library; there are no more. You see this chest?" He pointed to a large hope chest next to the desk. "It is filled with my father's things. I wanted to destroy them all at once so that I could be sure they were all gone. You wanted to look at them, didn't you? Well, now you can." With that, he took hold of my hand so tightly I thought my fingers would burst. He pulled me over to the chest. It looked like a beautiful antique trunk and had the name "Maria" etched on the side. I wondered if it was his mother's hope chest. He opened the lid while letting go of my hand. There were thousands of pages thrown haphazardly into the large trunk. I looked down and immediately took the first thing I saw. It was Debussy's unfinished masterpiece—the opera based on Edgar Allen Poe's *The Fall of the House of Usher*.

I was so fascinated that I almost forgot all about the Cardinal. I began flipping through the hand-bound manuscript. It all seemed to be there, every act, every scene. "You mean to tell me, this was finished? Debussy finished it?" I asked no one in particular.

The Cardinal frowned and looked a bit confused at that. "Who are you talking about?"

"This is an opera by Claude Debussy. Everyone thought this was unfinished. We only have about fifteen or twenty percent of it left in the Paris Bibliothèque nationale. We've been wondering for sixty, seventy years what the finished opera would be like. You know, Debussy wrote only one other opera, and it was very controversial in its time. This is invaluable. This is better than gold, it's…"

"I don't care about *music*," emphasizing the word "music" as if it were something utterly repulsive. He grabbed the manuscript out of my hand and tossed it back into the trunk with a gesture of disgust. I reached for it again, unwilling to let it out of my hands, but the Cardinal slammed the chest shut, almost taking my fingers with it. I cried out in dismay and fear. Carlos, Juan and Rafael remained on the floor, but out of the corner of my eye, I could see them flinch when the chest slammed shut.

"I care nothing about music," he continued in a soft whisper. "Or history, or historians. My father was a sinful man, and I will not have his sins tarnish me."

"What are you talking about? What sins?" I had to find out what he knew about his father and what had disturbed him so.

He looked at me and smiled. "You must have discovered by now who "F" was. I know you saw my sister today. I am not stupid. I know everything that goes on in this house. She always talks about her beloved Uncle Fernando, but she has no idea who he really was to my father."

"Yes, I knew, but it doesn't matter now if your father was homosexual, or at least bi-sexual. It was so long ago. You know the sins of the father, I mean…"

He was literally shaking with rage as he screamed, "It is an abomination. It is sinful and against the laws of God and Nature. I will not have it discussed so cavalierly in my presence. I am ashamed that I ever loved my father." The Cardinal turned and spat on the floor. "He is surely rotting in hell, as well he should. As you will be too, Miss Maxwell. You are a sinful woman and when I have Juan kill you, I will have purged the world of one more sinner."

I knew better than to interrupt him this time. Frankly, from my point of view, his father's crimes against the French government and his friends were more serious than his love for another man. The fact that Dadi was gay and had a lover was not a big deal. In fact, I felt sorry that he had had to stay in the shadows and to lie about his sexuality. It was cause to pity him, not hate him. And besides, I couldn't believe that the Catholic Church would ever find out, much less care, about the Cardinal's long-dead father. In the split second that I thought those things, I looked furtively around for some way out but couldn't see one.

"This is the last of it," he continued. "Everything is here and once I destroy it, no one will ever know." He picked up one of the larger wrought-iron candle holders and opened the chest again. I don't know what I was thinking but I screamed out and lunged for the candle as he was attempting to set the papers on fire. He pushed me away with what seemed to me superhuman strength. As soon as the candle touched them, the old papers caught fire easily. I started to shake from frustration, anger and the senseless loss of it all.

He looked at me and smiled. "It is a bonus that you should witness this, Miss Maxwell. No one will know about my father's sins after tonight. This fire will cleanse his soul and mine."

"Don't you understand?" I choked out. "You don't know what you're destroying! You will be judged by the content of your own character, not by the actions of someone else. You're destroying, not healing. Are you crazy?"

As the fire really took hold inside the hope chest, he had an enigmatic smile on his face. It seemed he hadn't heeded what I said; he was in a world all of his own. I looked again at the burning papers and was sure that he hadn't even considered the fact that the old trunk would also catch on fire. Smoke began to fill the room and my eyes started tearing.

He was still holding the candle in his right hand while staring, as if mesmerized, into the fire. Catching him off guard, I managed to grab the candle, but it caught on the chain from his cross and seared his goatee. He cried out, "No!" I let go of the candle and kicked him as hard as I could so that he lost his balance and fell against the chest and then onto the floor. Juan and Rafael scrambled up and dashed over to us. Juan ran to the Cardinal and kept saying, "Your Eminence, your Eminence, are you hurt?"

Carlos grabbed my arm and pushed me toward the door. He looked at me for a second, regret, fear, love all mixed in his glance. "Go. Go now," he said and turned back to the Cardinal.

Rafael looked up and headed toward me. "Carlos, get her," he said. Carlos stood in front of Rafael, and I turned to run. Once in the hallway, I glanced back and saw that the Cardinal was now trying to stop the fire by pouring water on it from a carafe, but the trunk had now caught and the old wood was already in flames. Juan was attempting to smother the blaze. Carlos held Rafael away from the door and they were yelling at each other, but I couldn't tell what they were saying.

I turned and ran down the steps as fast as I could and out the front door into the plaza. Juan must have gotten around Carlos and Rafael, because he was about ten steps behind me. "Stop," he bellowed. I kept running as fast as I could. What sounded like a firecracker split the air and my ear was suddenly hot. I put my hand up and it came back bloody. I almost stumbled from the realization that he was shooting at me. I reached the plaza just ahead of him and turned and headed for the restaurant where I had eaten lunch. As I burst into the restaurant, the bartender recognized me from lunch, but then looked shocked as he saw the blood dripping from my ear and onto my shirt and pants.

"Help, help me, please," I gasped.

Juan ran into the restaurant just then, holding the gun in his right hand and raising it to point at me. I crouched down and started to run behind the bar. A formidable looking bouncer, whom I hadn't noticed before, stood up and grabbed the gun from Juan in one fluent gesture. He took hold of Juan's other arm and brought him neatly to his knees.

The bartender called the police. Juan kept trying to get up, but the bouncer was in complete control and kept him on the floor with what seemed like superhuman strength. He said, "You will stay here and wait for the police–both of you." I was cowering behind the bar, and was unwilling to come out.

Juan said, "I work for Cardinal Dadi and I need to bring this woman back to the residence."

The bouncer answered, "I don't care who your boss is. You're staying right here."

Juan looked genuinely surprised that the bouncer didn't jump at the sound of the Cardinal's name. It was an impasse. At one point, Juan made a lunge to get out of the restaurant, but the body-builder arms of the bouncer made escape impossible. The police arrived a few moments later and wanted to take us both to the station for questioning. I was still bleeding and my breath was labored. As they came in, I stood up shakily behind the bar and the bartender took my elbow to support me.

"That man was shooting at me," I said pointing to Juan. "He tried to kill me," my voice cracking with emotion.

The police took one look at Juan, and then at my bloody ear and clothes and must have decided I didn't look the criminal type. The bouncer backed up my story by saying that I came running in already bloody, and Juan came in right after me and had pointed a gun at me.

The police were very efficient, taking the situation in hand, bagging the gun, putting Juan in handcuffs, and finally leading us both out of the restaurant. They didn't seem too concerned about the Cardinal either. I turned around and thanked the bartender and bouncer. They waved as if glad to be rid of the disturbance.

As I left the restaurant with Juan and the policemen, I looked over at the residence. There was smoke billowing out from windows on the second floor. I could see a few nuns coming out of the front door and Doña Maria was on the arm of one of them. The fire department was already there, but I wondered if the Cardinal was still on the second floor.

The police took me to a hospital to have my ear looked at. I felt like Evander Holyfield after the Mike Tyson fight. The doctors put large white bandages on my ear and kept telling me how lucky I was to be alive. Two policemen came to take my statement. I told them everything, from the robbery in Boston to the fire at the Cardinal's residence. They seemed skeptical but politely listened all the way through. They then asked to see identification and I rummaged around my purse for my passport. I noticed the Dictaphone and wondered when I had last turned it off. It was voice-activated so I sometimes forget to turn it off. I took it out and hit rewind for a few seconds, then pressed play. On the tape, the Cardinal could clearly be heard "He is surely rotting in hell, as well he should. As you will be too, Miss Maxwell. You are a sinful woman and when I have Juan kill you, it will purge the world of one more sinner." I switched it off. When I heard that voice, I started to shake all over again.

I handed the machine over to the police, not wanting any part of it at all. "Here is our conversation. You'll recognize the voice. You can ask Cardinal Dadi about it when you arrest him. He's insane, truly and deeply insane. I can't face him right now, but I'd like to press charges. He belongs in a hospital, if not jail, for the things he's done."

The policemen stood up. One of them said, "You should get some rest. The doctors say you'll be fine, but they'd like to observe you tonight. Injuries like the one you have can be surprisingly painful. We'll take the tape and transcribe it."

"There's also a conversation I had with the Cardinal's sister. That won't be of any significance to you. I'd like the machine and the tapes returned, please. It's for my research."

"Of course, Miss Maxwell. We'll see you in the morning." One of the policemen turned when he was at the threshold of the door. "Oh, and you needn't worry about the Cardinal hurting you. There were three casualties from smoke inhalation in the fire–three men. We're fairly certain that one was Cardinal Dadi." With that he turned away.

Just then a nurse bustled into the room and gave me a shot in the arm. I had no idea what was in it, and when I asked her, she said, "Something to help you sleep." I asked her if anyone from the fire was at the hospital. She didn't answer my question but just held my hand. At that moment, the lights in the room began to dim and she seemed very far away. I closed my eyes and slept for what felt like an eternity.

CHAPTER 20

▼

When I finally awoke, I saw my father's face. I must have slept more than twelve hours straight and I wasn't quite sure where I was.

"Daddy, what are you doing here?" I asked in a groggy voice.

"Shhh…You don't have to get up right now, you can lie back down."

"What time is it?"

"It's about noon."

The events of the previous night were coming into focus. "How did you know where I was?"

"I got a call at home from the nursing staff here last night. They found my name and number in your purse. I can't believe you actually filled out the "In Case of Emergency" form in your wallet. I got on the first plane this morning, and just arrived here about half hour ago."

"You're a sight for sore eyes. Thanks for coming."

He took my hand in his. "Hey, you're my baby. Any time you need me, I'll be there. You know that. How do you feel?"

"Tired and old. I'm still a bit out of it. What did they give me anyway?"

"I don't know but it was something that really knocked you out. How does your ear feel?"

I reached up and touched it. Thee oversized bandage was straight out of a Tom and Jerry cartoon. "It's throbbing, but not too bad. I wonder how bad it will look when they take off the bandage. Do you think I can get out of here this morning?"

"That's up to the doctors and, I guess, the police. When I got here, there were two policemen checking on you. They told me the whole story."

"Daddy, the Cardinal was really crazy, I mean absolutely insane. It was awful."

"It's okay."

"No, it will never be okay again," I answered. After a few minutes of silence, I continued, "Did anything survive in the fire? Oh my God, how is the library? It was right next door to the Cardinal's office."

"One of the rooms was completely gutted, absolutely everything in it was destroyed. That was where they found the bodies. The rest of the building is intact, it seems. You can see for yourself, once you're better."

At that moment, a nurse came in carrying a breakfast tray. She helped me up and to the bathroom. I got back to bed a little shaky but felt my strength returning.

"Daddy," I said slowly, "Was one of the bodies, I mean, did they identify the bodies?"

"I'm sorry, Leigh. Carlos died in the fire. I know how you felt about him."

I started crying. "You know, the strange thing is that I felt so close to him, but I guess I really never knew him. I still love Carlos, or at least the Carlos I thought knew. But who was he really? At the end there, you know, when I was running out of the room, he saved me. He saved my life. He stopped Rafael from running after me, and he let me go in the hall. I'm, I've…" I trailed off. My father was silent and all I could hear was the hum of the air-conditioning in the room.

A nurse came in and told me that I had a visitor. Raoul, the librarian from the Cardinal's Archive, shuffled into the room. I introduced him to my father and he sat on the chair next to my bed. He seemed uncomfortable and fidgeted.

"Miss Maxwell," he said finally, "I'm terribly sorry about everything that has happened. I feel responsible."

"Why should you feel bad? It was Cardinal Dadi who was doing everything, manipulating everyone, not you."

"I knew you might get into trouble seeing Doña Maria, but she's such a lonely woman, and I thought she'd like it."

"Raoul, that wasn't why he, ummm, well, why he tried to kill me. You had nothing to do with it. Neither did Doña Maria."

"Thank you for saying so." There was another long pause.

I didn't know what else I could say to him. He was feeling guilty for the actions of others. If he hadn't gotten me in to see Doña Maria, then I would never have figured everything out and would have been at a disadvantage when I finally saw the Cardinal last night.

He took a deep breath and let it out slowly. "Miss Maxwell, I'd be happy to help you in any other way that I can. I've just come from the Library, and I wanted you to know that nothing valuable was ruined. There's been some water damage but everything else looks all right. The rare books and even that codex that we looked at yesterday are absolutely fine. They were far away from the smoke and the water. If you ever want to see anything again, or know musicologists interested in medieval topics, I can certainly help."

I held out my hand and took his. "I want to thank you for everything you did. Actually, believe it or not, I have a friend who has been searching around for a good dissertation topic in medieval music and she's very interested in the liturgy. She'll get in touch with you, I'm sure. Can you tell me, how is Doña Maria? Was anyone else hurt in the fire?"

"There were only the three casualties. I think Doña Maria is still in shock but she'll be fine. She's with the sisters now and we'll be moving her to a country estate where she can live quietly. You could visit her there if you'd like. I do know she enjoyed your talk yesterday."

"Thank you, Raoul, and thank you for coming and telling me everything. Please give my best to Doña Maria next time you see her."

"I'll do that. I'm going back to the library now to work. Again, I am sorry for everything," turning toward my father he said, "It was a pleasure to meet you." With that, he slowly left the room.

After Raoul's visit, there was a long succession of doctors, nurses, and finally the police again. They were checking up on me and also wanted me to read through the statement that I had given them the night before. As I read through the report, the events of the previous night vividly came back to me. I knew then that the Cardinal would be in my dreams for a long time to come. In the late afternoon, I was finally free to go.

My father drove me back to the Caribe Hilton and we immediately checked out and took off for the airport. We didn't have a reservation but I told my father that I'd take any plane off the island and we could just go standby. Luckily, there was a flight to Boston due to leave at seven, and we were able to get two seats. They cost a mint, but I was way beyond caring. There was also a flight to Florida, and I told my father that he should just go home. I told him I'd be fine going back to Boston on my own. When he declined and decided to come with me, I'm sure the relief was evident in my face.

While we waited, I checked with the airline about my lost luggage. I told them I was leaving Puerto Rico and if my bags were found, the airline should send them to Boston. As I entered the office, I noticed some bags tossed along with mine, sitting off to the side. I spoke with the woman and opened my garment bag to make sure it was mine. There was my Picard T-shirt, right on top. I took out some of my old clothes and changed in the bathroom, throwing out the tan pants and shirt I had bought at the Hilton. I didn't want any reminder of that day. When I returned, I had pulled my hair back, and was wearing my jeans, Reeboks, and the Picard T-shirt that was ripped under the arms. My father shook his head and muttered, "Well, you look more like yourself now."

We boarded the plane and made it safely back home. I was relieved to pick up Jabba again and feel his soft, warm, purring heft in my arms. Throughout the evening, I kept crying now and then. I was an emotional wreck. My father slept on the couch, and I slept with Jabba.

The next day, one by one, my friends came to call—Jack, then Helen, a few friends from work and school. None of them stayed long, but all wanted to let me know that I could depend on them, if need be. It had been less than a week since the burglary but my life had changed in drastic ways.

I also got a call from the Boston police. They had found my hard drive and everything else. It was all dumped in Carlos' apartment. I explained what had happened in Puerto Rico. After I picked up my computer and diskettes at the police station, they escorted us to the apartment and I took a few of the things that I had left there. It was a hard emotional journey. I kept thinking back over the six months I had spent with Carlos. I kept asking myself if I could ever trust anyone again. I kept wondering how bad a judge of character I was.

My father was supportive and helpful throughout. He put everything away when we got home. He threw out all of Carlos' things from my house without ever saying, "I told you so." He even threw out the Harpoon beer and stocked my fridge with Harp—my favorite.

But it was also a relief when he left a few days later. I needed time to myself to figure out how and why it had all come to this. I wondered how much I should blame myself for my lack of judgment and my stubbornness. I was exhausted in every way possible but could not relax. I was edgy and nervous all the time.

I now understand that post-traumatic stress disorder is a very real phenomenon. A few weeks after I returned home, I started seeing a counselor for it, but I always have trouble sleeping and still can't eat much. I've lost about fifteen pounds, and while my friends tell me I look great, I smile. I still don't feel like myself. I have withdrawn from many social situations, only seeing a few of my closest friends once or twice a week.

The counselor agreed with me that perhaps the best way to work through my demons was to write the best dissertation I could. Since I couldn't sleep much anyway, and what I managed was marred by nightmares, I wrote at all hours of the day and night. I took a medical leave from the library, and lived on coffee and

Almond Joy bars. Often, there were days that I didn't even get dressed, and saw no one but the pizza delivery man. At the end of six months, I had finished my dissertation, and had a document that was truly groundbreaking. With the defense done and officially approved, I felt I could start thinking about returning to life. I even applied for some musicology jobs that popped up later in the year.

I would have given anything to go back in time and start all over again, to have the old Leigh Maxwell back.

Epilogue

▼

Seven months later:

I was adjusting my hat, which never looked quite right, when the phone rang.
"Hello."

"Is this Leigh?"

"Yes, Edna, is that you?"

"Yes. It's Edna–from the plane."

"I knew right away who it was."

"I'm so sorry, but I can't make the graduation this afternoon. I took a bit of a tumble coming down the stairs this morning, and I'm just not up for it. I hope you understand. I was so looking forward to meeting your father."

"I'm disappointed but you'll get another chance to meet him, no doubt."

"Has everything worked out? When I got your invitation in the mail, I was thrilled. How is that young man in Berlin and the widower? Is everyone doing fine?"

"Yes, everyone is fine. Johann is the head of the music library now. My cousin, Oskar, married his secretary only about eight weeks after Barbara's death. It was a blow to the family. My Dad and my sister are here now, and we're about to go off to the hooding ceremony. You should see me. I look so funny in this billowy robe. And the hat–well, you'll see the pictures for yourself. I'll visit you when you're up for it."

"Have a wonderful graduation, Leigh. I'm so sorry I couldn't be there to celebrate with you. And call soon, we need to catch up."

"Thanks for calling, Edna. Take care."

My father pointed to his watch and motioned that we had to leave. He's always an hour early for everything. I dutifully trooped out with my sister bringing up the rear.

Standing in the sunshine, waiting to file into the large yellow tent set up on campus for graduation, was more thrilling than I had thought it would be. The weather was perfect for a May day in New England, complete with puffy white clouds, a deep blue sky and a slight chill in the wind. I enjoyed looking at the stripes that I had earned on the sleeves of my gown. Now I understand why army officers have all those ribbons on their uniforms. They are a tangible acknowledgment of trial by fire.

The nightmares still come, unbidden, though with much less frequency now than before. Sometimes, I still wake, flailing to get away from tall men holding candles while we run through dark alleyways. I wake up gasping for air and holding my ear. My friends say that my ear looks fine even with the small chunk taken out of it. I probably look like a Tom Cat who has been in one too many fights.

My father and sister sat at the graduation toward the front, and they both smiled the whole time. Helen was in the first row in her own cap and gown and looked like a mother hen when my name was called. Jack was on stage and handed me my diploma. He kissed me on both cheeks and whispered. "You deserve it" when I smiled at him.

When it was time to walk down the aisle and out into the sunshine with the graduates, the eight new doctors all walked together. Not only was I the only musicologist in the group but I was also the only one who had a job for the following year. Jobs are tough to get in Academe, and they're especially rare in music history. My new job was only a one-year appointment in Illinois at a small school in Gainsberg, about three hours outside of Chicago. The university has a great reputation, and the course load and pay were decent. Basically, it was an offer I couldn't refuse. I had discussed it at great length with both Helen and Jack and I had decided that if I really wanted to be a musicologist, I'd have to spend some years paying my dues. Perhaps, after a few publications and some solid work experience behind me, I could come back to the Boston area and find work. Besides, it was the only job offer I had gotten, and I couldn't pass it up.

With my diploma in hand, I felt like I had finally been given keys that would give me entrance into the hallowed halls of Academe. Every now and then, I wondered if it was worth it.

As I left the graduation ceremony, my father came up and hugged me. "I'm so proud of you, Dr. Maxwell," he said beaming.

I smiled and said, "Thanks, Daddy. It sure has been an interesting ride. I wonder what Gainsberg, Illinois has in store for me now."

"That'll come soon enough," he said.

APPENDIX

▼

THE FIRST THREE PAGES OF LEIGH MAXWELL'S DISSERTATION

CITY UNIVERSITY OF BOSTON

GRADUATE SCHOOL

Dissertation

ENRIQUE DADI: THE MAN BEHIND THE VEIL

By

LEIGH J. MAXWELL

B.A., Yale University, 1985
M.A., City University of Boston, 1998

Submitted in partial fulfillment of the
requirements for the degree of
Doctor of Philosophy
2004

Approved by

First Reader

_____

Jack P. Wright, Ph.D.
Professor of Music
City University

Second Reader

_____

John Siegmund, Ph.D.
Associate Professor of Music
City University

Third Reader

_____

Matthew Berens, Ph.D.
Assistant Professor of Music
City University

Acknowledgments

There are a great many people I have to thank for their generous support, time and effort in helping me with this project. You can never do anything like this alone.

First, I need to thank Elena Rodriguez, head librarian of the Spanish Music Archive in Madrid. Her warmth, honesty and hospitality were the beginning of an adventure. In addition, Johann Spurber of the Berlin Library was most helpful in securing material for my final project, even if he was a little bruised at the end of my stay!

Thank you also is extended to Edna Martin whose great gifts with Wheel of Fortune helped me decipher the puzzles I found.

Helen Greenbaum, the head music librarian at City University, was helpful from the first moment I got it in my head to go chasing ghosts. She was an excellent boss, librarian and most of all, a great friend.

I wish to thank my family and friends who were always willing to help. Steffi and Heinz Uebler in Berlin will always have my gratitude and my love. I could not have continued my research without their help and guidance. (I'm so sorry I couldn't make the wedding, but my best to Conrad!)

My cousin, Barbara, who gave more than she ever realized she would for me, will always be in my thoughts and prayers.

My readers, Matthew Berens and John Siegmund, were most helpful during the final stages of writing.

I'd like to thank my father, whose knowledge of history is beyond compare and whose generous spirit helped me through. I must also thank Jack Wright, my advisor and friend, was always willing to help and was especially necessary in the editing stage of my work. I finished this work in record time, thanks to him.

It is to my father, Hank Maxwell, and Jack Wright that I dedicate this work.

Elizabeth A. Seitz
19 Thomas Street
Jamaica Plain, MA 02130

0-595-31782-0

Printed in the United States
24192LVS00003B/308